The earth is the Lord's, and everything in it,
the world, and all who live in it;
for he founded it on the seas
and established it on the waters.

—Psalm 24:1–2 (NIV)

The Island Bookshop

ROSEANNA M. WHITE

Guideposts

A Gift from Guideposts

Thank you for your purchase! We want to express our gratitude for your support with a special gift just for you.

Dive into *Spirit Lifters*, a complimentary e-book that will fortify your faith, offering solace during challenging moments. Its 31 carefully selected scripture verses will soothe and uplift your soul.

Please use the QR code or go to **guideposts.org/spiritlifters** to download.

The Island Bookshop is a trademark of Guideposts.

Published by Guideposts
100 Reserve Road, Suite E200
Danbury, CT 06810
Guideposts.org

Copyright © 2025 by Guideposts. All rights reserved. This book, or parts thereof, may not be reproduced, stored in a retrieval system, or transmitted in any form or by any means, electronic, mechanical, photocopying, recording, or otherwise, without the written permission of the publisher.

This is a work of fiction. Apart from actual historical people and events that may figure into the fiction narrative, all other names, characters, businesses, and events are the creation of the author's imagination and any resemblance to actual persons, living or dead, or events is coincidental. Every attempt has been made to credit the sources of copyrighted material used in this book. If any such acknowledgment has been inadvertently omitted or miscredited, receipt of such information would be appreciated.

Scripture references are from the following sources: *The Holy Bible, King James Version* (KJV). *The Holy Bible, New International Version* (NIV). Copyright © 1973, 1978, 1984, 2011 by Biblica, Inc. Used by permission of Zondervan. All rights reserved worldwide. www.zondervan.com.

Cover design by Müllerhaus
Interior design by Müllerhaus
Typeset by Aptara, Inc.

ISBN 978-1-961442-60-3 (softcover)
ISBN 978-1-961442-61-0 (epub)

Printed and bound in the United States of America
10 9 8 7 6 5 4 3 2 1

The Island Bookshop

To Leslie and Gee Gee
of Books to Be Red and Buxton Village Books—
thank you for your willingness to pull back the curtain...
and especially for your amazing stores, that combine
my two favorite things: books and the beach!

Chapter One

Washington, DC
Present Day

White gloves tugged into place, Kennedy Marshall reached for the treasure before her—old leather, careful gilding, delicate paper. She drew in a deep breath as she slowly opened the cover and let her gaze roam the end leaves. Not purely because she loved the smell of an old book, though she always swore it was the sweetest perfume in the world, but to check for a not-so-sweet smell. Mold, the archnemesis of books and hence of her. The same thing her eyes scanned for.

No discoloration met her eyes, and no odor affronted her nose. Good—and a little miraculous given the age of this volume. She flipped to the title page, her examination beginning again. Her pulse kicked up a notch when she read those beautiful, precious words. The words that meant this book might actually be what the original owner had claimed, a rare first edition.

The Whole Booke of Psalmes
Faithfully
TRANSLATED into ENGLISH

Metre.
Whereunto is prefixed a discourse
declaring not only the lawfullness, but also
the necessity of the heavenly Ordinance
of singing Scripture Psalmes in
the Churches of God.
Imprinted, 1640

Her breath caught, her pulse thudded at those last two words. She'd known, of course, that was what the page would have on it. That was why it was here now, in her hands, bequeathed by the billionaire book collector who had died two months ago.

But everyone always claimed the books they donated to the Library of Congress were valuable—and all too often, they were lying through their teeth. Okay, fine, more likely they were just mistaken. People saw the date and, if it matched the year in which a title was first printed, or didn't have "Second Edition" typed right there to see, they just assumed. The general populace didn't know the difference between an edition and a printing, didn't know the hallmarks to look for in each book to know if it was *really* the most valuable version.

Kennedy's job was to never assume. Her job was to know which details to look for in each title they received, to examine every inch of every tome, to evaluate, to grade, to restore where possible, and to store accordingly.

Some books would enter their permanent collection, where any library visitor could view them. A few were so valuable they would be on display, but were not to be touched without her hovering over them, white gloves ever present. Some would be stored in the parts of the library that regular patrons would never see, when the books were too fragile to be exposed regularly to light and humidity. Others would be sold or given away, when they weren't good additions to the collection for one reason or another.

This one she had high hopes for. Ephraim Kensington had invited her to a dinner party at his estate last year for the sole purpose of showing off his rare book collection, and she'd pegged this little book as the gem—if it turned out to be what he claimed. Unlike most people, Kensington would have done his homework. *The Bay Psalm Book* was the first book printed in the Massachusetts Colony, back in 1640, and if this was really one of that first printing...

"Take a breath, Kennedy," Melessa Taggart teased from the worktable beside her own.

"Can't." Kennedy exaggerated the breathlessness of the word, just to make her friend chuckle. "Too nervous. If this is one of the eleven surviving copies of this book..."

"What, you're not used to handling books that auction for tens of millions of dollars?" Melessa had another of the donated books in front of her, but, much as she loved her best friend in DC, Kennedy hadn't been willing to let anyone else touch this one. That was the perk of her recent promotion, after all—she was the boss in this room. Her new position meant that, once in a while at least, she could snatch the best books for her own perusal.

Still, she obeyed the advice and made herself take another long breath—not to smell for mold this time, just to steady herself.

She knew all the elements to check for, after spending two hours already this morning refreshing herself on the hallmarks of a first printing of this text. Having familiarized herself with Kensington's documentation regarding each book of his collection, Kennedy knew that another specialist had authenticated the book fifty years ago.

But the Library of Congress required everything entering their permanent collection to be verified again, of course. Not to mention she needed to document any changes to the book since its last evaluation. *Please, Lord, let the condition still be excellent.*

Yes, Kennedy prayed against mold and mildew and rips and tears and paper decomposition. Melessa always razzed her for it, but she figured the Lord loved books too, right? Why else would He have instructed His people to write them?

Okay. One more deep breath, and she was ready to slowly turn another page, then another and another, watching and listening for any creaking of the binding, fingers noting the feel of the paper through the gloves. Heart still skipping along like a kid in a candy shop as she saw that, unlike the last version of this book to go to auction, there were no handwritten markings marring the margins, no crumbling along the edges.

"It's clean," she whispered, knowing Melessa would hear the glee in her voice.

Melessa abandoned all pretense of doing her own work and moved to Kennedy's side with a little squeal of delight. "Man. If this went to auction, it could probably surpass the fourteen million for the last copy that sold."

"It's in better condition, for sure. I still can't believe Mr. Kensington willed his collection to us instead of his family."

Melessa shrugged, making her black braids bounce around her face. "I guess when your family doesn't value the books for what they are and only see the price tag..."

"I guess." Kennedy couldn't even imagine. But then, she came from a family of booklovers. She glanced over at her friend. "Wanna do the notation for me, since you're standing here? Then we can switch for yours."

"Sure." Melessa pulled the laptop forward from where Kennedy had left it at the side of the table.

They went through the book page by page, with Kennedy noting every telltale oddity that marked it as the first printing, as well as any of this tome as its own unique variation—discoloration of the paper, the tone of the ink, places where the binding was loosening. Melessa typed it all in as they went. As frequently as they worked together, it was easy to fall into the comfort of a rhythm, even on a project as unusual as this one.

When finally they finished, Kennedy's neck ached a bit from the tension she'd been holding, and she took a moment to roll her head and loosen it again, letting out a long exhale. She still couldn't quite believe it. It was *real*—authentic. Everything Kensington had claimed.

Melessa gave a sigh of her own. "Well. My date tonight is going to have a hard time topping *that*."

The grin that tugged at Kennedy's lips was partly for the book—and partly for the reminder that Melessa would be going out on date number three with a guy they had high hopes for. Kennedy had been teasing her for weeks about having cartoon stars in her eyes.

"This is just the best day ever." She moved *The Bay Psalm Book* back into its box, clipped the airtight lid in place, and slid it onto one of the metal shelves behind their worktables. "Rare first editions *and* you have a date with Mr. Cutie."

"At Filomena's. Last time I got in, I swear I saw George Clooney." Melessa moved back to her table and the book still sitting out.

Kennedy followed her, reaching for Melessa's laptop. "Never mind the celebrities. I just want their ravioli again. Those things are big as pillows and *so* good." Even thinking about the pasta made a mockery of the salad she'd packed for lunch today. Her stomach rumbled a protest.

She tabbed to the correct document and set her fingers on the keyboard, ready for the dictation.

"You should have let me set you up with Mr. Cutie's brother," Melessa said in a sing-song tone. "Then you could be going with us tonight."

Kennedy grinned. But shook her head. "No more blind dates. You remember what happened last time, right?"

Her friend gave her a narrowed-eye glare. "That was *not* Marcus's fault. He's a perfectly nice guy."

Kennedy pressed her lips together. Melessa wasn't altogether wrong. There hadn't been anything wrong with the man from her friend's church. He'd just been…or rather, *she'd* been… She huffed a sigh. Honestly, the problem was that she'd just returned from a trip home for her dad's birthday. Which meant thoughts of Someone Else were in the forefront of her mind. His grin. His laugh. The way he hugged her so tight. How he called her "Kenni" even though no one else on the face of the earth had ever done that.

She'd spent the whole double date comparing the unfortunate Marcus to Wes Armstrong, and even knowing it was unfair to her new acquaintance, she hadn't been able to stop herself.

But maybe she should have let Melessa set her up with Mr. Cutie's brother. She hadn't been back to Hatteras since Christmas, so she'd once again succeeded—mostly—in pushing all thoughts of Wes aside. Until he texted or emailed or called. Which he did at least once a week. But she was fine dealing with those interactions and still remembering they were only friends. It was when she *saw* him that all those old dreams pummeled her again, even though she'd long ago resigned them to the "never gonna happen" file.

Kennedy had known it since they were sixteen, when he'd chosen Britta instead of her. Had done a great job of believing it while he and Britta were married. But these last two years, after Britta's death, when Wes took to calling and emailing and texting nearly every day for a while? Yeah. Her stupid heart hadn't done so well with it then. One would think that a woman who'd just celebrated her thirty-first birthday would be able to forget her first love, but…

She and Melessa got through that book and one more before lunch. They'd left the clean room and were en route to their offices when Kennedy's cell buzzed in her pocket. She wasn't surprised to see her aunt's number on the display—Aunt Grace called during her lunch hour once or twice a week, just to chat and keep Kennedy updated on the goings-on of life in the sleepy seaside town in North Carolina that had once been home. However, today was Friday, and her aunt usually volunteered at the art gallery on Fridays.

Waving to Melessa, Kennedy answered the call, stepping into her office as she said, "Hey, Aunt Grace."

"Oh, good, you're there! Something happened to Lara."

Four words, but they made Kennedy freeze just inside the door, her hand hovering over the light switch. She'd heard words like those before. *"Something happened to your mom"* had been her aunt's panicked words eight years ago, pulling Kennedy out of a graduate studies lecture to tell her that Mom had had a heart attack—Kennedy hadn't even made it home in time to say goodbye. *"Something happened to Britta"* was Wes's choked greeting two years ago when he called, sobbing, to say her best friend, his wife, had been in a fatal car crash—on her way to visit Kennedy. *"Something happened to Grandma"* had been the last one, nine short months ago and again from Aunt Grace, telling Kennedy that her eighty-six-year-old grandmother was in the hospital, declining suddenly and fast. She had at least gotten there before it was too late, that time.

Her throat wouldn't work. Her heart, she was pretty sure, couldn't decide whether to pound or stop altogether.

Not Lara. Nothing could happen to her sister. *Please, God, please. Not Lara.*

She couldn't say anything, gasp as she might for breath.

Aunt Grace didn't wait for her to speak anyway. "She fell off the attic ladder somehow—at the bookshop. Thank God that Shaleen was there to call the ambulance. I'm following it now."

Ambulance. Ambulance, with her aunt trailing it, meant that Lara was alive. Kennedy dragged a breath into her lungs. "How bad is she?" *No need to panic*, she told herself. Even something as non-life-threatening as a broken leg would require a trip to the hospital in Nags Head. They only had a few small urgent care clinics on Hatteras Island, nothing that could handle anything remotely serious.

But her aunt was silent for a long beat. "I don't know, Ken. She was still unconscious when they loaded her up. Her face is a bruised mess—they think she has a concussion, and the EMTs were pretty concerned by how unresponsive she was." Thunder rumbled loudly enough on her aunt's end to come through to Kennedy, making her eyes dart to her window.

Raindrops streaked the glass, but it was a rather gentle late-spring rain here in DC. She knew they were getting pounded in the Outer Banks. Lara had texted that morning, like she did every day, and mentioned rather grumpily that the roads were flooding. Again. Seemed like every time a system rolled through these days, the barrier island's low-lying roads went under. Kennedy had replied, THEN HAVE A NICE SWIM TO WORK!

She squeezed her eyes shut. How had they gone from grumbling and snarky morning texts to this? "I'm on my way."

"Oh, baby, you don't have to—"

"It's *Lara*. Of course I have to." If the situation was reversed, Lara would be in her car already, plowing through the water to reach her. And if the water was too high, she'd be in a boat. And if she couldn't find a boat, she'd sprout wings and fly by the sheer force of her will. Nothing in the world would keep her sister from rushing to her side if she was injured, so how could Kennedy do any less? Since Mom died, they'd been more than sisters, more than best friends. They'd been each other's lifeline. "I just need to…"

What did she need to do first? Her mind spun in a dozen different directions. She had to take the rest of the day, let her boss know. And Melessa. Catch the metro. Pack for the weekend, find a gas station, pray that she'd beat Friday afternoon traffic out of DC, which was an absolute nightmare this time of year.

She forced a deep breath in, back out. "I'll let you know when I'm on the road. Keep me updated, okay? How long till you get to Nags Head?"

"Just another ten or fifteen minutes at this point. The road's washed out, so we've been crawling, but we're just coming up on the Jug Handle Bridge. Should be fine from here. I didn't dare take my attention off the road long enough to call you in all that water, even with my hands-free."

Kennedy finally reached out to hit the lights, striding toward where she'd stashed her purse and messenger bag that morning. "Any closures on Bodie that will affect me?" Bodie Island was where the hospital was located, north of her family's home on Hatteras Island.

"Not that I've heard. They're not even closed here, and you know we get it worse than they do at the northern beaches. But be careful, baby. If there *is* any flooding, that little car of yours..."

"Mitzi and I will be fine." She forced a smile into her voice, hoping that referring to her car by its name would make her aunt smile too. "She's tougher than she looks."

"Just like you girls. I'll call with updates whenever I have them."

"Thanks. See you soon, Aunt Grace. Love you."

A moment later she was hanging up her cell and reaching for her office phone. But her mind was already hundreds of miles away, back in the one place she tended to avoid—home. Because as much as she loved Avon—that tiny little town nestled between the Atlantic Ocean and Pamlico Sound, on a spit of sand barely wide enough for a road and a couple rows of houses—being there was just too hard.

Maybe it was where tourists went to get away from it all and bask in the beauty of the beach community. But for Kennedy, it was the place that reminded her with each crashing wave and scuttling cloud that dreams too often slipped through your fingers.

And people did too.

Chapter Two

The rain had finally stopped, but the world was thoroughly waterlogged. As Kennedy stepped out directly into a puddle, she wished she'd taken the time to change out of her dress shoes and into something more suited to the parking lot of the Outer Banks Hospital—like waders. Or at least rubber boots. She loved the comfy-but-stylish dress sandals for walking between the library and the metro station back in DC, but they did nothing to keep out the water.

At least the sun was attempting to bully its way through the clouds, promising a few more hours of daylight yet. Ordinarily, she would have tilted her face up to bask in it. She loved these first weeks of June. The weather was finally warm, and the sheer number of daylight hours felt lavish after winter's short days.

Today, she was just glad that night hadn't already encroached during the drive. And that she'd missed the worst of the Friday-afternoon-in-the-summer traffic jams. And that the next call from her aunt during the drive had brought good news. Well, good*ish*, anyway. *"She's awake! And there's no spinal cord injury, she can move everything. But she's in terrible pain and not very coherent, probably from the meds. They said it's a severe concussion, and since she was* *unconscious, it gets the Traumatic Brain Injury name instead of Mild Traumatic Brain Injury, like she's had before in her soccer days."*

Kennedy's gaze flicked over the façade of the hospital. It was a far cry from the ones she saw most often in the capital area—first, because it was a fraction of the size, but second, because even the hospital down here was so...*beachy*. Sunny yellow window shades, peaceful blue accents, all against white-sand bricks. As if even this building were trying to convince every passerby that they were in paradise.

Inside, on the other hand, it smelled exactly like what it was. A place full of medicine and disinfectants and cafeteria food.

She hated hospitals. Which meant that every time she got a whiff of one, every bad memory came flooding back. How frail Grandma Janey had looked in that hospital bed nine months ago, when an obstructed bowel ended her decades of stellar health. How Dad had sat in one of those uncomfortable chairs, shoulders hunched and quaking with sobs when Kennedy finally made it to her mother's room after the heart attack, twenty minutes too late. How Lara had rushed to meet her, to wrap her arms around her, to hold her so tight that she knew the sandy ground under them had washed away in the rain, and they were both just clinging to a life preserver.

Aunt Grace had already told her where to go, but Kennedy's stomach tightened into knots as she aimed her feet toward the ICU. She found her father in the waiting room, his hand tight in Deanne's—his wife as of last year.

Her lips wanted to smile a bit at the sight. She loved seeing Dad happy again, loved that he and Deanne, a longtime friend of the family, had found their second chances together. And she loved knowing that Dad—who had been at loose ends after he retired—had a new lease on life now that he was helping run Deanne's boutique hotel on Ocracoke Island, just a ferry ride away from the family home in Avon.

She just didn't like to see them clinging to each other's hands *here*. "Hey."

"Kennedy! You made it." He surged to his feet, Deanne right behind him, and came forward with arms outstretched.

"So did you. You hadn't, as of when Aunt Grace called." She walked straight into his embrace and held on tight, thankful when Deanne's arms came around them both. "I worried you wouldn't be able to. She said the ferries weren't running and there was a small craft advisory."

"There was, but I pulled a few strings with my Coastie buddies." He eased back enough to wink down at her. "They brought us to Hatteras, and then we had Joe drive us to the bookshop. Took Lara's car from there."

Leave it to Dad to call on the Coast Guard—many of whom he knew from his years in the Ranger service. She was glad he had. "Have you seen her yet?"

He nodded, flicking his blue eyes toward the doors separating them from the ICU proper. "We just came back out a few minutes ago so Aunt Grace and Uncle Tim could have a turn. I'll text her and let her know you're here. They've already been back once before. I know Tim won't mind trading places with you."

While he pulled out his phone, Deanne edged closer and cupped Kennedy's elbow. Her eyes said she understood how much Kennedy hated being in this place. Hated needing to be. But wouldn't have chosen otherwise for anything. "You look nice, Kennedy. Did you come straight from work?"

By reflex, she glanced down at her blouse and trousers. Both were designer—though purchased from a second-hand site. Working as she did with rich donors and special guests to the Library of Congress, she had to look the part of a beltway powerhouse. It was a far cry from the "island chic" her family favored: shorts, flip-flops, and a choice between a T-shirt or a tank top, this time of year. Once in a while the ladies would break out sundresses, and Dad would reach for a golf shirt.

Every time she came home, Lara would pull her in for a hug and say, "You're overdressed."

And Kennedy would hug her back and say, "You're just a slob."

Tears stung her eyes, as unexpected as they were unwelcome. Man, did she want that banter today. To hear her sister's continual prodding to shuck the "straightjacket of city life and come home where you belong."

For her stepmom, she nodded. "I only stopped at my place long enough to pack an overnight bag then hopped in the car."

"Not exactly the weekend home we were looking forward to you taking." Deanne rubbed her hand up and down Kennedy's arm. "Run into much traffic?"

She was partway through answering when the doors swung wide and Uncle Tim came through, holding it open. "There you go, Ken. Room four."

Good thing Deanne wouldn't be offended by her half-finished answer. Kennedy rushed toward the door, shooting her aunt's husband a tight-lipped smile as she passed him.

The smells were worse back here. And the *beeping*. She knew all the monitors and machines were good things, but...well, but needing them wasn't, and those stupid tears welled for real when she stepped into room four and saw her sister hooked up to an IV and the monitors and who knew what else.

Worse was the condition of Lara's face. Her left eye wasn't just black, it was mottled purple and swollen shut, the bruising and swelling extending all down the side of her face and along her jaw. Bandages hid what Kennedy assumed were lacerations on her sister's cheek. Even the dark hair they shared looked like it hurt, trapped as it was under a wrapping of white gauze.

Kennedy had to pause for a second and drag in a calming breath. Her big sister wasn't supposed to be like this. She was the capable one, the force of nature, the outgoing personality who could get strangers laughing in two seconds flat. She wasn't supposed to be lying so still on a hospital bed, looking like it pained her just to blink.

"Lara?" She tried for cheer, but it sounded flat and strained even to her own ears. She moved to stand beside Aunt Grace, who turned in her seat to greet her with a tired smile.

Her sister moved her head a bit, but it must have hurt, because she winced and stopped. "Ken?" she whispered. "What are you doing here? You were tackling a big project today."

"Yeah, well, my attention hound of a sister totally upstaged that with her dive off the attic ladder." Kennedy perched on the edge of the bed and reached for her sister's hand with the O2 sensor on her finger, but without an IV snaking from her arm. Hopefully her grin looked more convincing than the cheer in her greeting had sounded. "You look miserable."

The twitch might have been intended as a smile, but Lara's face was too swollen to pull it off. "Good a word as any. Other concussions didn't hurt like this."

"You were a few years younger the first two times. What were you even doing in the attic?" It had been bothering her the whole drive. They *never* went into the attic of the old house their grandmother had converted into the Island Bookshop twenty years ago. Kennedy could remember maybe two times they'd tugged the ladder down from the ceiling and made the climb—and it certainly hadn't been in the summer, when the temperature up there stayed only a few degrees shy of the Sahara.

Lara's uninjured eye squinted a bit. "I don't know. I can't remember anything after I got to work today."

"Shaleen said something about a roof leak," Aunt Grace said. "You'd called Joe to take a look and fix it, then gone up to see how bad it was up there."

Though her sister's expression showed no memory of that, Kennedy had no trouble interpreting the frown that pinched her brow. Roof repairs weren't in the budget this year. If they had to pay for that—*please, Lord, let it just need a patch and not a whole new roof!*—then the interior renovation they'd been saving for would have to be postponed again.

Kennedy's stomach knots twisted in a few new ways. She might not be part of the daily business of the bookshop, but Lara had been running it for years after Grandma finally admitted it was too much for her, and Kennedy and Lara were co-owners—Grandma Janey had willed it equally to both of them nine months ago—and Kennedy was as active as she could be from DC. They planned everything together, did the budget together, made big decisions together. She had her heart set on that renovation every bit as much as Lara did.

Well. If it came down to it, she would just postpone her own home improvement projects she'd wanted to do this summer and pay for a new roof for the shop instead. She didn't really *need* to terrace her postage-stamp of a backyard—she rarely went out there anyway. But the shop definitely needed a leak-free roof.

Lara would object, but they could argue about it later, after Joe gave them whatever estimate he came up with.

Her sister was still frowning. "I think…I think Shaleen's going out of town this weekend. Did they say when I'll be able to go home? Someone needs to be there to open tomorrow."

Leave it to Lara to be more concerned with opening the shop than with her TBI. "You know I'll do that."

"And there is no way you're going to be released straight from the ICU, Lara." Aunt Grace shook her head, heaving a sigh. "You'll probably be here all weekend, at the least."

Lara groaned. "I hate hospitals. They smell funny."

Kennedy breathed a laugh, just because in some ways, at least, they were so alike. "That's *my* line."

Her sister focused her good eye on Kennedy again, another tired twitch of a smile trying and failing to find a place on her lips. "You're overdressed."

Thank You, God. Kennedy lifted her brows and sniffed a teasing reproach as she pinched a fold of the hospital gown Lara wore. "You've achieved new levels of 'slob' with this ensemble, I'm afraid."

Lara chuckled. "I don't know what you're talking about. I can totally pull it off." But her good eye blinked heavily and shut. She sighed. "Tired."

"It's the meds they have you on," Aunt Grace said. "Go ahead and sleep. Rest is the best thing for you, they said."

At Lara's first concussion, Kennedy had been shocked to hear that sleep was okay—evidence that she'd been reading far too many historicals, apparently. These days, the experts didn't tell you to keep the injured person awake, it seemed, which flew in the face of everything teenage Kennedy thought she knew thanks to old novels.

Lara, being the stubborn creature she was, pried her good eye open again and focused on Kennedy. "You'll run the shop until I get out of here?"

They couldn't afford to close for a whole weekend during high season, that was for sure. "Of course. My boss knows I might have to take Monday too. It'll be fine."

Lara let out a long breath and squeezed her sister's fingers. "I know I keep harassing you about coming home more—but this wasn't planned. Promise."

A laugh bubbled up and spilled over. "I don't know. You're pretty devious, sister mine. Wouldn't put it past you. You were probably up on the roof last night poking a hole to let the water in, just so you had a reason to go up and investigate."

"You found me out." Another fleeting, weak attempt at a smile, and then Lara let her eye slide shut. "Love you, Ken."

"Love you too, Lar. Now go to sleep."

She hung out until she was sure Lara had done just that, spent a few minutes chatting softly with her aunt, then returned to the waiting room. If she was going to open the shop in the morning, she'd better drive the last hour to Avon tonight—and if the roads were flooded, she'd better do it before it got dark. So she only granted herself another half hour with Dad and Deanne and Tim before she hugged them all farewell too and left the hospital.

The salt breeze wrapped around her as soon as she stepped outside, teasing her bangs and bringing with it the smell of food from some nearby restaurant or another. Her stomach growled, reminding her that she hadn't ever eaten that salad she'd made for lunch, and the granola bars she'd grabbed as she flew out the door hadn't exactly been full meals.

She'd eat when she got to the house—no time to grab anything now if she meant to beat the darkness.

When she'd come home at Christmas, the roads had been all but empty, the wind had been biting, and most of the faces she'd seen were locals, quite a few of whom she knew—even here in the bigger towns of Nags Head and Kitty Hawk.

But it was the first week of June, which meant the roads were clogged with vacationers, and everywhere she looked were people with sunburnt skin, bathing suits, and wagons full of beach supplies. As always, she breathed a sigh of relief as she pulled away from the last stoplight and turned onto Virginia Dare Trail, heading south. The crowded houses in their bright colors or cedar shakes fell away, leaving only low scrub trees stretching for miles toward the Oregon Inlet.

Kennedy leaned back in her seat, a bit of the afternoon's tension seeping away. She loved this stretch of the drive, where it was all open skies—currently beginning to tint red and orange as the sun sank toward Pamlico Sound—unmolested nature, and water stretching out on either side, beyond the dunes.

There were no scenes like this in DC, she could admit that. No time of year when parks were empty, no place where you could take a solitary walk and not see a single person for miles. She never thought she missed this, not until she was here again, smelling the ocean air and seeing that water that went on forever.

She never had trouble finding God in the hustle and bustle of the city. He was always right there, whenever she turned to Him. But here...here she never even had to turn and look. Here, she saw Him everywhere. In the cry of the gull, the graceful sweep of a pelican's wings, the glistening of light-diamonds on the too-high water. Here, even, in the ache in her chest that got a little stronger with each mile she drew closer to home.

Coming home always made her cling to His hand. Because coming home hurt, every single time. Made her keenly aware of all the people who were missing. Mom, Grandma Janey, Britta.

Wes. Always missing, even though he was still there.

Her fingers tightened on the wheel at the thought of him. This time would be better. She'd be too busy taking care of the shop and visiting Lara to even see him, probably. And if she did, it wouldn't be like it usually was. She had Lara's injury to fill her thoughts. And worry over the leaky roof. And the excitement of *The Bay Psalm Book* to replay in her mind.

And really, she should take a few minutes to do a video from the shop for social media while she was here. Her viewers always loved it when she took them to different places for a "tour of the shelves" episode. Usually she only talked about rare books on her little video channel, often featuring the ones private collectors hired her to authenticate and evaluate in her side hustle, after-hours work she did from home—which, as a government employee, she could do only because she had their permission and had already established herself as an expert before getting on at the Library of Congress. But whenever she traveled, she always popped into a bookstore or specialty library and did a quick little video tour of her favorite parts. And she always got a ton of comments when she took them to *her* shop and told stories about Grandma Janey and her legendary love of books.

It was proof that the charm of the Island Bookshop appealed to more than just vacationers. Even now, she could imagine its cheerful white siding, the welcoming porch, the brightly-colored flowers that would be hanging in pots. And inside—inside was a feast of the senses. Scents from the locally made candles and lotions, plush toys, beach-and-book-themed T-shirts and tote bags begging for a hand to run down them, soft music playing in the background, and of course, books. Every wall of every room covered in colorful spines that promised escape, entertainment, education, and maybe a little bit of enlightenment.

Plenty to keep her occupied while she was here for the weekend. She zipped over the Oregon Inlet Bridge, admiring the view of choppy waves and sun-painted clouds, then dragged in a long, slow breath as the bridge delivered her home.

Hatteras Island. The last stretch of road between her and all her memories, through the villages of Waves and Rodanthe and Frisco… then the long stretch of undeveloped island, too narrow for anything but a road and the sand dunes. Then Avon. Buxton. Hatteras.

The communities she knew best. Loved and hated. Where the visitors this time of year would outnumber the locals more than ten to one. But whose every local she knew—or at least knew *of*.

She drove through a few deep puddles in the towns, but it was on the empty stretches of road between them that things got dicey. The line of vehicles slowed to a crawl as water rose inch by inch. Kennedy gripped the wheel and straightened her spine, willing her low-slung car to lift onto its tiptoes.

Water flowed, every car's wheels making little waves that lapped at her bumper. "This is stupid," she whispered to no one but Mitzi. "Why do people live in a place that floods multiple times a year?"

Of course, in her head she could hear her sister's rebuttal. *"Why do people live in a place with DC's crime rates? Where you can't turn around without bumping into someone? Where a couple acres of trees in a park is all the nature to be found?"*

She closely watched oncoming traffic for other small cars, just as proof that they were making it through. There were more trucks and SUVs and crossovers than anything, but a few sedans gave her hope.

The water had to be eight inches deep in some places, making her stomach go so tight she was glad she hadn't stopped for food. This would have been so much easier in Uncle Tim's truck.

The car in front of her slowed. "No! Keep moving, keep moving..." Didn't these people know that if you stopped, that was when the water could sweep you off the road? "Please, please, please, please, please." She didn't know if that plea was for the line of traffic or for God—but He answered, anyway. Even when she came to a halt in the high water, Mitzi's tires didn't lose traction. She exhaled when they started moving again.

But it was without doubt the longest drive on the island she'd ever made, and by the time she finally pulled into the driveway of the bungalow she'd grown up in, her fitness tracker watch was telling her to do some breathing exercises because her stress was too high. "No kidding," she mumbled to the watch as she dismissed the alert.

Then jumped halfway to the ceiling when her door was wrenched open.

"How is she?"

Kennedy slapped a hand to her chest. "Good grief, Wes, don't scare me like that!"

And *this* was why her self-talk about how she wouldn't have to see him this time always crashed and burned in minutes. Because, of course, Wes Armstrong lived right next door, sandwiched between the house Lara now claimed and the home belonging to their aunt and uncle. Not seeing him wasn't an option.

But if he would just stop *grinning* like that, making the stupid dimple in his left cheek wink to life, she'd have a chance of surviving it with her heart intact. Maybe.

"Sorry." He didn't sound—or look—sorry as he kept right on grinning. He held out a hand as she unbuckled, like she couldn't get out of her own car without assistance. Stupid, gallant Wes. "Should have knocked before opening the door."

A snort of laughter slipped out. She put her palm in his because she knew from experience that he wouldn't actually back away from her door and give her room to exit until she let him help her. And given how shaky her legs felt after that scuba-drive, she was kind of grateful for the help.

At least until he went and folded her into one of his tight hugs. "You okay? Lara okay?"

He smelled like cinnamon and vanilla, which should have been weird for someone who wasn't either a baker or a grandmother, but he totally pulled it off. He likely had something delicious next door that he'd offer her any minute, so she returned the hug. "She's awake and coherent. No spinal injury, but it's pretty serious. Traumatic Brain Injury—and the doc warned that the symptoms could be worse, given that it's her third concussion. Sounds like they're hoping to move her out of ICU in the morning but will probably keep her all weekend."

"And you?" He pulled away and clapped his hands to her shoulders so he could survey her.

She could only guess at what he saw. "Glad to be on dry ground." She glanced to her feet, where the driveway was, in fact, under a half-inch of water. But it was better than the roads. "Okay. Dri*er* ground."

"You need a cup of tea and some coffee cake. Let me help you get your stuff in, and I'll bring it over. Have you had dinner?" He released her and moved to open the back door so he could reach for her suitcase. "Anything in the trunk?"

"No. And no. I can get that."

He shot her a look. "Don't insult me. I'll let you carry your monster purse though."

"Generous of you." She grabbed it off the passenger seat—and admitted only silently that it was as heavy as the toiletry bag he'd slung over his shoulder. But what could she say? If a purse wasn't big enough to hold a book, it was useless to her.

"I made enchiladas for dinner. I'll bring you one of those too." He led the way up the stairs to the front door. Unlike many of the newer houses on the island, the old family home wasn't on full stilts, just raised about six feet on brick pillars. They did the job for small surges like this one, but every couple of years a hurricane would come through that would get inside. The family had long ago learned to keep all valuables on high shelves—and to constantly add money to the Sheetrock Fund. Insurance, sky-high as it was, only went so far.

Wes was already fishing his own copy of the key out of his pocket—because neighbors *always* had "emergency" copies of each other's keys down here, which hadn't struck her as odd until she moved to DC—so Kennedy didn't bother fishing hers out of her purse. She just followed him in a moment later, unable to hold off the wave of exhaustion that struck the second she stepped inside the house she'd grown up in.

It should have been a good day. The best day. The Kensington collection, *The Bay Psalm Book*... It should have been the kind of day that confirmed she was exactly where God wanted her, living out her passion, building the life she'd always hoped for.

Yet here she was, back in the place she'd worked so hard to escape, the man she didn't want to love taking care of her just like he always tried to do, but never like she wanted him to. Her sister in the hospital, their bookshop roof leaking.

Wes took her bags to her room and was back again by the time Kennedy had unstrapped her soggy shoes. He planted his hands on his hips and raised his brows. "So...what was the real estate emergency Lara called me about, anyway?"

She paused, frowned. "What?"

"She left a message for me this morning while I was on the other line. Sounded pretty panicked, but all she said was that she had a real estate emergency and to call her when I could. But then before I got a chance, your aunt texted about the fall."

Kennedy shook her head. "I have no idea. What exactly would even constitute a 'real estate emergency'?"

He chuckled. "Got me. It's not a phrase I've ever heard before. I kinda assumed it was just Lara being dramatic."

That would be typical. But still... What could she have meant? It couldn't be the roof leak. That warranted a call to their maintenance guy, not to a real estate agent. She shrugged. "No idea. And Lara, as of when I was there at least, couldn't remember anything after arriving at the shop this morning."

"I'm sure it's not *really* an emergency." He grinned again. "I'll go grab you some food."

"Thanks." She turned toward the kitchen, thinking tea sounded good—but she'd opt for the cold variety she knew Lara would have in the fridge.

Of course, Wes didn't let her walk on by while he showed himself out. He intercepted her for another hug and held her close. Pressed a kiss to the top of her head. "Glad you're home, Kenni. I've missed you."

And this was why she stayed away.

Chapter Three

Avon, North Carolina
June 2, 1938

Freedom tasted like salt air on her lips and a hot summer sun beating down on her head. Ana Horvat adjusted the brim of her straw hat and looked around the docks, praying Marko was somewhere among the workers but knowing well he might not be. Her husband couldn't know what day she'd finally arrive. He'd said in his last letter that he would check every day, but if he'd found a steady job—*please, Lord*—then working might prohibit him from being able to.

Even so, she hoped and prayed for the familiar bob of his dark hair through the milling sailors and merchants, the even more familiar flash of his smile.

The last three months had felt like a lifetime without him by her side.

She'd known, had agreed, that the plan was wise. For him to immigrate first, to find a place for them, find a job. Get their new life set up. Perhaps she would have argued, if it weren't for the little one swelling with life inside her abdomen, but as sick as she'd been those first months...travel was the last thing she'd felt up for. Even if this precious life inside her was the whole reason for it.

They wouldn't raise their child in Mussolini's Italy. They wouldn't subject their baby to the same persecution they'd endured all their lives in the Dalmatia region—too Croatian for the Italians, too Italian for Croatia, in a region contested and fought over constantly, but whose people were always, always outcasts.

Ever since the World War, things had been fraught with tension. But since Mussolini's takeover? Violence was running rampant. She wished her whole family, Marko's whole family, had been able to leave too...but with so many of them losing employment because of their ancestry, there wasn't money for that.

There wasn't money for much at all. Their families had contributed to her and Marko's escape, and the guilt of it pricked at her constantly.

"It is not just for you," they had all said, clasping her in embrace after embrace as they'd seen her to the ship in Dubrovnik that would take her away from the only home she'd ever known. "It's for the baby. Make a new start, Ana. For all of us."

When she closed her eyes, she could almost pretend it was the salt air of Dalmatia she smelled, that the sun's embrace was her mother's, her father's, her in-laws'. She could almost pretend that this little fishing village she'd just used some of her last coin to reach was the one she'd grown up in.

Except that the voices ringing through the air weren't speaking Croatian or Italian. *English*. They were English words coloring the breeze, in an accent she'd never heard before. In Europe, the English spoken and taught was clipped with British cadences. Here, though…the vowels were long, the consonants lazy and stretched. She'd spent most of the last two days trying to adjust her ears to it, but those long vowels were even more pronounced here than on the mainland.

How had Marko been doing with the language? She'd been teaching him ever since they decided to come to America, but she'd only been able to instruct him in the English she'd learned from her father. Which consisted, of course, of the British inflections *he* had learned at university. She knew, as she glanced around at the sun-bleached hair and Western European features of the men on the docks, that their Mediterranean looks would set her and Marko apart. Croatians tended to be taller than the Italians who had annexed them, at least. And perhaps the English inflections would serve them well.

She could hope. She had to hope.

"Ma'am?" One of the sailors from the little boat she'd taken from the mainland wheeled her steamer trunk over to her with a smile and tip of his hat. "Here you are. Find your husband yet?"

She offered him a smile, her hand resting of its own volition against the swell of her stomach. "Not yet. I imagine he has found work that keeps him from meeting each boat, but I shall inquire. Do you know who may be able to help me?"

The man motioned toward a white-haired chap talking to another sailor beside a rickety looking building of weathered wood. "Ain't nobody come through here that Cap Barlow don't meet. Reckon he's your best chance there." *Ain't…reckon…*these weren't words her father had ever taught her, but she'd already pieced them into her vocabulary, given how often she'd heard them over the last two days of travel through the American South.

She dipped her own head, trying to ignore the trickle of sweat down her neck. "Thank you."

"Need help with your trunk?"

"I can manage, I think. But I do appreciate your helpfulness." She gripped the handle and tugged it onto its casters.

Hard to believe that her whole life was stored in this trunk and the small carpetbag on her arm. Twenty-six years whittled down to two pieces of luggage. So many memories left behind. So many treasures left in the hands of her sister, her mother, her father, her aunts and uncles and cousins.

Just thinking about them made the tears, always so close to the surface since she became with child, sting the backs of her eyes. She blinked them away and gave them up in prayer. Worrying over her loved ones, under that oppressive regime, accomplished nothing. She had to trust that the Lord would preserve them. And that if He chose not to, then they would know sweet peace in heaven with their Lord. She had to trust that this path He had led her and Marko on would bring them exactly where He wanted them to be.

She had to trust. But standing here alone in the scorching, humid heat made her every weakness feel so much heavier than her faith.

As her feet pointed the way toward Cap Barlow, she remembered the words Papa had whispered to her before her first morning teaching, as she'd stood quaking in the empty classroom about to fill with pupils. *"This is just one step in your life's adventure, Ana. Some things will go wrong. Others will go right. But that's what makes the adventure. Grasp it with both hands, knowing that nothing will pluck you from our Good Father's palm. He has made you for this."*

He had been right then, and the advice was just as apt now. Things would go wrong. Others would go right. Regardless, she was in the palm of God's hand, and He would see her through it all.

As she approached the white-haired man, the sailor he'd been speaking to went off in a different direction, and the captain must have noticed her approach. He turned to her, his brows drawing together.

Ana's fingers tightened around the handle of her trunk. She'd already been dismissed time and again as she made her way from New York's Ellis Island to the various trains that would take her south to

North Carolina. So many took one look at her olive skin and dark hair and muttered phrases she'd never heard before under their breath. She'd even caught sight of help-wanted signs in shop windows that said "Irish and Italian Need Not Apply."

She was more Croatian than Italian, but she had a feeling those shop owners wouldn't have cared about the difference, wouldn't care that her little coastal region had been so disputed for so many decades. She had a feeling they'd have spat on her shoes, if not in her face.

Not so different from home, as Mussolini sent more and more of the "right" kind of people to take over any position of power in Dalmatia.

But it was supposed to be better here. America was the land of opportunity, wasn't it? She knew better than to believe the old promises of streets paved with gold, but what of all the stories of the glorious melting pot, where people of all nations and creeds could come for freedom and equality and the chance to better themselves?

That couldn't just be a fable. It *couldn't*.

"Can I help you?" Cap Barlow said the moment she was within earshot. His voice carried on the incessant breeze off the water, reaching her easily enough.

She drew out the smile she'd learned to give those Italian officials, the one that promised she was an upstanding young woman, and picked up her pace so she didn't have to shout back. "I hope so. I'm looking for my husband, who arrived on Hatteras Island about a month ago and then sent for me to join him here. Marko Horvat. A kind man who worked the boat I just took from the mainland said if anyone would know his whereabouts, it would be you."

The captain's scowl didn't lessen any. "Look like you?"

She held on to her smile by sheer willpower. "If you mean with a Mediterranean complexion, then yes. Though he's a good ten inches the taller, and he wouldn't have been wearing a dress."

For a moment, amusement flickered through his eyes. He banked it quickly. "His English wasn't as good as yours."

That meant he'd spoken to Marko, knew him. Praise God! Her smile needed no help in going brighter. "I've been speaking it the longer—my father is a university professor, a linguist. He taught me and my sister English from the time we were tots. My husband only began learning a year ago."

He'd done well in his lessons, despite trying to tell her that he was just a fisherman, not suited for academics like she was. And he'd looked at her in that way he always had, as if she were so much above him, as if she belonged on the pedestal he'd always put her on, as if she were the biggest blessing of his life.

Sweet, silly man. He'd never seen himself as she saw him. The heart as big as the sky, the goodness as deep as the sea, the kindness and charm as endless as the world. Marko never met a stranger, could make friends with anyone. She, on the other hand, had always been more at home surrounded by books than people. Or, when people were a must, she preferred the smaller ones to their parents. Children were always so much more willing to dream.

The grown-up before her grunted. "He came in about a month ago, as you say. Poked around for work, took a few day jobs here and there. Haven't seen him for about a week though. Assumed he moved on, probably back to the mainland. More of your kind there for him to blend in with."

Your kind. Her shoulders edged back, her chin edged up. "He would not have left the island before my arrival, sir. Not without leaving me word. This is where he instructed me to meet up with him again."

Cap Barlow shrugged. "Only telling ya what I know, ma'am. Ain't seen him around for a week. Coulda moseyed down to Hatteras Village, maybe. Or up toward Frisco."

Having studied the map of the island that he'd sketched for her in his last letter, she let her shoulders sag again. Hatteras Island was dozens of miles long, and Hatteras and Frisco were at opposite ends—this little village, Avon, about in the middle. To get to either end without transportation, and with a babe six months along in her belly, seemed daunting indeed just now.

The captain's gaze twitched down to where her hand rubbed at her stomach, then back up to her face. Did he soften a bit, or was it just the shadow as a fluffy white cloud skuttled in front of the sun? "Reckon it's possible he signed on with one of the fishing trawlers. Couple were taking longer trips along the coast. You go on into the village, you'll find the Armstrongs—Miz Caroline will know if he found work with her husband. She'll likely know if he signed on with Kit or Dave too. Just head to the church. She's usually around there this time of day."

The church ought to be easy to find, so she nodded. "Thank you so much for your help, Captain."

"Sure. Hope you find him soon."

As did she. And she hoped Marko had found a cottage or a flat, at least, somewhere, and that this Miz Caroline Armstrong knew where it was. Because from what she saw as she wheeled her trunk away from the dock and along the dirt road toward the smattering of buildings that made up the village, there wasn't a hotel or boarding house in sight.

She'd been alone since she boarded the steamer three weeks ago. Alone as she crossed the Atlantic, alone as she made her way through Ellis Island. Alone as she took the trains south that Marko had instructed her to take.

But she'd been alone in crowds, then. First in crowds of people like her, who spoke her native tongues. Then alone in crowds of other immigrants, or at least of other travelers. She'd seen people with every shade of skin, from fairest white to darkest brown. Every shade of hair, of eyes. Her own looks hadn't been so out of place in any of those places, any of those parts of the journey. Her dwindling coins had been enough to provide food and shelter at any number of vendors and small hotels.

Here, though, the world looked so different. Yes, Marko had deliberately sought out a small fishing village in a place southern enough to feel like their Mediterranean home. It was what they'd decided they wanted. A place where, yes, they might stick out at first, but where they could get to know their neighbors, integrate themselves into a true community.

Neither wanted to remain in the larger cities, where more Croatians or Italians could be found. They weren't city people. They were rural people, used to small villages like the one that tumbled before her, between the sound and the sea. They were used to the smells of fish and brine, of morning walks along the coast, of salt air and a world that revolved around the tides.

A big city like New York or Baltimore could never feel like home. Not to them. She'd visited the bigger town near their village often, since it was where Papa worked at the small university that she herself had attended, but it had never felt like home either. Just where they went for school.

Just now, however, she doubted their wisdom. The few people she passed as she walked looked at her with a careful sort of curiosity. They nodded a greeting, but no one spoke to her. No one asked her who she was or who she was looking for or what they could do to help.

But soon a white steeple pierced the blue sky, and a bit of the tension eased from her shoulders. Cap Barlow had said *the* church, so she had to assume there was only one in the village, and that she was looking at it.

As she drew nearer, she listened for the sound of voices and watched for any movement that might indicate Miz Caroline was about. She didn't spot anything promising outside, not at first, but she wheeled her trunk around the walkway that circled the church, wondering if she ought to try the big front doors or a smaller back entrance.

She had her answer as she rounded the final corner and spotted a smaller back door. On its step was a most blessed sign of life indeed—a little girl, sitting on the concrete step with a book in her lap and a straw hat shading her from the sun.

Another knot of tension unraveled. Children put Ana at ease in a way adults rarely could. "Hello," she said softly, stopping several feet away so as not to alarm the child. "What are you reading?"

The little girl looked up, but not with a start, and no fear entered her eyes at the sight of a stranger. She just grinned and lifted the book, revealing the title. *Alice in Wonderland.* "It's my favorite. I've already read it four times."

"Four times!" The girl couldn't be more than six or seven, so that was pretty impressive. "You have me outdone. I've only read it three times. What's your favorite part?"

"The tea party with the Mad Hatter." The girl scooted to the side and patted the place beside her in clear invitation. Her blue eyes had gone wide. "When did you read it? When you were a girl?"

"For the first time, yes. Probably when I was about your age. But my most recent reading was just last year. I read it to my students."

"You're a teacher?" The girl's eyes went wider still. "School's my favorite thing. But Mr. Walker had to go back to his family, and we don't have anyone to take his place yet, so I don't know if it'll start back up on time in September." Her rosebud lips moved into a pout. "And he took his books with him. Now I only have the ones Mama gets for me, and I've read them all over and over."

"That just makes them dearer friends." Ana eased herself down to the low seat, wondering how she'd manage to get up again without a helping hand. "I've reread my favorites so many times, I have many passages committed to memory. Although…" She tugged her trunk closer and unlatched it, opening it up to reveal the drawers and shelves within.

Her mother had shaken her head when she insisted on filling some of her precious cargo space with books. But what else was she supposed to do, leave her most precious belongings in Dalmatia? She'd rather try to replace dresses and stockings in this strange new place than her books.

Especially this set, which had always been her favorite. *The Secret Garden* by Frances Hodgson Burnett. First in its original English, then in French, Italian, and finally German. It was how her father had instructed her in the languages he knew—by having her read children's books in each.

It was even, in some strange way, what had convinced her she wanted to come to America. The book was set in England, it was true, but the author was American. And something about an American writing about a place other than where she'd grown up made her think that such things were possible here. That people were open to new places, to learning about them and putting themselves in the shoes of those from other countries.

That was the sort of place they would need. The sort of place that could someday be home.

"Have you read this one yet?" She pulled out the English version and handed it to the little girl.

Her companion first slipped a ribbon into her place in *Alice in Wonderland* and then reached with eager hands for the book. "I haven't!" She traced the gilt title and smiled at the matching illustration beneath it, on its field of green. "What's it about?"

"Well. It's about a little girl who grew up in India, who has to go back to England and live in the country with a distant relative, who isn't even there to greet her. He lives on a big English estate, and he has a son who is a cripple. She discovers that there's a garden that has been locked away, because the man's wife used to love it, but after she died, he couldn't bear to see it anymore. But of course, the little girl finds a way in. First she meets her maid's brother, who understands all of nature, and they become fast friends. And she soon meets her cousin, who is terrified of being a cripple all his life and is spoiled absolutely rotten. And together, the three of them bring new life to the garden—and to themselves."

The girl opened the cover. "It sounds lovely."

"It's a wonderful story. You're welcome to borrow it, if you like."

Blond brows shot up. "Honest? I would take real good care of it, I promise I would! I'm always very careful with my books, especially any that aren't mine."

"I can tell. Just look at the pristine condition of *Alice*!"

The girl clasped the new treasure to her chest. "I'll have to ask Mama first if it's okay."

Right on cue, footsteps sounded from inside, and the door behind them creaked open. "Susie? Who are you talking—oh! Hello there."

Ana gripped the metal rail beside the step and used it to haul herself back to her feet, smoothing her cotton dress with one hand and touching a nervous hand to her wind-torn chignon with the other. She turned to face the doorway, expecting to find suspicion in the woman's expression.

It wasn't there. Just an open smile as sunny as the sky, and eyes as blue as the little girl's. She was already reaching out a hand—the one not resting on her own baby-swollen middle. "Caroline Armstrong. It seems you've already met my daughter, Susie."

"She is a delightful child—and we share a love of books, it seems. I am Ana Horvat."

Caroline's face positively lit. "Marko's wife!"

And just like that, the unease inside uncoiled so fast it made her shoulders slump in relief. "You know my husband?"

"Of course! Jack signed him on for his fishing run after a few day trips together. Which—oh." Her face fell. "They won't be back for several weeks. This is their big summer run, and Marko had just been letting a room by the week. He didn't know whether or not to keep it, not knowing exactly when you'd be arriving, and hadn't wanted to spend the money for an empty room. He seemed to think you wouldn't beat him here."

"I'd had some trouble booking passage at first. My last letter indicated as much, but then a berth opened up last minute and…" She trailed off, her shoulders sagging in something other than relief now. "Perhaps you could direct me to this room? If it's still available?"

The pretty blond pursed her lips. "I have an even better idea. Why don't you come home with me for now? It's awful quiet in the house with only me and Susie, and I could use the company." She rubbed her stomach, grinning like a schoolgirl herself. "We can swap stories. Is this your first?"

Ana nodded. "It is. But I couldn't possibly impose—"

"Nonsense! It's no imposition at all. There's far too much room in that big ol' house, and I know once Marko gets home, he'll want to find a cottage for you."

Little Susie had stood too. Now, she bounced on her toes. "Please come! We can read the book together, and I can show you my dollies and all my other books!"

Something about the identical looks of hopefulness on mother's and daughter's faces stilled the arguments in her chest. This was what she had been praying for, wasn't it? Someone who knew where Marko was, someone who would befriend her. Someone who would show her that she was where she belonged, and not so alone as she'd felt after all.

Ana drew in a long breath and smiled. "It would be an honor to keep you company while our husbands are at sea. You are a true answer to prayer, Mrs. Armstrong."

The woman laughed. "Oh, none of that, now. Married women go by 'Miz' and their first name down here. So you'll be 'Miz Ana,' if that's all right with you. Though among friends, we drop the 'Miz' business too. Just plain ol' Caroline is fine."

Mere minutes' acquaintance, and Caroline was already prepared to dub her a friend? It was more than she'd dared to hope for, even as she'd prayed the Lord would make the way straight. It lit a flame inside her that burned like the candles she knew her mother was lighting for her in their home parish. Prayers, shining their way heavenward. Her fickle eyes wanted to fill with tears again, but she smiled to try to hold them back. "And Ana is perfect for me. Thank you. You can't know how much a relief this is."

Caroline pulled the church door shut and grinned. "We Southerners pride ourselves on hospitality, you know. And it seems you've already lent my Susie a book, so clearly we're destined to be friends. Come on—we're right down the road here, just a couple-minute walk. Can I help you with your trunk?"

Ana turned to relatch it, its weight suddenly seeming like nothing more than a breadbasket.

Maybe Marko was right—maybe this place was meant to be their forever home.

Chapter Four

Wes pulled the door closed behind him, somehow not at all surprised to glance next door and find that Kenni's car was already gone from her driveway. Seemed like whenever she was home, she made it a point not to be *home* whenever she could. The bookstore didn't open until ten, but she'd be there by seven, stocking shelves with yesterday's deliveries and tidying everything.

He liked books as much as the next person. And loved the shop that the Marshall family had poured so many years into. But sometimes he wondered if his old friend wasn't using it to hide from whatever it was she didn't want to face.

His phone dinged in his pocket, and he pulled it out while he jogged down the stairs toward a car parked under the raised house. Wynn—no surprise there.

Stop by Sunshine Bakery on your way in and I'll scratch two items off my Reasons Wes Is Wrong list.

He chuckled and swiped a reply.

Way ahead of you. So make it three items, because I didn't need to be told.

Don't push your luck, little bro.

He rolled his eyes at the moniker—his twin sister had been lording that five minute gap over him all of their thirty-one years. At this point, she was also claiming to still be twenty-eight, so she often called him "big brother" when it suited her.

After pulling open the door of his SUV, he tossed his bag into the passenger seat and hopped in. Cicadas thrummed from the grasses, a reminder that summer heat would bake the puddles into clouds of humidity by midday, despite the calendar insisting it was barely June. He slid into his seat and grabbed his sunglasses. He loved Avon in all its seasons—moody and stormy winters, brisk and biting springs, glorious lazy autumns. But summer was when the island showed the world its best.

Long beaches, long days, long sunbeams making vacation dreams come true for fifty thousand people every week. A far cry from the sleepy, empty roads of the off-season—which was why he couldn't dawdle on a Saturday morning. Outbound traffic would be a bear in the morning, and incoming would escalate to nightmare rates by afternoon. He always made it a point to be in the office by eight and generally didn't leave again until after six on summer Saturdays.

The water had mostly receded overnight, leaving nothing but a few puddles to splash through as he aimed south. The family's main office, Kenni's bookstore, and the bakery were all that direction, and the bakery came up first on his right. He parked in the mostly empty lot and was inside in seconds.

Cue all the mouth watering. He was a decent cook and baker, thank you very much—because he liked to eat, and Britta had hated to cook—but he could readily grant that he was no professional.

And that sometimes, you just needed one of the pastries that Sunshine set out every morning. They looked like edible art, from the flour-dusted ciabatta rolls to the sugar-dusted confections.

"Hey, Wes."

He smiled at Harper Dailey—fellow graduate of their class at the high school and recently returned to the island to help out after her dad's heart attack a few months back. "Hey. Wynn says I earn bonus points for stopping in this morning."

His old friend laughed and leaned onto her end of the counter. "What does she fancy today? Muffin? *Pain au chocolat*? Bagel? Sandwich?"

He blinked. "You've met my sister, right?"

"Okay, fine," she said on a laugh, before turning toward the pastry display. "Sweet for her, then. But what in particular?"

"Lucky for me, there's no bad choice." He eyed up the selections, pointing to a few. "Give me a dozen mixed donuts for the office, throw in one of the chocolate croissant things…and one of those new muffins in a separate bag for Kenni. I'll take the ham and cheese on ciabatta."

Harper had already been reaching for a box but paused, spun. "Kennedy's home?"

His brows drew together. "You didn't hear? Lara fell off the attic ladder yesterday, gave herself a nasty concussion. She's in the hospital."

"What? No!"

"Kenni, of course, rushed down. She's running the shop this weekend."

Harper drew in a long breath and then moved to fill his order. He couldn't look at her without remembering how Britta used to say she'd love to have hair her color—a rich red, currently pulled up in a sloppy bun. Though he'd eventually realized his late wife only said it so that he'd assure her he loved her blond hair.

He waited for the pang, the one that used to be a throb whenever he thought of his wife. It had dulled, but it was still there. That ache that said, *You're alone now. You're never going to get used to it. Never getting the chance to work things out with her. So get used to the pain.*

He'd never been alone, not until that horrible day just over two years ago. He'd been a kid living at home, then a college guy living with friends in the dorms and apartments, then married to his high school and college sweetheart. Sometimes the quiet still got to him. Sometimes he still rolled over in the morning and expected an eyeful of that sunny blond hair. Sometimes he still came home in the evenings and wondered why there was no other car parked under the house, why Britta wasn't home yet, why there was no one snapping at him to put his shoes away.

"Is Lara okay? I mean, other than having a concussion?" Harper shifted from the box of sweets to the ciabatta rolls. "Want this toasted?"

"Sure. And I don't really know. I mean, I talked to Kenni last night when she got in. Lara's awake and everything, but it must have been pretty serious. She was in ICU, up in Nags Head." He moved over toward the register while she slid meat and cheese onto the roll and popped it into the toaster oven. "I'm sure we'll hear more today."

"Tell Kennedy I'm praying. I'll try to pop over to the bookshop later today." While the toaster did its thing, Harper moved to her side of the register and tallied up the order. On—he couldn't help but note—a *tablet*. Not the ancient register her family had been using since the eighties. At least.

"Whoa. Look at that. Is that, like, twenty-first-century technology you've got there?"

Harper smirked and flipped the screen around on its nifty little swivel head. "Just came in last week—but don't tell my parents. I paid for it myself, because I can*not* handle that old thing anymore. Total's on the screen. Select payment method and follow the prompts."

"Nice." He selected credit, put the card right in the tablet, added a tip, and signed. "And your secret is safe with me, though I don't know how you intend to keep it."

"Oh, they'll find out soon enough, but by then, I'll have the old machine packed up and hidden away." She gave him a grin and moved to get his sandwich when the toaster dinged.

Wes chuckled. He and Wynn were lucky that their parents had already handled all the major updating at the family's real estate office, long before he and his sister started taking on more and more of the work so their parents could cut back their hours. The last big upgrade happened just a couple years ago—exchanging physical keys at all rental houses for keypads. Converting every single rental house had been a nightmare at the time, but now that it was done, everyone loved it. The staff because it cut back drastically on the crush during check-in and check-out for all the weekly rentals, and the vacationers because they didn't have to wait until four o'clock for their keys to be available. They could just get their code as soon as housekeeping was done cleaning each house.

Saluting Harper with his bags, he stepped away. "Thanks. See you around, Harp."

"I wish you all fortitude for the weekend."

The sun had cranked up another notch—it felt like the temp had gone up five degrees just while he was in the bakery. But he only had to drive another mile, splashing through a few more puddles, before he was turning in at the Island Bookshop, where Kenni's red Mazda was indeed already parked out of the way of the customer lot. Joe Wright's truck was there too, and the sound of hammering met Wes's ears the moment he stepped out again.

A few strides and he was on the porch that stretched across the front of the building, fragrance from the hanging flower baskets hitting his nose. On the door, the artsy Closed sign was still face-out, but he knew well it would be unlocked. The bell over the door jangled merrily as he let himself in. He looked around, seeing the usual shelves of books, displays of local art, and inviting bric-a-brac, all set against the bright and airy walls and windows…but Kenni wasn't in sight. He knew she'd emerge when she heard him, ready to smile and inform whatever customer hadn't paused to read the sign that she wasn't open yet.

Of course, when she came from the kitchenette—where she'd no doubt have put on the first pot of coffee of the day—her pleasant professional expression turned to that look he always thought of as pure Kenni. One part welcome, one part curiosity, four parts distraction. No unexpected visit from him could ever derail her from the to-do list she'd composed.

In the city, folks probably would have called her floral capris and coral top casual. The sleekness of her bob would have been expected. Down here, she looked ready for church, and he knew well his sister would have been muttering that the state of Kenni's hair, unfazed by humidity and wind, was just not fair.

But that was Kenni. She'd always been drawn to the sort of sophistication that the tides usually washed away on the islands. It was how he'd always known she wouldn't stick around. And he was proud of her—he was. She'd made something of herself. Chased her dreams. To look at her, even to listen to her, one would never know that she'd spent the first eighteen years of her life on an island nestled up against North Carolina's shore. She'd lost the accent, she'd lost the perpetual tan, she'd lost the laid-back style.

No. She'd just never had them—well, other than the tan. While Lara drawled with the best of them, Kenni had always mimicked the flat speech they heard on TV and the radio. Where most of them opted for shorts and tees, she'd always gone for dresses or tailored slacks and blouses.

But at least she knew the vocabulary of home. "Hey."

He grinned and held up the little white paper bag Harper had put her muffin in. "Breakfast."

Only Kenni would greet such a simple thing with a veritable hurricane of emotions flickering through her eyes. "You didn't have to do that."

"We both know you haven't eaten yet, and that you only brought yourself lunch, but that you'll be hungry by nine thirty because you won't actually pause to drink that coffee you say fills you up while you're dealing with the morning stuff."

She narrowed her eyes in a playful glare and snatched the bag from his fingers. "Can't we at least *pretend* I'm mysterious?"

He chuckled and moved to his usual chair in the gift section. Something about the arrangement of artwork, the cloud-soft skeins of yarn, and the mixed scents from various candles always put him at ease. "It's from Sunshine Bakery. New recipe Harper brought with her from Savannah, apparently, when she came back."

Pulling out the muffin, her eyes went wide. "Harper's back?"

"Yeah. Her dad hasn't been able to do his usual work since the heart attack, so she's running the bakery. Even got a fancy-schmancy POS system for check-out." He nodded toward the very similar point-of-sale tablet at the bookstore's own counter. "She said to tell you she'll try to stop by this afternoon."

"Nice. I haven't seen her in ages." Kennedy turned the muffin in her hand, examining it from all sides. "This thing's almost too pretty to eat. Cinnamon streusel?"

"With cream cheese filling."

She was already peeling back the parchment and breaking off a piece. A look of adorable awe washed over her face as she popped it in her mouth. "I'm in love with a muffin."

Wes laughed and pulled his sandwich out of his own bag. "What did Joe say about the roof?"

She already had a second bite in her mouth. "Should be fixable with the spare shingles, praise God. Said the wind must have just ripped a few off, then the sheer volume of rain wreaked its havoc, but the under-roof looked fine."

"Good. Hear anything on Lara yet today?"

She shook her head, her eyes moving toward the windows, as if she could see all the way to the hospital. "I texted Dad, but the doctors hadn't been in yet, and she was still sleeping." Even as she broke off another bite of muffin, she sighed. "You just never know, do you? When an ordinary day will go so wrong."

His throat went tight around his own bite. He could still remember like it was yesterday how he'd been laughing in the office when the state police walked through the door. The way his stomach had dropped when Kyle met his eyes. He'd known something had happened to Britta. Known it must have been fatal, since they'd come to find him in person instead of just calling to tell him what hospital to go to.

He just hadn't known in that moment that it would be forever seared into his memory—the smell of coffee and the Italian sub someone had been eating for lunch, the song playing in the background, the way the AC had just kicked on and given him a chill. A normal day, except that Britta had been heading to DC to spend the weekend with Kenni.

He'd been looking forward to it. Looking forward to a break from the mood Britta had been in. A weekend hanging with the guys. He and Asher were going to take a long bike ride, get some wings, and then go for a sail with Beckett the next day.

Then the words that had changed everything. Absolutely *everything*. "Wes—I'm so sorry. There was an accident on the highway, near Norfolk. Britta was killed."

He blinked it away. Thank God that yesterday's accident hadn't been as bad. Though a severe concussion was bad enough. "I know. But we all know how hard Lara's head is, right? She'll be fine."

Kenni breathed a laugh, and, more importantly, her shoulders relaxed a little. "True. Just an elaborate scheme of hers to get me down here, she said."

His lips twitched. "If she was joking already, then you *know* she's going to be okay."

"I know." But her voice said she didn't. Her voice said that she, too, knew how quickly life could be snuffed out. She'd not only been through it with Britta, she'd lost her mom.

Had their chairs been closer together, he would have reached over to squeeze her hand. Since they weren't, he had to settle for a small smile, the kind that said he knew how it hurt. "It's a Saturday in the summer—so you know what that means, right?"

One of her dark brows lifted. "Don't try to make a left turn?"

"Ha. Yes. But also, fish fry at Mom and Dad's after the office closes. Plan to come over—you'll need to eat."

He could actually *see* the arguments forming on her tongue, so he stood up before she could say them. "You will *not* be too tired, postponing your quiet for an hour won't kill you, and you know very well if you don't come, everyone in Avon's just going to be calling you all evening anyway to get the update on Lara. Admit defeat now and save yourself trouble."

She stood too, but that cute little crease was flashing in her left cheek, the one that only winked to life when she pulled that side of her mouth between her teeth. "I am so not mysterious."

He laughed again and moved to the door. "I don't know, you seemed it in that last video of yours, where you were talking about that volume of Shakespeare. I had to watch with a dictionary by my side."

She rolled her eyes and trailed him toward the door. "You did not. And why are you even watching my videos? Did you become a rare book aficionado when I wasn't looking?"

"Hey." He splayed his free hand over his heart. "I am hurt. Can't a guy watch one of his best friend's book videos just to learn something?" And he did, every time. How she could remember all the things she knew about old books was beyond him—but he watched every video she posted, just to hear what she'd say this time. To read the comments and see how impressed people were. To think that was his Kenni, all educated and flourishing.

"Yeah, yeah. You're just still helping me pad my views."

At the start, sure. But at this point, his one measly click and view was a drop in her audience bucket. "I watch because I like it." He pulled open the door and stepped out onto the porch...but rather than move toward his SUV, he just pointed himself south and sighed.

Wynn and her list of why he was wrong would be waiting for him at the office. And while the usual anticipation to get to work buzzed in his veins, along with the excitement over this new offer, dread curled its way around his shoulders too.

Kenni followed him onto the porch, frowning as she studied him. "What's going on? You okay?"

Never could pull one over on her. And if she hadn't already been on her way here by the time he got off work yesterday, he'd have sent her a long email already, or called her. "You ever use VaKayBo?"

When she tilted her head like that, her hair made a thick, dark curtain. "Melissa and I did last summer to book the Tahoe cabin, yeah. Why?"

"What did you think of them? I mean, compared to the other big online booking sites."

She shrugged, her frown not lessening a bit. "Felt more corporate than the ones run by the owners, but they had a good selection, and there weren't a bunch of fees tacked on at the end. And we weren't expected to clean before we left."

He snorted a laugh. "Though you did anyway."

"Well, *yeah*." A grin smoothed out her frown. "You don't grow up with the way of things here without the habit persisting. You're supposed to strip your beds and vacuum—it's just proper."

He wasn't about to argue. Rental agencies had a limited number of housekeepers and only so many hours in a day to turn every single house for the next occupants. Every little bit helped.

"Why do you ask?"

At that, he had to sigh again. "Yesterday—the reason I couldn't take Lara's call? I was on the phone with VaKayBo. They...they're looking for an in with the Outer Banks market and are wanting to buy out a local agency's rental side. We're their top pick."

"Wes! That's..." But she gaped rather than finish her sentence, eyes drilling into him. "I don't honestly know what that is. Exciting? Flattering? Horrifying? Tell me what I should be feeling here."

His smile felt slow this time, weak around the edges. That was the question, wasn't it? "I don't know either. Wynn's excited—I mean, we don't know what they'd be offering yet, but it could potentially be enough to let Mom and Dad really retire, and possibly pad the company for years. But...my gut reaction is to say no. They did make it clear they'd run it all from their corporate headquarters, which means we'd have to cut office staff, if we're only running the sales division. And...I don't know."

She stepped closer, rested her hand on his arm—she must have left her muffin inside. "Yes you do. That's the side you run, and the part you always loved—the hands-on stuff with the clients. Welcoming them all to Hatteras Island, making their stay special."

Because this strip of sand was the best place in the world, and he wanted everyone to think so. Wanted to make their week here the highlight of their year, because living here, helping run Armstrong Realty—that was a gift straight from the Lord. He lived in paradise, in a house he didn't even have to buy, because it had been in the family for generations. How could he *not* want to spread the blessing?

"Yeah. So...yeah. They asked us to get back to them within two weeks on whether we'd want to open negotiations, which would mean bringing in lawyers and disclosing all the financials. I just don't know. It's a big decision for us."

She gave his arm a squeeze and then dropped her hand. "I'll be praying for wisdom as you all decide. It *is* big. And of course," she went on, offering a smile that looked strangely forced, "if you need a sounding board, you know where I am."

Yeah—hundreds of miles away in DC, most of the time. Here now, but he could hardly impose on her time while she was only home because of Lara's fall. Phone calls and emails would have to do, like they always did.

It was enough. It *had* to be enough, because it was all she'd ever give him. And he'd take it, because any little bit of Kenni was better than no Kenni at all. Life without her...nope, not even worth contemplating. He'd suffered it before, and it had been miserable. He'd sworn years ago never to let her put distance between them again. No matter what.

He pasted on a smile of his own and nodded. "I know. I better get going and get out of your hair." He took a step toward the stairs, though he still paused again to level a finger at her nose. "Fish fry tonight. Don't try to get out of it."

Whatever had been forced eased again in her face as she rolled her eyes. "Fine. But only because that sounds *so* yummy."

He grinned and moved toward his car. "We'll take your company however we can get it."

The story of their friendship these days.

Chapter Five

Kennedy awoke on Monday morning and had to blink long and hard at the ceiling in her old room. It was still the same white it had always been, the ceiling fan still turned in its lazy circles, the sun still beamed through her east-facing window and made patterns through the slats in her blinds.

Last day here. And only a partial day. Lara had been released yesterday, praise God, and Aunt Grace and Uncle Tim had driven her home. She'd still had a killer headache, but she was asleep even now in the next room over. Bruised and swollen, but out of danger. Kennedy would spend some time today prepping meals for her sister for the week—Shaleen was back and would open the shop this morning—and then head out early afternoon for the drive home.

Tomorrow, normal life would resume. Kennedy would dive back into the collection from the Kensington estate. Have lunch with Melessa and give her all the updates, see how the third date with Mr. Cutie went. Organize her schedule for the week. Just a few more hours here. She could do a few more hours.

Pushing herself out of bed, she hurried through her morning routine, eager to get through her to-do list. She'd stopped at the supermarket last night and stocked up on easy foods for her sister's breakfasts and lunches, as well as what Kennedy would need to make dinners for the fridge and freezer.

They had other help covering Lara's usual shifts in the store this week—it seemed wise to assume she wouldn't be up to her usual workload. But hopefully she'd be feeling well enough by the end of the week to go in and do office work. Maybe even by midweek. Kennedy felt a little bad about leaving her alone here so quickly, but Lara had been the first to point out that Aunt Grace and Uncle Tim were right next door, as was Wes. If she needed anything, they had her covered.

As if in proof, Kennedy had barely flipped the lights on when a knock came at the door. She knew very well it would be her aunt, and let her in with a sleepy smile and a whispered, "Morning. Lara's still asleep."

"Good." Aunt Grace slipped in and shut the door behind her, toeing off her sandals. "Thought I'd come help with the food prep. What can I do?"

Kennedy pointed to the coffee pot. "First things first. Coffee and Bible."

"You got it." Aunt Grace gave her a mock salute and moved to the counter, shooing Kennedy toward the kitchen table where her Bible still sat from yesterday.

Soon the coffee was dripping happily into the pot, she'd finished her morning Bible reading, and Aunt Grace scrolled through the news on her phone. Once they'd both taken a few fortifying sips of coffee, they headed for the fridge.

Aunt Grace pulled out ingredients and handed them to Kennedy. "What first?"

"I'm thinking the soup. While it simmers, we can move on to the Swiss cheese chicken and potatoes. Then the steak for the fajitas, which is already marinating."

"Sounds like a plan." Her aunt divvied up the veggies while Kennedy pulled out two matching cutting boards. Within a few minutes, Aunt Grace was softly humming and they had most of the dicing done.

"Morning, Ken. Aunt Grace."

Kennedy hadn't heard Lara coming over the sizzle of oil in the stock pot, but she looked up with a smile. "Morning."

Aunt Grace spun to face her with that hawk-eyed concern she had perfected decades ago. "How's the head?"

"Head?" Lara rubbed at her temple. "Pretty sure you mean the… you know. The thing in a forge that they hammer on."

Kennedy frowned and exchanged a glance with her aunt. Yesterday when her sister had gotten home, she hadn't done much talking. She was in too much pain, and the doctor had warned them that she could be pretty out of it for about a week, that she'd likely do a lot of sleeping. If he'd said anything about an inability to find words, the warning hadn't made its way to Kennedy. "Anvil?"

Lara pointed at her in a "that's it" way and shuffled to the coffee pot. But rather than grab a cup and fill it, she just stood there, staring at the machine.

"Lara?" Kennedy moved to her side. Her sister blinked, turning her face toward Kennedy. The swelling was going down around her eye, but those eyes looked…glazed. Like they had in the hospital but, during that time, Kennedy had chalked it up to drug side effects.

Still could be, maybe? They'd sent Lara home with a prescription for some "good stuff" to get her through this first week—and cautioned her not to drive while on it. This behavior might well be the reason. "Did you take your pain meds yet?"

Lara shook her head. "Figured I'd...with food."

Pasting a smile onto her face that she was far from feeling, Kennedy put an arm around her sister's waist and steered her to the table, earning a nod of approval from their aunt. "How about you just sit down and let us pamper you a little this morning, okay? Aunt Grace will get your coffee and one of Harper's amazing muffins that I picked up yesterday for you."

"I should..." But rather than finish her sentence, Lara trailed off and let Kennedy herd her toward a chair. She sighed as she sat down slowly. "What are you two cooking?"

"Several things. Chicken tortilla soup is what you're smelling and hearing now, but I also have stuff for Swiss cheese chicken and steak fajitas that we're going to put together for you."

"You really don't have to do that, you know. I'm perfectly capable of cooking." She sounded groggy even as she said it.

Aunt Grace snorted her opinion into the fridge she'd opened again, no doubt in search of Lara's favorite coffee creamer, which she held when she closed the door.

"Hey, I was stuck in the shop all weekend and didn't get to fuss over you in the hospital—let me feel useful." Kennedy moved to the counter, where the container of muffins sat. "Besides, since when do you argue about Swiss cheese chicken?"

"Good point."

Kennedy grinned and set a muffin on a plate, delivering it to Lara just as Aunt Grace came over with a cup of coffee.

"I'll go grab your meds." Before Lara could object, Kennedy hustled to the bathroom, where she knew the bottle of pain pills had been put. And yes, she counted them first to make sure Lara hadn't already taken one and just forgotten. But the bottle was only missing the one she'd taken before bed last night, so Kennedy shook another into her palm. When she delivered it, Lara was slowly chewing a bite of muffin. She'd pulled her Bible forward but, so far as Kennedy could tell, she wasn't actually looking at any of the words on the page she'd opened to.

Kennedy squeezed her sister's shoulder and returned to her cutting board beside their aunt. Aunt Grace gave her a wide-eyed look that voiced the concern her mouth wouldn't, not with Lara right there. They finished chopping in silence and added the veggies to the onions sizzling in the pot. Whenever Kennedy glanced over, Lara's eyes weren't tracking across the page, though she was staring at it. "You okay? Reading giving you a headache?"

"I...maybe." She sighed and pushed the book away. "I don't know, I just...I can't seem to hold the words in my head."

Alarm screamed in Kennedy's ears as Aunt Grace cleared her throat and said, "Don't push yourself too hard. The doctor warned that since you've had concussions before, the symptoms could be bad this time. I thought he said you could be a little better in a week or so, but normal things might be hard right now. Things like reading could make the headaches worse."

Lara gave a listless nod. "Too tired anyway. Maybe I'll..." She motioned toward the sliding glass door. "With my coffee."

The fact that Lara willingly gave up even a moment of reading told Kennedy how bad her sister really felt. With a silent nod to Aunt Grace to take over in the kitchen, Kennedy hurried to intercept her as she stood. "Let me help carry your stuff out."

"I can handle my own coffee cup, Kennedy," she snapped.

Kennedy lifted her brows. And took both the coffee and the muffin, seeing how her sister wobbled. "Humor me. I still owe you for the way you nursed me back to health that time I got sick in college, remember?"

A gust of breath passed Lara's lips. She didn't so much agree as relent, but Kennedy didn't regret insisting, given the way Lara reached from one object to another to steady herself as she walked. Come to think of it, she'd been trailing a hand down the hallway wall as she stepped into the kitchen earlier too.

To be expected. Balance was a delicate thing, after all, and hers could well be off for a while.

Lara pulled the sliding glass door open and stepped outside. From a step behind her, Kennedy felt the wave of heat roll in and hurried to follow so she could shut the cooler air in again. "Upper deck or table?"

"Upper."

That was Kennedy's favorite place to have her coffee too, where she could sit on one of the benches built onto the deck and see either ocean or sound, depending on which way she turned her head. Though she hadn't taken the time to go up there this morning.

She probably should have—she hadn't all weekend, and she'd regret it when she got home and was relegated to morning coffee with a view of nothing but the townhomes across from her.

Or maybe...she chewed on the corner of her lip. Maybe she should take the week. She had the vacation days to spare, and the way Lara took one step up, knuckles white on the railing, then stopped, made unease prickle along Kennedy's nerves. She turned slowly, reaching for the opposite railing, and stepped back down, blinking rapidly. "Actually, the table makes more sense with the muffin."

Right. It had nothing at all to do with the way her sister swayed. Kennedy smiled and moved to slide the coffee and breakfast onto the table to the left of the door, so she could offer a steadying arm if Lara needed it for the trek over the open deck.

Which she did, though when Lara took Kennedy's arm it was with a vague smile. "I'm humoring you."

"And I thank you for it." Even if she seriously doubted it. She made sure Lara was safe in a chair before heading back inside.

Once the door was shut between them, she drew in a long, unsteady breath and locked gazes with Aunt Grace again. "Tell me the inability to find her words, the unsteadiness on her feet, that hollow look in her eyes...it's just those 'more serious' symptoms they warned us about, right? It'll all clear up in the next few days?"

The shake of her aunt's head wasn't so much denial as bafflement. "No idea, Ken. We can only pray so."

Shoulders slumping, Kennedy moved back into the kitchen. Had the doctors given them all false hope? All along, she'd planned to only stay a couple of days. Clearly Lara wasn't herself. Even if some of the severe symptoms did clear up in time, what about those next few days? "She shouldn't be here alone if she can't navigate stairs unaided or remember how to pour her coffee."

Her aunt put her knife down and moved to slip an arm around Kennedy. "You know I'll be here. I'm only two doors down and—"

"And you have obligations, commitments." Yes, she knew her aunt would drop everything to help. But how could Kennedy just leave it all to her?

And she would feel better if she were here to keep an eye on Lara herself. Otherwise, Lara would likely soften her reports when Kennedy asked—she always did. It was that big sister thing. She always thought she had to protect Kennedy, even from the truth.

Aunt Grace rubbed a hand up and down Kennedy's arm and then moved back to the counter. "I think the real issue here is that you're just not ready to go home yet. And I can't blame you for that. But you have obligations too. We should pray about it."

Well, there was no time like the present. "Lord," she whispered as she dumped more soup ingredients into the pot, "what should I do? Any guidance would be welcome."

Aunt Grace grinned at the simplicity of the prayer and said, "Amen." She glanced out the window, presumably checking on Lara.

The question simmered along with the pot as they finished the soup and pulled the chicken ingredients out of the fridge. Kennedy's phone rang just as she was reaching for the glass baking dish she'd need. "My boss," she said for her aunt's benefit. She swiped to accept the call and smiled into the phone. "Hi, Pam."

"Morning, Kennedy. Just wanted to check in. How's your sister?"

Her gaze flashed to the glass door. No Lara making her way inside to overhear. "Honestly? Not great. I mean, she's out of the hospital, but she's unsteady on her feet, can't seem to remember what she was doing, and can't hold what she's reading in her head."

"Is that common with a concussion?"

"They warned us she could have some bad symptoms for the first week or ten days, given that she's had prior concussions—soccer player. Took one too many cleats to the head in high school."

"Do you need to take a few more days?" Kennedy could hear mouse-clicking in the background. "Doesn't look like you have any meetings or tours this week. If you need to stay down there, it's a good time to do it. Melessa can keep working through the Kensington collection."

Obviously able to hear both sides of the conversation from where she stood a step away, Aunt Grace grinned and mouthed, *Answer to prayer?*

Sure seemed like it to her. She let out a long breath and did the math. For now, she'd take the doctors at their word. Even if it took the full ten days for the last of the symptoms to clear, that would put things at the end of next weekend. "You know, I think that would be a good idea. Lara would never *ask* me to stay, but I don't like the idea of leaving her alone when she's having trouble with the basics like that."

"And you know I'm all about family first. You've got lots of vacay yet, right?"

More than she ever used, honestly. Why take vacations when she loved her job so much? "Tons. Can you put it in for me from there, or should I log in?"

"I gotcha, Kennedy. You'll get an email in a minute, but no worries. You just focus on your sister, and we'll see you next week."

"Thanks, Pam." She disconnected and turned to the stove.

"See there?" Aunt Grace said, chuckling. "Ask and ye shall receive an answer before your sister even comes back inside."

Kennedy smiled, but her mind spun far beyond the kitchen. *Family first.* Those were words Pam said time and again, to any member of staff when they had pressing issues at home. Kennedy had always nodded her approval, because *of course* family should be first.

But something like guilt tickled the back of her neck. She'd never actually had to make the choice to put family first, not really. Because her family had never asked—or needed—her to choose them over her career and her life in DC, other than coming home for Grandma's funeral. Sure, they teased about how rarely she came home...but they also understood. Aunt Grace would have canceled all her own plans for the week to stay here with Lara, had Kennedy decided to return to DC today. Dad had never done anything but cheer for her as she sought out her dream job and chased her goals.

And Lara—Lara was the one person in the world who knew her *other* reason for avoiding Avon. She had in fact been the one to hold Kennedy while she sobbed when Wes and Britta got engaged after freshman year of college. The one who had taken on the no-nonsense tone of Older Sister and given her the advice she'd lived by ever since.

"You can't be in love with your best friend's husband, Ken. If you can't squash these feelings, then you give it to God and you honor both them and Him by steering clear. Stay away from Wes until the feelings die. And they will."

Kennedy's response had been something snotty and snarky, if she recalled. Something along the lines of, "How do you know that? You've never been in love."

But her indomitable sister had just lifted her chin and looked her square in the eye. *"I'm not speaking from experience. I'm speaking from faith. God promised that you'll never be tempted beyond what you can bear. Wes is your temptation, so you bear it, and if you can't, you do what Paul said to do—you flee."*

She'd fled, as much as Wes and Britta had let her. Mostly. There was that one time she'd tried to voice her doubts about them...and *that* had gone so well that she'd decided Lara was right. Her only option was to steer clear of Wes, which meant steering clear of the whole island.

Except, even following that horrible conversation a month after the engagement, Wes didn't seem to get it. He continued to call and text and email whenever they weren't in the same place—usually group threads that Britta was in too.

But after the accident two years ago?

Kennedy sniffed, blaming it on the onions when her eyes burned, even though their sting had faded twenty minutes ago. She'd been doing well, up until then. Mostly. She went months at a time without any pangs, and the ones she experienced were understandable, she'd thought. Only when Britta would do something so...*Britta*. So thoughtless and selfish and downright horrifying. Like when she'd send Kennedy a photo of some hot guy she'd been flirting with. Kennedy had always just replied with *You're married.* But internally, yes—she'd had thoughts of *You don't deserve Wes. He never should have married you.*

But she'd managed to stop her thoughts before they turned to *He should have chosen me.* She trained herself to pray for them, for their marriage, in those moments. She wouldn't say she'd *conquered* her feelings, but she'd wrestled them into submission. When she was home, she focused on Britta and only ever saw Wes in a larger group. When in DC, she'd never shied from meeting new people and going on dates, knowing well that finding her *forever* love could be the thing she needed to get over her *first* love. She'd done exactly what her sister had advised, and she'd reaped the benefits.

Until Britta died. Until Wes had turned to *her* for comfort. Talk about opening Pandora's box...but she kept shoving the lid back on.

Because even if Britta hadn't deserved him, he'd still loved her. He *did* still love her. He didn't know how horrible his late wife had been to him, he didn't know...any of it. And he wouldn't. Kennedy had tried—once—to speak to him about Britta's behavior, and Wes had lobbed a painful accusation at her: *"You're just jealous."* She had no intention of trying again.

While Aunt Grace arranged the chicken she'd been trimming in a baking dish, Kennedy popped the top of a can of cream of chicken soup and spooned it into a bowl. He'd been right, then, and she couldn't risk speaking the truth until she was sure that was no longer the case.

A text buzzed, and she glanced at her smart watch to see it. Melessa. Mr. Cutie may well be Mr. Right! We had the best weekend!!!

Kennedy smiled and wiped off her hands so she could reach for her phone. I want to know everything.

Dancing dots soon turned to a reply. Too much for text. When will you be home? I'll just stop by.

She sighed. She typed in her reply. Staying here for the week. Lara's pretty out of it, I don't feel comfortable leaving her yet. Pam just approved it. Maybe a call later?

Of course! Tell Lara I'm praying for her!

"Well, that's a nice smile. Who you texting? Some cute guy?"

Kennedy's head snapped up. Lara was stepping back through the sliding door—her hands blessedly empty, at least, since by the time Aunt Grace rushed over, she was already inside. "What cute guy do you think I'd be texting?"

"I don't know. Didn't you say Melissa was trying to fix you up on a double with her new boyfriend's brother?" Lara motioned toward the phone. "Maybe you went out with him and haven't told me yet. Is he going to welcome you home tonight with…you know, those flowers you like? The red ones that are cliché."

Kennedy had definitely made the right call. This was not at all similar to the way Lara had been three days after her last concussion. "Roses."

"And a six-course meal."

Kennedy pushed aside the concern and smiled as Aunt Grace assisted Lara to one of the chairs at the breakfast bar. "I declined the double date, so alas. No flowers or elaborate meals waiting for me in DC. Which is just as well."

"Why would that be just as well?" Lara frowned and positioned herself carefully on the chair, somehow managing to smile a thanks for their aunt without smoothing the question from her brows for Kennedy.

"Because…" Her sister was going to argue. She knew she would. But there was no help for it. "Pam called and suggested I take the whole week—it's going to be slow there. Given that I have way more vacation days than I need, I agreed." With a bit of luck, the new smile she donned would look bright and innocent. "So you're stuck with me all week."

Lara's frown became fierce. Or maybe just looked that way because of all the bruising. "No way. You are not postponing your life for me, Sis. Aunt Grace, tell her."

Their aunt's expression was pure innocence too. "Why? I'm glad she's staying. We don't see enough of her." She punctuated it with a loud kiss to Kennedy's cheek as she passed by, on her way back to the baking dish.

Lara sighed. "I am perfectly fine—"

"Don't insult me," Kennedy said. That shut her up. Momentarily, anyway. "If it were me with a concussion, where would you be?"

Lara held her scowl a moment more, then sighed. "That is totally different."

"Why?"

"Because I'm your *big* sister. It's my *job* to take care of you."

Kennedy rolled her eyes and added milk to the bowl, Aunt Grace chuckling beside her. As she whisked, she said, "You are a whole fifteen months older than me. And what's more, you've done such a great job of it, I actually turned out pretty well. Responsible adult, organized, totally capable of rearranging my schedule for a week so that I can return the love." She gave an exaggerated bat of her lashes. "Argue with me. I dare ya."

Instead, Lara held up her hands, palms up. "Okay, okay. I relent. Mostly because...I'm really glad you're staying too. I mean, I'm sorry you'll be missing so much of going through those books from the rich dude. But I feel better knowing you're here."

She knew how hard it was for Lara to ever admit needing help. So she gave her a cheeky smile as she poured soup over the chicken cutlets in the baking dish. "That's just because I'm making you Swiss cheese chicken."

"Making *us* Swiss cheese chicken." Lara leaned back against the rungs of her bar stool. She tried a cheeky smile of her own, though it still looked shadowed. "But not only that. There's a big shipment of books arriving on Tuesday too."

It felt good to fill the kitchen with laughter. Maybe her decision to stay wasn't for a reason any of them would have wanted—but it would be good to spend the week with her family.

Usually, the early morning setting-to-rights was Kennedy's favorite part of the day in the shop. Not that she didn't love the time spent with customers too, but there was something satisfying about opening all the boxes of treasure that had been delivered the previous afternoon, scanning each book into inventory, and then finding their proper places on the shelves. About tidying up any mess from the previous day and making sure the store looked beautiful and ready for today.

On Wednesday, however, Kennedy's mood was far from sunny, and it had nothing to do with the aching back muscles from the truly enormous shipment of books that arrived yesterday, nor with the humid heat assaulting her as she bent down, baggie in hand, to pick trash from the gravel of the parking lot.

Sweat dripped into her eyes as she found a cluster of cigarette butts and food wrappers. What, had someone just stood out here chain-smoking and eating while another member of their party browsed for hours? How had this much garbage accumulated since she last checked the lot after closing up on Saturday? And why couldn't people walk the ten feet to the trash can?

"Wow, that is quite a scowl. Should I come back?"

She straightened, letting her face relax and then smile as she spotted Harper rolling in on her bicycle. "A distraction is quite welcome." Harper had never been in the Kennedy-Britta-Wes trio, but she'd always been a good friend. They had in fact roomed together for two years during college, and though for some years now they hadn't seen each other in person, they kept in touch.

Harper parked near the porch and left her bike in its shade. "What's up?"

"Lara." Deciding that was enough litter cleanup for now, she tossed the baggie into the trash and motioned for Harper to join her on the glider on the small porch. "She had a follow-up appointment yesterday with her primary care. Aunt Grace is with her now."

"Yeah?" Harper sat beside Kennedy, concern knitting her brows. "How did it go? Did you mention Lara's problem finding words, the poor balance and spaciness?"

For a moment, all Kennedy could do was nod. She stared out at the parking lot, at the narrow strip of road, at the houses beyond. The shop was on a little ridge that was about as high as ground got around here, close to the sound and farther from the ocean—meaning that, in all the time this had been family property, the house-turned-shop had never flooded in a storm.

They'd weather this too. She knew they would. She just couldn't picture what that would look like right now, as the proverbial rains were lashing down. "Dr. Lee had done some research and was pretty concerned about it, especially since she hasn't really seen any improvement in that or in her motor coordination. Said that it's possible…it's possible she has brain damage."

Harper sucked in a breath. Reached for her hand. "Seriously? Like…irreparable?"

Kennedy shrugged. "Too soon to know, but he said she might need therapy, if it continues. And even then…" She had to pause, swallow, look to the heavens for fortification. "Given the severity of the injury and the fact that this is her third concussion, he said it could take months if not years for her to get significantly better. That she may be close to nonfunctional for a while. He referred her to a specialist in the city. Lara, of course, doesn't think she needs to go."

Lara had tried to prove it, when they got home from the hospital. Prove herself capable of handling what she'd always done. She'd sat down with her laptop and pulled up the shop's books, and…half an hour later, she'd been sobbing.

She couldn't make sense of the numbers—she kept interposing them when she tried to type them in, even though she swore she knew what she *wanted* to put in. And reading…she'd been trying to do that in the afternoons, but she always gave up after a few minutes, saying she felt nauseous. Lara didn't seem to draw the connection between the reading and the nausea, but it was obvious to Kennedy.

Then there were the times she just stared blankly at something, even though she clearly *thought* she was working. She'd taken an hour yesterday morning to answer an email that should have taken five minutes, and she'd felt so sick afterward she'd had to go lie down. She *said* her dizziness was better, but she was still leaning on walls as she walked, especially up any stairs.

There was no way Kennedy could leave her like this. She wasn't in any condition to live alone, and while they had family that could help with that part, what about the shop? There was no way Lara could handle the business portion right now, and their clerks hadn't been trained to do that side of things.

"But it *could* get better?" Harper's fingers went tight around Kennedy's.

Even though she nodded, tears still stung her eyes. "Yeah. And we'll be praying it does, of course. But…but it's not better *now*, and it won't be by Monday, barring a miracle. It may not be for *months*."

For a moment, the only sound was the traffic on the road and the gulls crying overhead. Harper would understand what Kennedy wasn't saying.

That there was no way Lara could manage the Island Bookshop right now. That they had no idea when she'd be ready to again. It could be in a couple weeks. Or it could be in a couple months.

She might never get better.

Kennedy had said all the things she could think to say to Lara yesterday—that the doctor had said her injury *may* improve quickly, as the last of the swelling went down. That it *might* just be temporary. And even if it wasn't, they'd learn to adjust. There were workarounds to each problem. She'd already looked them up. Special glasses to help with the disorientation, shaded ones to help with the pain from bright lights, noise-canceling headphones, screen-readers for phone and website.

This wasn't the end of the world. Lara was a fighter. She'd overcome this.

Heat wrapped around Kennedy even in the shade of the porch, and it felt like fear in her stomach. Fear for her sister, for all of Lara's dreams. And a selfish bit of fear for herself, and for *her* dreams.

Because she knew what she had to do, and she didn't want to do it. She didn't want to move back to Avon. She didn't want to leave her life in DC. But what was the alternative? If Lara couldn't run the store...then what? Sell it? Their grandmother's legacy, the thing they'd both grown up loving, the place that had always been a safe haven for them both? She couldn't do that.

As Harper reclaimed her hand, Kennedy looked over at her friend. She might be the only person who could understand this, given her own situation. "How did you do it? Make the decision to come home? I mean, I *know* how, I know it's your family, but..."

The turn of Harper's lips was more commiseration than smile. She tucked an escaped strand of hair behind her ear and looked off toward the sea grass that waved beyond the parking lot. "I had to do a lot of telling myself that it wasn't forever. That coming now doesn't mean I can never reclaim my life in Savannah. But honestly? It stinks. I had to give up my apartment. Quit my job. And *those* things are never going to be there again, most likely. I'll find another job, another place to live, but not the same ones. That's hard. I worked for years to get there, you know? In a lot of ways, this feels like I'm back at square one. Back at my first job."

Exactly. That was exactly what it felt like. Like regressing. And Kennedy didn't just have an apartment, she had a *house*, with a thirty-year mortgage. She had enough in savings that she could afford to keep making her payments for a few months if she wasn't getting a paycheck from the library, but not beyond the summer.

Even if she took more of a salary from the shop, they couldn't afford to pay both her *and* Lara, so that money would have to cover their living expenses here.

"But," Harper said on a sigh, "I'd make the same choice again. Maybe Sunshine isn't as glamorous, but it's a community institution, and we have people who come in and say they choose Hatteras Island as their destination every year because it wouldn't be vacation without our pastries. And of course, it helps Mom and Dad out, which is the most important thing." The wind sang through the chimes hanging at the corner of the porch while Harper took a long breath. "They mean for me to take it over, of course. In a few years. I've always known it, but I thought it was another decade away, maybe more. Far enough out that I could just not think about it."

Kennedy nodded. "I honestly thought I'd just be the silent partner here forever. Helping with decisions, lining up authors to visit, handling some of the management stuff that can be done from a distance...but Lara's the one who's good with people and loves the daily tasks." She said yet another prayer that the brain injury would heal fully—and quickly. Then glanced at her watch. She had to get back inside soon, before Shaleen's shift ended at three. "Enough serious stuff. Distract me."

It was an old joke, from their college days—they'd unintentionally distracted each other so much that they knew they could rely on each other for the task when one of them just wanted to put off homework.

Harper laughed, her face brightening. "Well, as it happens…I came by today with ulterior motives. I had an idea."

"Oh, your ideas are always good." She angled herself to better face her friend. "Hit me with it."

"I was thinking that you could stock some Sunshine goodies in your shop, back in the kitchen area. You could charge the same amount that we do, but keep a percent. It wouldn't be a lot, but it would be more exposure for us, and it would keep people in the shop longer."

"I love that, actually." She stood, angling for the door and motioning Harper to join her. Thinking about something like this felt like progress—on the bookshop front, at least.

She led her friend through the front room where four adults browsed, down the bookcase-lined hallway that housed the young adult books, where a teen girl had her nose in a historical mystery that Kennedy had read and loved, and finally into the kitchen. Which was currently the only room without customers, despite the free coffee.

There was clearly room to improve this area. She surveyed the shelves with their cookbooks and other house-related topics, like gardening. They had a great selection, but these books didn't move as fast as others.

She spun toward the stretch of counter they'd left intact when they remodeled, which currently looked a bit forlorn with only a coffeepot on it. "We've talked for a while about doubling down on the kitchen area and making it more of a coffeeshop nook with goodies for sale. We just hadn't pursued the idea enough to think through where to source the goodies. This is perfect, though. We were thinking of changing out the coffee pot to a super-automatic too, capable of espresso as well as regular coffee, and then charging for it."

"I think that would be a great upgrade for you guys." Harper grinned and appeared to size up the counter space with her gaze. "You've got plenty of room for some pastry displays, and the mini fridge will do for your coffee creamers and milk and such. Run it by Lara, of course. And then when she says yes, just let me know when to start deliveries."

Kennedy laughed. It didn't change the hard decision she had to make…but it did give her something concrete she could accomplish. One small thing she could control.

Chapter Six

Though the beaches would be crowded before midday, at five thirty on a Friday morning they were all but empty—just how Kennedy wanted it. She'd gotten down here in time to watch the sunrise, breathing in peace as God painted the sky with the most beautiful colors on His palette.

She'd made the right decision. The best one she could make. The family had a long talk last night over pizza from Gidget's—she and Lara, Aunt Grace and Uncle Tim, even Dad and Deanne after ferrying over from Ocracoke. Lara, of course, had tried to object and tell Kennedy she couldn't give up her life in DC for an injury that would surely improve in a couple weeks…but her sister hadn't been very convincing, given the splitting headache that made her wince and the sunglasses she'd had to wear inside for the last few days.

The ocean was glassy this morning, the wind a barely-there wisp that danced around her as she walked northward, toward the uninhabited stretch of dunes. She kept her pace brisk enough to count as exercise, glancing down every few feet to look for any truly special shells that caught her eye. Those finds would join the collection that surrounded the bushes and flowers in front of the bookshop.

Pam had known Kennedy would be talking to her family last night and had told her to call her cell once she'd made a final decision. Lara had already brainstormed the options with her, and it had been her boss who had come up with the one she'd decided on—to take a leave of absence for the summer. It would be unpaid, but it would mean the job would still be hers if she came back by September. It was a kindness Pam hadn't been required to offer, and one Kennedy couldn't turn down. Three months would give them enough time to know whether Lara could step back into her role at the bookshop, and in what capacity. And Kennedy would be able to continue making house payments without a paycheck during that period.

She hadn't told Melessa yet, or any of her other friends in DC. Melessa, she meant to talk to in person this weekend—she had to go home long enough to pack more than the few outfits she'd thrown in her bag last Friday. Pack up her plants. All the other things she'd want for the next few months. She had to open the shop today, but another of their clerks, Caitlyn, would come in at noon and close out. Kennedy would leave then and drive home, spend the night there, and pack up tomorrow.

Not that she'd be able to fit much in her car, and Lara's was no bigger. She'd ask Tim if she could borrow his truck, but he kinda needed it every day as a contractor.

A wave tumbled to shore and raced toward her with enough energy to make her dance out of its way, lest it soak her shorts. The water was warm this morning, making her smile—unlike two days ago, when it had been so icy that it sent shards of pain through her feet whenever it caught her. That was the Atlantic in early June for you—couldn't make up its mind from one day to the next whether it wanted to be arctic or Caribbean.

Her watch buzzed that she'd walked a mile, so she did an about-face and turned south, the Avon Pier now in her view where it stretched out into the water. She'd yet to pass anyone else walking, but she saw several figures in the distance now, and at least one of them seemed to be heading her way. The form, little but a silhouette from this distance, soon resolved into a man—and further into a familiar one, jogging toward her.

She sighed. She knew, of course, that Wes did his morning run on the beach around now, but she'd done a great job of avoiding him thus far. He usually headed to the pier, since these dunes would be roped off any day now to protect the nesting birds, and people would be forbidden to even walk the waterline, to keep from disturbing them.

She'd hung out at his family's fish fry on Saturday for an hour, but she'd mostly talked to Harper and Wynn. And though she'd expected him to drop by another time or two to talk about the VaKayBo offer, his visits had only been long enough to check on Lara and drop off a meal his mom had made for them, and then he'd vanished again. Suited her fine. Sort of. It *should* have, anyway.

Just as she should hope he'd simply jog past her with a smile and a wave…but she was instead stupidly happy when he slowed, circled around her, and fell into step beside her. "I thought you jogged," he said, voice teasing, as he slipped his earbuds out of his ears. "What's this slow amble you're doing?"

"It is *not* a slow amble. I don't like running in the sand."

"There are sidewalks."

By the road, sure. "Can't see the ocean from the sidewalks. I figured walks would suffice this week." All summer, though? She'd have to pick. Or get over her aversion to getting sand in her shoes.

"Heard you were driving up this afternoon to pack."

Which meant he'd also heard that she'd be home all summer. Not surprising, given the light-speed capabilities of the island gossip chain. "Yep. I'll be back tomorrow with all my stuff—so if you want to help me carry it all in..." She flashed him a grin and gave an exaggerated bat of her lashes.

He grinned right back. "Do you one better. We can take my SUV. It'll fit more than the two boxes you could squeeze into your little car."

"Wait—we?" Did he just say *we*? "You can't come. Tomorrow's Saturday."

His laugh was so very Wes—not at all offended at her rejection, just full of amusement. "I am aware of the day of the week. But it's my Saturday off."

She raised her brows and untangled a strand of hair caught in her sunglasses. "And you want to spend it on the road?"

"With you? Absolutely. The week turned so crazy we've barely had time to catch up."

And see, *this* was why her stupid heart was still stuck on him after all these years. He said things like *that*.

"Your house has a spare room, right? And I can finally try that pizza place you swear is as good as Nino's and Gidget's. Then you'll have my extra muscle to haul everything for you, and you won't have to drive ten hours in the course of twenty-four."

The help *would* be nice…but this was a bad, bad idea. "I was…going to get together with a friend while I was home."

His eyebrows flew up. "Like…a date?"

Did he sound jealous? For a moment, she could almost convince herself of it. But she knew better. It was wishful thinking, nothing more. That note that she wanted to think was jealousy was just surprise. Which was not a great boost to her ego, especially since it *wasn't* a date. "No. Just Melissa. She said she'd help me with the packing."

"Right." He grinned. "I still haven't met her. Perfect opportunity."

Kennedy made a point of not looking over at him. Melissa had long wanted to meet her "beach guy friend" too, but Kennedy had always found a reason not to bring Melissa home with her. She'd never admitted why, not out loud.

But she knew. She'd already had to watch Wes fall in love with one of her best friends. She couldn't do it again. And yet she knew it could happen. Melissa was wonderful—how could he *not* see that and start falling? Sure, there was Mr. Cutie now, but that was still in the early stages and could easily be derailed by someone better coming along. The only thing that might prevent it was the fact that they lived so far apart.

How many times had Melissa joked that she'd give it all up to live somewhere like Avon, though? Every time Kennedy went home for a visit, Melissa made some comment about how if that was where *she* was from, no fancy job would have lured her away. *"Most people work like a dog all their life so that they can* retire *to a place like that, Ken. Why in the world would you give it up just for a job?"*

She wasn't about to admit her insecure and selfish thoughts to Wes—just like she hadn't admitted to Melessa that it was far more than the job keeping her away. Better to just dismiss it entirely. "The point being that Melessa will help, so there's no reason for you to make the trip."

His dubious look was so sharp, she felt it poking into her face until she gave up and glanced at him again. Yep. Not convinced at all. "I have no doubt she'll be helpful while there," he said. "But the fact remains that Mitzi can barely hold your purse, much less the boxes of books we both know you'll bring home with you."

Her chin came up. "So lend me your car."

He didn't even deign to respond to that, though the suggestion was perfectly logical to her mind. "And while we're on the subject of your social life—"

"We are *not* on the subject of my social life."

"Let's discuss when you *did* last have a date."

If he wanted to just ignore her reasonable comments, she could do the same with his nosy ones. "You know I'm a good driver. I can be trusted with your SUV."

He sighed. "I know you think it's none of my business, but I worry about you, Kenni. I worry that the time and effort you've put into chasing your career dreams comes at the cost of your personal dreams. I don't want you to wake up one day and realize that life has passed you by. You're thirty-one."

She glared at him for that oh-so-helpful reminder. "Lara's thirty-*two* and single. Do you give her this speech?"

He rolled his eyes. "Lara lives in a place with a local population of four thousand. Eligible bachelors aren't exactly in abundance." Of course, this being Wes, it was only a second before another grin flashed. He slung an arm over her shoulder. "Maybe she should send to the mainland for a mail-order groom. Sounds like one of your books, doesn't it?"

It kinda did, which meant she was laughing again instead of returning to the argument as to why he shouldn't come with her. Though she did shrug out of his one-armed embrace under the guise of evading an enthusiastic wavelet set on splashing them.

Which meant he returned to the subject before she did. "So what time are we leaving today?"

"*We* are not."

"Don't be stubborn, Kenni. You know you want my help, and it'll be fun. Isn't driving with a friend way better than making the trek solo?"

Totally. "I was going to listen to an audio book."

"And we still can, if you want. That's more fun with a friend too. We can talk about it. Our own little book club."

She watched a line of pelicans glide over the waves, and though she shook her head at his argument, she knew he wasn't going to give in. He never did when he'd decided he wanted to help someone. She'd just have to hope that Melessa was seriously serious about Mr. Cutie. "Fine. We leave at twelve-thirty. But we do not discuss my love life or lack thereof. That's my condition."

"Fine. Though that means you owe me cannoli along with the pizza."

"Done."

He glanced down at his watch. "I better hustle if I mean to finish my run. See you at twelve-thirty."

Kennedy waved him off and picked up her own pace too, since they really had slowed to an amble as they talked. Soon she was letting herself back in the house, showering, and gathering everything she'd need for the morning at the shop. Lara still wasn't awake, but she knew Aunt Grace was going to check in on her sister before going in for her shift at the museum, so she contented herself with a little peek into Lara's room, then headed out.

The bookshop was all golden light and stillness as she let herself in, making her smile. Maybe this wasn't the life she'd chosen, but walking in here *did* still feel like coming home in the best way. There was something about rows and shelves full of books on a quiet, sunny morning that spoke peace into her soul.

The summer wouldn't be so bad, Wes-related difficulties notwithstanding. She did love time spent in the shop. And if she was going to take over Lara's usual tasks for the summer, then that justified taking over the office too, right? After shelving the new arrivals, she stepped into the office and flipped on the light, smiling with perhaps a bit too much glee.

Lara had plenty of firstborn tendencies—like bossing Kennedy around and being over-protective—but the organizational gene that Lara had inherited, in what one might deem a normal amount, had come to Kennedy at double strength. She'd been itching to rearrange the office for years but had never dared. She'd long ago learned not to mess with Lara's systems, even if they *could* be improved.

But now...

She snapped photos of each area so she could reference them when she turned it all back over—which she had to believe would happen in a few months—then rubbed her hands together and got to work.

Twenty minutes later, she was shoving the desk to its new home in front of the window when Harper appeared in the office doorway, brows raised. "Guess that's why you didn't hear me come in. Need a hand?"

"I wouldn't refuse it."

Harper took one side, making it far easier to get the vintage desk into position. She then looked around with furrowed brows. "I assume this will eventually result in *more* order, but it looks like a hurricane swept through."

Kennedy laughed. She had, of course, emptied out all the furniture before she could hope to move it all around on her own, so there were currently piles and boxes in the middle of the floor. "It'll be neat as a pin by the time we open. Did you get the goodies set up?"

Lara had agreed wholeheartedly—if groggily—with the plan to add baked goods from Sunshine Bakery…and even to upgrade the coffeepot. They'd picked out a Jura Automatic together last night, which should arrive on Monday.

And by the time they'd finished scrolling the website together, Lara was feeling nauseated and had a headache. Kennedy had taken note, even though her sister dismissed her concern—the doctor had told Lara to avoid screens for a week or so, until the glare stopped hurting her eyes. Lara had said it didn't anymore, but…well, Kennedy honestly didn't believe her. Not given how it made her feel after a few minutes of browsing.

"I just dropped them off and came looking for you, actually. Figured you'd have opinions."

Kennedy snorted another laugh. "It's like you know me or something. Help me with the filing cabinet real quick, and then we'll detour to that so you can get back to the bakery."

They scooted the last big piece of furniture to where Kennedy indicated and then moved to the kitchen. When Grandma Janey had redone the house into a store, they'd taken out the big kitchen equipment and many of the cabinets, but left one wall with a counter, its cabinets, and a mini fridge where the dishwasher had been. The rest of the space had been turned into shelving for cookbooks and other home-related titles, as well as a reading area where the table used to be.

Harper had brought some cute little racks with her to display individually wrapped muffins and the like, and Kennedy had dug out a domed glass cake pedestal for donuts and a cupcake display, both from the store of party supplies Mom had collected over the years. She'd already checked health code regulations months ago for selling things like this, and knew they'd be fine as long as nothing was open to the air—it all had to be either wrapped or in a closed display.

As they decided where to put everything and filled the displays, adding price cards or stickers, Kennedy shared about the short trip back to DC to get her things—and how Wes had invited himself along. Harper didn't know about her stupid lingering feelings, but she got a good laugh out of Wes's determination to help even when he was dismissed.

"You should make him listen to some totally girly rom-com in the car," she proclaimed, trailing Kennedy back to the office rather than making her excuses and heading back to her own shop.

Kennedy grinned and picked up an armful of hanging files to reload into the cabinet—she'd been careful to stack them in order, to make for easy refiling. "I have a few waiting that would accomplish that goal."

Her friend really must not be in a rush. She plopped down in the cushy leather executive chair and made herself comfortable. "I like the rearrangement in here. Why didn't Lara have the desk facing the window to begin with?"

"She finds it too distracting." But Kennedy had worked hard to rate an office with a window in DC, and she wasn't about to deprive herself of the perk now. She loaded another armful of files, and another, until the cabinet was full again. She slid the desk drawers back into place, then turned to the items she hadn't catalogued so easily. Namely, unmarked boxes Lara had piled up in a corner.

Knowing her sister, one held random computer parts and wires and cords and spare keyboards and the like. She wouldn't be surprised to find another containing office supplies. The one on top, however, made her frown. It was clearly an old box, dusty and even carrying a few cobwebs on the corners, and when she pulled the lid off, a stale smell reached her nose, along with the scent she'd been trained to recognize at first sniff—paper mold.

Interesting. "I wonder…"

"What?" Harper, apparently still as game as ever for even a hint of mystery, propelled herself closer in the chair.

"I wonder if Lara pulled this out of the attic." Had there been boxes stored up there? Kennedy honestly couldn't say. It had been so long since she'd been up there, and she'd never lingered long enough to explore—something about the shadowy space with its bare bulb had struck her as creepy as a kid, and the tight space had made her wonder if she was more claustrophobic than she thought.

The box was packed with books, which wasn't exactly a surprise. She pulled out a few pulp paperbacks whose covers made her think they were from the 1960s or so...and of course, she had to flip one open to check the copyright page, just to see how close she was. The smell when she did so was enough to make her wrinkle her nose and set it aside.

"Old books?" Harper leaned in to get a better look. "Anything good?"

Kennedy pulled out the rest of that stack of paperbacks. "I don't recognize any of the titles. Just look like mass market romances and mysteries. I'm guessing they must have been favorites of Grandma Janey's, if she kept them—though I don't know why she left them here, rather than moving them when she came to live with us."

She took out another paperback from the next pile, but the books beneath it were hardcover. She set the soft one aside and drew in a sharp breath. The hardcover on top was definitely *not* from the 1960s. It looked older than that to her eyes, and her eyes were pretty good at these things. She lifted it out carefully, smiling at the gold design on the green fabric. "*The Secret Garden.* Looks like..." She flipped the cover with careful, trained fingers, and turned the first page, eyes seeking out the date. "Yep. First edition."

"Nice. I assume."

"It is—but it doesn't mean it's particularly valuable, monetarily speaking. For one thing, it was stored in a box with molding books—I don't see any infesting it in the obvious places, but the spores could still be there." She fanned a few pages close to her nose. Not as strong an odor as the others, which could mean it just had residual smell from them, but...well, everyone knew how mold liked to spread. "And this was clearly a well-loved copy. Look how worn the pages are." Soft as velvet on the edges—which was lovely from a tactile perspective but not what a collector would want to see.

Harper grinned. "Should I get out your phone and record this for your video channel?"

Kennedy breathed a laugh. "Sorry. I can't see an old book without snapping into professional mode."

"Hey, I get it. I can't eat bread or dessert at another restaurant without trying to name all the ingredients and figure out the ratios." Her friend leaned into the arm of the chair. "*The Secret Garden*. I know I read that as a kid, but I don't remember much. I mean, I know there was a garden. And the girl started out as a brat. And... something about eating potatoes outside that were roasted over a fire or something."

This time, her laugh was fuller. "Wow, that is quite a summary. 'Brat of a girl finds a garden and eats potatoes.'"

"Also, 'Read it, I remember liking it.'" Harper reached toward the next book in the stack, and her smile faded. "That one doesn't look like English."

"Hmm?" Kennedy hadn't even looked at what was beneath *The Secret Garden* as she drew it out—that training again. Her eyes had been focused solely on the item in her hands. But she frowned too as she read the title. "*Der geheime Garten.* German. For...*The Secret Garden*, if I'm not mistaken. That's a little odd, isn't it?" She pulled it out and handed it to Harper. Then shook her head. "*Il giardino segreto.* Pretty sure that's also *The Secret Garden*, just in Italian."

"If the next one's the same book in Swahili, I'm going to be really impressed."

Kennedy removed the Italian version and laughed. "How about French?"

"Not quite as exotic, but I guess it'll do." Harper flipped the German version over in her hands. "Why would your grandmother have had the same children's book in four different languages? Did she know them all?"

"I don't think so. She talked about taking Latin in high school, and she knew a few words in Italian, but just the usual ones—greetings, good night, that sort of thing." Definitely curious. She opened the Italian copy, surprised to see a folded piece of paper inside. A letter? The paper looked awfully thick for such a thing. She set the book down and unfolded the sheet—two sheets, actually.

Her eyes went wide. "Wait. This is...this is a *deed*. To this house. Dated 1938, listing it as the property of...Ana Horvat?" She moved that sheet to the back and saw a second deed. For the same property, dated 1957.

For a moment, the blood rushing into her head was all she could hear. They'd been looking for this deed ever since Grandma Janey passed away nine months ago, so they could close out the estate. Given that there'd been no one to contest the will, their lawyer had assured them there wasn't a huge rush on finding it and filing it in their names, but if they couldn't locate it by the year mark, he'd said they'd have to make a trip to the Register of Deeds office for Dare County—which was up in Manteo—and pay for a duplicate to be made of the one filed there. Not a big deal, just enough of an inconvenience that Lara hadn't taken the time to do it yet.

And now she wouldn't have to. Which was good, because it had totally slipped Kennedy's mind, given that she wasn't the one here dealing with this stuff every day, and Lara was in no state to remember any such details right now.

Her eyes scanned over the information, catching on the name.

She'd been crouching, but at the sight before her, she fell back onto her rear.

"You okay, Kennedy?"

"Who's Marija Horvat?"

"What?"

Kennedy thrust the paper toward her friend, a strange tightness in her throat. "Grandma Janey said she'd gotten this place from her mom when she turned eighteen, which would have been in 1957. But this deed is dated 1957, and it's made out to Marija Horvat."

Harper took the sheet, her expression more cautious than panicked. "Maybe…I mean, then this has to be your grandmother, right?"

"Her maiden name was Marshall too, just like her married name—didn't you ever hear that story? How hilarious it was when she went to college in Raleigh and fell in love with a man who had her same last name? Marshalls on both sides of the family, though no relation. My grandparents never tired of telling that one." And *Janey* certainly wasn't a nickname for Marija—which she assumed would be pronounced like Maria, despite that *j* in there.

Janey Marshall—that was all she'd ever heard her grandmother called. It's what she called herself in all her stories, what they'd put on her tombstone, for crying out loud. Wouldn't Dad have known if his own mother's real name was something else?

Kennedy rubbed at her forehead, letting her eyes slide shut. She had a feeling she knew what "real estate emergency" Lara had called Wes about last week. But what in the world did it mean?

Chapter Seven

"Kenni, don't panic." Wes cradled the phone between his ear and shoulder so he could use his hands to haul the last box of welcome totes to the back door, where their housekeeping staff would drop in throughout the afternoon to grab the quantity they needed. "There is no way your grandmother was living all those years in a house owned by someone else."

"So then she's lied to us all her life about her real name?" Given the disbelief in her voice, she didn't think that was a better option. "Come on. She preached honesty above everything."

"I'm sure there's a perfectly logical explanation." He slid the box onto the table by the door, flashing a smile at one of the housekeepers approaching even now. He pushed the door open for her before she could reach for it, stepping out into the muggy heat to make room for her. Angling the phone away from his mouth, he said, "Morning, Lisa. You're in early today."

She gave him a wide smile and patted his arm as she walked by. "Got a busy afternoon with the grandbabies. Figured I'd better pick these up now."

Ordinarily he'd have offered to carry them to her car for her, but he knew she only had five houses on her schedule this weekend, which meant one box. He'd be just as helpful holding the door. "Tell Corey and Halee I said hello."

"I sure will."

In his ear, Kenni was saying, "I am a perfectly logical human being, but I cannot think of what this 'logical explanation' could be. We've been looking all over the place for this deed. It wasn't in Grandma's little safe-box with her car title and bonds and bank info, which never made any sense. What if...what if she was hiding it? That she didn't actually own the house?"

An incredulous snort slipped out before he could stop it. "Kenni, come on. That makes zero sense."

"Oh, you talking to Kennedy?" Lisa stepped back out, pleasure on her face. "Hi, Kennedy!" she said loudly toward the phone. "Hear you're home for a while—stop by and see me sometime."

"Is that Lisa or June? I can never tell them apart on the phone."

The two sisters did sound an awful lot alike. "Lisa." Anticipating what she'd say next, he said to Lisa, "She says hello, and she'll swing by some time after work."

"*So* not mysterious." Kenni sighed.

Lisa was smiling. "I'll have cookies for you, sweet thing."

Lisa *always* had cookies. Which was one reason no one ever minded obeying when she commanded them to stop by. Another was her sparkling personality, of course, but that went without saying.

"She says she's drooling just thinking about them," he said, though Kenni hadn't said anything more.

Lisa moved off toward her car, whose trunk was already open and waiting for the box of totes. Wes stepped back into the cool interior of Armstrong Realty, refocusing on the topic at hand. "Look, if you're worried, let's just stop at the Register of Deeds office on our way up the road today."

"Manteo isn't exactly on the way."

"Closer than we usually are to it though. It won't be that big a detour." Frankly, he didn't know why Lara hadn't done that months ago—the very thought of not settling the estate because it required an hour's drive was just ridiculous.

But Lara hadn't seemed to be in a rush, and neither had their lawyer, apparently. So Wes had told himself it was none of his business and stopped asking.

Although… "If you're truly concerned about this, you should be calling Mack, not me. Which is what I would have told Lara a week ago."

"You really think she'd want to go to a lawyer and say, 'Hey, what if we don't actually own the house we've been occupying for the last few decades? What happens then?' Um, no. That makes it all, like, legal and stuff."

Patrick McDonald might be a lawyer, but he'd also been going to the same church as the Marshalls and Armstrongs for…well, forever. He was a friend first, lawyer second. But even so. "You're his client. He's not going to report you to whatever authorities you think are just waiting to snatch your bookstore from you—he's going to help you sort it out."

"I just…" She trailed off, huffed. "Let's do Manteo. I'm sure there's just another, newer deed on record. I don't know why this one was in the attic, but maybe it came with the place…or something."

Which made no sense at all, if it was dated 1957 and Janey had gotten it from her own mother in that year. But pointing that out clearly wouldn't keep Kenni calm. So he simply said, "Perfect. It shouldn't take all that long, and then we'll be back on the road. Still get to DC in good time."

"Okay. Thanks—I'll let you get back to work. I see customers pulling in anyway."

He glanced at his watch as he turned into his office. It was still half an hour before the shop supposedly opened, but they'd always operated on the principle of "if the door's unlocked, I won't turn away anyone who comes to it." They were a bit more structured here, but it was a different sort of business. "All right. See you at noon-thirty."

She laughed a bit at how he phrased it, said goodbye, and disconnected.

He set his phone on his desk and sat down. He barely had time to do more than wake his computer from sleep with a shake of his mouse before his sister strode in and flopped into one of the client chairs across from him.

"Wanna trade me weekends off? I need a break." She let her head fall back, stretching out her legs.

She did look tired—no doubt the fault of Hannah, his adorable nine-month-old niece who still wasn't sleeping through the night. Ordinarily, he'd have agreed to the switch without a second thought. He didn't care which weekend he had off, or even if he had any. Not like there was much luring him home anymore. "Can't. Riding up the road with Kenni to help her move home for the summer."

That snapped Wynn's head back into normal position—and brightened her eyes too. "Kennedy's moving home for the summer?"

He tsked and shook his head. "Wynn, Wynn. You are seriously disconnected from the gossip chain if you haven't heard that already. It's been the plan for a whole day now."

She rolled her eyes—the same blue as his. By nature she ought to have had the same medium-brown hair too, but she had "remedied" that a decade ago with the help of an overpriced salon and regular applications of dye that gave her instead a headful of auburn hair with some blond-ish highlights. He thought it was a little silly, but he could grant it looked good.

And Everett clearly agreed—the day trader relocating from New York had taken one look at his new real estate agent and tumbled straight into love, he said. Everett and Wynn married a year after they met, four years ago now. They'd just presented the grandparents with their first grandchild nine months ago.

Another pang Wes forced from his mind. He and Britta had been trying for a year before she died. He'd wondered time and again if their failure to get pregnant had been part of what put Britta in such a mood those last few months, part of what was building walls he'd kept trying to scale but had never managed. She'd never talk to him about it.

Wynn leaned forward, eyes twinkling. "So...you're driving all the way to DC with her? To help her move?"

He knew that tone of voice. Knew it all too well. "Don't."

"What?" No one could feign innocence like his twin sister. She had it down pat, right down to the hand splayed over her chest. "I'm only *asking*."

"You're never only asking." She'd been on a crusade the last six months to set him up with someone, anyone, everyone. Any single woman between the ages of twenty and forty seemed to be fair game in his sister's mind, and she never listened when he told her he wasn't ready to date again.

The all-innocence hand dropped. "But Kennedy would be *perfect* for you, I've always said so. You should have asked *her* out in high school instead of—"

"*Don't.*" This time, the snap in his voice made her lips press together. It was one thing for her to have insisted in high school that he'd asked out the wrong best friend. She'd had the good sense to stop saying it after she'd failed to talk him out of proposing, after they got married. But the fact that his wife was dead didn't mean she could start questioning his wisdom in marrying her all over again.

Heaven knew he'd questioned it enough himself. No one else got that honor.

She had the grace to wince. "Sorry."

"And it's irrelevant. I didn't ever consider her then for the same reason I wouldn't consider her now—she was never going to stick around here, and I never want to leave. Basic incompatibility." A truth that hurt no less today than it had when they were fifteen.

Kennedy might love him like a brother, but not enough to stay. Never enough to stay.

When Wynn held her hands up in surrender, her expression shifted enough that he believed it. "A valid point. So I will instead simply encourage you to talk over the VaKayBo deal with her while you drive. She's always had a good head on her shoulders and should be a good sounding board."

Which, in Wynn-speak, meant she thought Kenni would convince him to take the deal. "Already intended to." He glanced, as he did multiple times a day, at the paper with the VaKayBo logo he'd printed out and had sitting on his desk.

They had one more week to express interest. And yeah, he knew that opening negotiations didn't mean they were saying yes. They had to see an offer before they could decide, even if he were as excited as Wynn. He knew that signing this confidentiality agreement was a perfectly reasonable thing to do. Get the ball rolling, see what they were thinking. See if it was worth it.

He just couldn't think of a number high enough to tempt him. He *loved* this work. Not just helping people find their dream homes when they were looking to buy, but helping them find it for a week's stay. A sliver of escape or fun or relaxation. He loved scheming what to put in the welcome totes that would bring a smile to the vacationers' faces. He loved giving them passes to the company's pool and seeing how many people reserved the same house year after year because they loved it so much.

And how would it even work, to only run the sales side? So many of their homeowners went on to list rental properties with Armstrong Realty. It would be weird to help buyers settle their purchases and then just say, "Yeah, sorry, you can't list the rentals with us."

"Wes, I can *see* you overthinking this again." Wynn leaned forward and rested her hand over the confidentiality agreement. "It doesn't hurt to see what they're offering. We're not committing to anything. But don't you want to *know*?"

Discover what some company headquartered in New York City thought their family's legacy was worth? Not really. "I don't think it matters. I don't want to give this up."

"You don't even know if you'd have to! They could well want to keep our staff running things on the ground."

Unlikely, from what poking around he'd done online last week. "That doesn't seem to be how they run things. All their service calls are routed through their main number."

"Which could dispatch to a local office from there. You don't know. You're just creating objections based on assumptions." She met his gaze, held it. "I love this place too. I love what our family has built, and I wouldn't just sign it away for a shiny enough penny. But this has the potential to change the lives of everyone here. I think we should at least hear them out."

How could Wynn understand? She had *more* to her life now than Armstrong Realty. She had a husband, a daughter, and would likely try for another baby in the next year. This wasn't her whole world anymore, not like it was his.

The thing was, if he said as much, it would only make his family more determined, because they all insisted it *shouldn't* be his whole world.

Honestly, they had a point. It hadn't always been this way. He'd had a wife before to pull him home…even if she wasn't always there and wasn't always engaged when she was. He had no delusions about his marriage—he knew they'd had their problems. But he also believed they would have weathered them. He never would have given up, and Britta wouldn't have either, out of stubbornness if nothing else.

But that wasn't his reality now, and he didn't know when or if it ever would be again. He just couldn't…couldn't imagine investing that much in another person again. Not because he didn't want to, but because he still felt so numb, so often. He wouldn't have traded the years with Britta to avoid the heartache of losing her, but that didn't mean he was eager to invite that heartache again. And he knew all too well that life offered no guarantees.

This office, this business, this legacy. It had no guarantees either, of course, but it was the one thing in recent years that was stable, solid. It was what got him up in the mornings, what kept him going all day. Maybe the reason he was resistant to learning more about the VaKayBo offer was because he didn't want to shake that. Didn't want to rock the boat even a little. Not when it served as his life raft.

Wynn patted the paper and stood. "Talk it over with Kennedy this weekend. We'll revisit on Monday." The way she said it, he knew very well that she was actually thinking *We'll sign the form and get the ball rolling on Monday.*

He offered a tight-lipped smile. "I will."

They strode out of the Register of Deeds office into glaring afternoon sun, Wes leading the way back to his SUV while a too-quiet Kenni marched behind him. He could feel her simmering with pent-up questions, with all the unknowns nipping at her.

Kenni didn't do well with unknowns. It was why she loved her work so much. She could ask all the questions, find definitive answers, and use that information to deliver a certain answer to her clients. She could value a book based on set criteria. She could investigate, use her knowledge to make decisions. When there were rips and tears, she could fix them. Preserve what was worthy.

But the copy of the deed they'd just looked at had given her none of the answers she wanted—it was an exact match to the one from the attic.

Wes waited until they were buckled into his SUV with the AC blasting before he ventured a glance at her profile. "Well...now you know where to focus your investigation, anyway. You're trying to figure out how your grandmother was really Marija Horvat. That's the only explanation. There's no way she was living all those decades in a house that didn't belong to her. That kind of thing just doesn't happen in a community as small as ours, not without everyone knowing."

Kenni sighed and adjusted her air vents, then slipped her sunglasses on. "Then shouldn't they also know who she really *was*? I've been wracking my brain trying to remember any mention of Horvats, but I'm coming up empty. I called Dad, and then talked to Aunt Grace, but they both said the same thing—that they had no memories of it, and Grandma Janey just didn't talk about family history all that much. They asked her why, once, and she just said, 'Well, I guess we just don't talk about some things.' That's all they could get out of her."

Wes frowned, backing up and maneuvering out of the parking lot. "My grandparents were the same way. I remember being shocked to learn a couple years back that my mom's cousin lived with them for four years during their childhood. Apparently the situation that required it wasn't a happy one, so...they just buried it, in a way. Didn't talk about it at all. Mom just made some off-handed comment about it, then seemed almost embarrassed when we asked what she meant. I guess maybe it's a generational thing."

She gusted out a sigh. "A rather inconvenient one, thank you very much. I don't even know where to start with this."

He flashed a grin at her, looked both ways, and pulled out onto the highway. "Just pretend it's a book."

With a laugh, Kenni said, "I don't think my usual resources will help me with this one."

"No, but there are other resources instead. Online newspaper archives, family documents, even other old-timers who might remember. Which means a great way to plug back into the community this summer—and I'm going to pretend I don't see the way your face twists up at that."

Another glance showed her cheeks flushed. "It's not that I don't love the people."

"Just that you don't want them to suck you back in? Attach those anchors to you?"

"Seriously, Wes. Just *pretend* you can't read my mind now and then, won't you?"

He chuckled and tapped his in-dash display to start the navigation to her townhouse. "Hey, now. I spent a lot of years perfecting my Kenni-mind-reading skills. You can't ask me not to use them."

She stuck her tongue out at him.

He laughed. "So sophisticated."

But she grinned and settled in, relaxing a bit. That was something. "What can I say? You make me revert to my thirteen-year-old self."

"Things were simpler back then, weren't they? Nothing but lounging on the beach and ice cream runs."

"You have a very selective memory. Or else being a thirteen-year-old boy is far different from being a thirteen-year-old girl. I distinctly remember body image issues, social anxiety, fighting with my parents about the amount of time I wanted to spend curled up with a book, arguing constantly with Lara…"

"You clearly misplaced the rose-colored glasses I sent you a decade ago."

Her laugh was a beautiful thing, always had been. "Actually, I still have them. They're just not all that useful in a southern summer sun. They're at home."

By which she meant where they were headed, not where they'd come from. "Well, pack 'em up, Kenni girl. You might need them."

"And how about you?" She angled a bit toward him, though he kept his eyes mostly on the road. "How are you feeling about the VaKayBo thing?"

He drew in a deep breath and shared his thoughts, along with Wynn's and their parents'. She listened in that active way she had, asking for clarification here or there without offering any thoughts of her own until he'd run out of his.

Then she sat for a long moment, contemplation evident even in her profile as he glanced over briefly. Finally, she drew in a long breath of her own. "Well, here's my take. I think you should at least see their offer, if for no other reason than your family will always wonder what it would have been if you don't. That doesn't obligate you to anything."

Wes nodded, because he knew she was right. In a family business, he couldn't just focus on what *he* wanted, not in something like this. Certainly not at this stage.

"That said," she went on, "I think your family will have to keep in mind that the rental side of things is *your* baby. Wynn focuses more on sales, so this will impact her less than you, and your parents have already taken some steps back and do general oversight more than hands-on in one particular area. If you go through with this deal, *you* are the one most impacted. That means your voice and opinions get a little more weight, at least from my perspective."

And just like that, a bit of his anxiety eased. Because *yes*, that was why he felt this differently than his sister would. He just hadn't quite pinpointed it that clearly—but Kenni had always been able to read his heart and mind as easily as he did hers.

Well. Mostly. There were a few things he'd made it a point to guard from her. But those things weren't what they were talking about. "Good point. You wanna be the one to tell them that?"

She laughed and leaned her head against the rest. "Sure, if you need me to."

"And while you're at it, you could parry a few swipes for me about making work too much of my life. Not that Wynn said it outright, but she's hinted that this could be good for me *because* I spend so much time on it."

Kenni shook her head, lips pursed. "Maybe you *have* sunk yourself into work a lot these last couple years—but what do they honestly expect? I'd think they'd cut you some slack and be glad you've had something good and meaningful to focus on. And it's not like you've cut off your friends or anything. Right?" She faced him. "I know you keep in touch with me, and I have to assume you do the same with everyone else."

He nodded. But then shrugged. "The guys aren't as good at text and email as you, but I try to get together with at least one of them once a week. It's hard juggling everyone's schedules, but I'm no recluse."

"Then I'm happy to tell them to back off, if you need me to." She gave him a grin. "Always easier to stick up for someone else with their family than argue with my own."

He could chuckle at that.

Their conversation moved into more general catching up, but never flagged enough for her to break out the audio book she said she'd picked for them. They laughed, they talked about the collection she'd been working on at the Library of Congress before she got the call about Lara, he shared some funny stories from the office… normal stuff. Stuff that made his chest feel lighter than it usually did. And even when they got into beltway traffic, he felt better than he had since the first call from VaKayBo had come in.

Kenni had that effect on him. Always had. It was what made him count her as one of his best friends, even though she only came home twice a year and he'd rarely visited her in DC. It was what made him wonder, time and again, what might have been, if she'd ever for a moment considered staying home.

But then he saw with his own eyes what drew her away. He gave a whistle when she pointed to her red-brick townhouse. "Nice digs. You're really big time now, aren't you?"

Her laugh was sunshine and birdsong. "For a librarian, sure."

He shot her a glance and pulled into her driveway. "You're not a normal librarian, Kenni. Not that I don't love a good librarian, mind you, but you do way more than that."

Which she obviously knew, but still she shrugged. "I am merely pointing out that this is hardly one of the giant houses you sell and rent, but it's exactly what I was looking for. Three bed, two bath, nice living and kitchen space, but little exterior yard to manage. Nice neighborhood without being too posh for my pocketbook."

"I like the feel of the neighborhood, for sure." He threw the car into park and got out, eager to stretch his legs and get a better look.

She'd just shut her own door when someone called out "Kennedy!" from a car parallel-parked along the street.

Melessa, he'd bet, based on the woman's enthusiastic wave and quick steps toward them.

"I got your text," probably-Melessa said as she drew near. Proving she *was* Melessa, to his mind. She was the only one Kenni had mentioned texting. "I'm ready to get packing." Her gaze, of course, tracked to Wes.

Well, no one had ever accused him of being shy. He came around, hand held out. "You must be Melessa—Kenni's told me all about you." More or less. "I'm Wes, her best friend from home. Grew up next door and volunteered to play pack-mule for her."

They shook, and Melessa's smile turned curious as she moved it from him to Kennedy. "Wes...Armstrong, right? I've heard about you too. Glad you were able to come lend a hand. Though Kennedy didn't mention she was bringing reinforcements."

Kennedy fished a keyring out of her purse. "The day turned kinda crazy. I'll tell you all about it while we get to work." She sent Wes a look he couldn't quite interpret.

Cautious? More like warning. But why she thought she had to warn him about Melessa he couldn't figure out, despite all her claims that he could read her mind. She knew well he'd be nice, right? Polite. Friendly. What did she think she had to warn him of?

Before he could figure it out, the three of them were moving inside, and he decided not to spend any more time wondering. For now, he'd focus on getting Kennedy back to Avon for the summer. And on trying to convince his stupid heart not to hope she'd stay this time.

Chapter Eight

Avon, North Carolina
June 13, 1938

Ana closed her eyes, let the warm summer breeze caress her face, let herself breathe in the familiar scent of sea and salt and pretend it wasn't coming from a whole other sea in a whole other country. Let herself think, just for a moment, that she was *home*.

There were parts of this new place that, over the last ten days, had become familiar enough to make it possible. The laughter of little Susie wasn't so unlike the laughter of her nieces and nephews. Conversations with Caroline were warm and heartfelt, if in English instead of Italian or Croatian.

The paths from porches, across dunes, and to the surf looked different and yet welcomed her like the ones she'd tread all her life.

Marko hadn't chosen this spot for them to settle without thought. She learned a bit more each day as to why this was the place he'd chosen, this the home he wanted to give their little family. It was a quiet community, a peaceful one, filled with beauty. And to Marko—who had never met a stranger—it was no doubt one filled with friends within a day or two.

Ana had never had quite so easy a time of that. She was more comfortable with a book in her hand than in a crowd, and even if her English was technically better than her husband's, he never hesitated to try bantering in it, even if he risked saying something wrong.

She rubbed a hand over her stomach, where the little one within poked her with foot or elbow or knee. A smile tugged at Ana's mouth as she massaged the spot. "Be gentle with your mama, now," she chided softly, the whisper in Croatian, even though she'd tried to school her tongue into remembering English. Sometimes, first thing in the morning, she had to indulge just a bit. Just with her baby. Just in her prayers. A bit of who she'd always been, before she had to stretch into whoever she'd become on these new shores.

The little one moved even more, tracing an arc across Ana's belly that made her grin. How much longer till she got to hold her bundle of joy? They'd calculated that the baby would be born in mid-September, but Mama had said she looked to be a little further along than that, before she'd left. She wouldn't argue if her baby joined her sooner. Would it be the son Marko dreamed of? A daughter for her to usher through all things feminine? Either way, a blessing.

And to think—this child of theirs would be born an American, just by arriving in the world on this little island in North Carolina. This child wouldn't know the horrors of Mussolini's regime or the fear of being judged and hated because of where their family lived. God willing, he or she would never stare down hate-filled eyes that threatened death just for being born the "wrong" ethnicity.

The screen door screeched, bringing Ana's head around to see which Armstrong girl was coming to join her. Caroline emerged, using her hip to open the door. Both hands were filled with steaming mugs, and the wind was quick to catch the scent of the coffee inside and bring it to Ana's nose.

She smiled and rose to reach for one. "You didn't have to do that. I was coming back in soon to get a cup."

Her hostess dismissed Ana's comment with a wave of her now-free hand, just as she had yesterday. "Habit. I always bring Jack his coffee out here in the morning, summer or winter. Rain or shine. Isn't a day at home that he doesn't start out here, at least briefly."

"You have such a lovely view." The Armstrong home was one of the larger ones she'd seen in the village, raised up a bit from the ground with lattice covering the open space. The height gave them a view over the dunes toward the Atlantic. "The wind must be slicing in the winter."

"Horribly. I never last more than a few minutes on those mornings—but Jack, he loves it. No matter the temperature." Caroline settled beside Ana on the swing, cradling her cup and looking out at the sea. "I hate this long summer trip of his. A whole month apart! I know it's necessary, but I still hate it."

Ana took a sip of the coffee that Caroline had already learned her preferences for. A splash of milk, the tiniest pinch of sugar. They made the brew weaker here than her family did, but she didn't mind. Just lessened the amount of milk she used. "I know exactly how you feel." They'd already shared so much, these last ten days. That Ana and Marko had been apart for three months already, and why. She'd told her new friend all about Dalmatia and its unrest, about why this move had seemed the best choice.

About her fears, as she crossed that vast sea on her own, and how much she longed to step into Marko's embrace again and know they'd be okay, that their family would flourish here. Ana and Caroline had talked about their families, their educations, their hopes. They'd traded childhood stories and marveled at the differences between their worlds, as well as the similarities.

They both knew the vagaries of life near a shore, of growing up in a fishing village where everything depended on the tides.

But Caroline had never had to fear for her life, just because she wasn't enough of one thing or too much of another. Her home had never been fought over by rivaling political forces. She'd never been denied food or shelter or education or basic rights because of her last name.

And now, Ana's child would never know that life either. They'd made certain of that, she and Marko and their families.

Caroline sipped at her coffee—which she preferred lighter and sweeter than Ana's—and let out a sigh that sounded more contented than wistful, despite her husband's absence. "I keep telling Jack I just married him for this view," she said, lips turning up.

Ana chuckled. From what she'd gleaned from her new friend, theirs had been a love match through and through. Much like Ana and Marko. She was so looking forward to meeting her new friend's husband—her own husband's friend. To building a life near this lovely family and knowing their children would grow up together. "It *is* quite a view." She and Marko would no doubt have to settle in a smaller cottage, likely with no water view. But that would be fine. She'd always had to walk to the water when she wished for a glimpse of it.

Anything would be fine, so long as they were together again.

The door squeaked open, and Susie slipped out, still in her nightgown. A familiar green spine peeked out from beneath her arm as she moved to the swing and nestled in between Ana and Caroline.

"Morning, sugar," Caroline said. "You need milk or breakfast yet?"

Around a yawn, Susie shook her head and opened *The Secret Garden*. She'd already read it through once but had immediately restarted it. It had made Ana smile, seeing the girl flipping those pages she'd flipped so many times herself.

Susie only turned one page now, before pausing to look up at Ana. "Didn't you say you learned English reading this?"

Ana nodded and reached out to tuck one of Susie's curls behind her ear. "There were other lessons too, of course, but this was a favorite method. I'd read a sentence in Italian—which I already knew—and then the same sentence in English."

"And you have a French version, right?" Susie turned her sweet little smile from Ana to her mother. "Can I learn French like that?"

Caroline's eyes went a bit wide. "Well, sweetie…I don't know any French…"

"Miz Ana does." The girl looked up at her again, all hope and brightness. "Could you teach me? Jill and me, we think it would be awful fun to know French. We're gonna go to Paris someday and live in the big Eiffel Tower thing."

Caroline pressed her lips against a laugh.

Ana smiled. "I think learning French would be a wonderful thing for you and Jill. Even if you don't visit the Eiffel Tower, there are many people in North America who speak French as well. In Louisiana, in Canada...and it is used in much business in Europe."

"Plus it sounds *so* pretty!"

Ana laughed. "It does indeed. A very beautiful language, and I would be delighted to help you learn it. If," she added, moving her gaze to Caroline, "that's okay with your mother. And Jill's mother would have to approve too, of course."

"I think it sounds lovely." Caroline toyed with her daughter's curls too—they were just irresistible—and took another sip of her coffee. "Something to keep your mind busy over the summer."

"And won't everyone be so surprised when I come into school speaking French?" Susie laughed in delight and reopened her book. "I'll tell Jill after breakfast. We could start after lunch, if her mama says it's okay."

A hundred thoughts raced through Ana's mind at the prospect. It had only been a month since she'd taught her last class in the little village school, but she hadn't thought she'd get to plan any more lessons for quite some time. The idea of doing so again, even if it was only for a child or two, made happiness bubble up inside her chest.

She'd have to get some paper and pencils—or slates would be even better, with chalk. They'd have to start with some basics before they launched straight into the books...though she'd still let them try out a sentence. She knew how eager kids were to dive right in, and even when they needed a foundation first, it had always worked well for her to let them get a taste of what they'd be doing.

Ana would need to explain conjugations and endings, masculine and feminine nouns and adjectives, how French letters were pronounced...

Oh, this was going to be so much more fun than simply sitting around waiting for Marko to come back. She'd been helping Caroline with chores, of course, both at the house and the church. She'd been knitting and sewing in preparation for the coming baby. She'd been writing letters home. But that had all felt like marking time, treading water until Marko returned.

This, though. This felt like *living*, like doing the thing she most loved to do.

Caroline met her gaze over Susie's head. "This is awfully nice of you. You don't need to feel obligated to spend your summer tutoring—"

"Oh, please, Caroline! It would truly be a delight. Teaching is one of my greatest joys."

Her friend's face went contemplative. "And we're currently lacking a teacher. Some summer tutoring wouldn't go amiss for others too, I daresay. Especially if we don't find a replacement for Mr. Walker soon—though, obviously once your little one comes along, continuing to teach will be a bit difficult."

True. She'd have had to stop teaching once the baby came, even if they hadn't moved an ocean away. But tutoring in French would surely fit in around diaper changes and feeding and naps. At least if she stayed close by. "I would be happy to help out however I can. Certainly over the summer, in French or anything else the children need. I taught in the village school for the last five years, back home. Reading, writing, mathematics…I worked with the younger children, mostly."

"Well. I certainly won't turn down French lessons for Susie. Maybe I'll sit in on them myself. What all do you need to get started? I can round up some supplies."

They chatted it over while they finished their coffee. When Susie dashed inside to get dressed and eat breakfast so she could go and see her friend, Ana compiled a list of things that would help. Paper, pencils, slates, chalk. They could do their lessons at the dining room table, for the most part. She briefly considered outdoor lessons, but the constant wind would make that challenging, if they were using paper.

It was easy to get lost in the familiar routine of planning lessons. Easy to hum one of her favorite songs and organize a little corner of Caroline's dining room, which could be tidied and moved out of the way if they needed the space for a meal. For the most part, the three of them had been eating in the kitchen, at the smaller table there. Caroline and Susie had gone to her husband's parents' for Sunday dinner, but Ana had bowed out, claiming—truthfully—that she needed a nap. If ever Caroline hosted the weekly meal here, it would be a simple thing to move all the school supplies.

By the time Susie bounced in from outside for lunch, her friend Jill with her, Ana was surveying her work with a smile. Even if the girls lost interest in a day or a week, this had been fun. Something to remind her that even on another continent, she could still be *her*. She could teach, she could help children grow, she could encourage their minds to blossom.

Perhaps...perhaps she ought to ask someone how to get a teacher's certificate in North Carolina. She'd completed the schooling she'd needed in Dalmatia to qualify, but would that matter here? Or would she have to take courses and exams all over again?

Part of her thrilled at the idea—she loved a classroom, whether she was the student or the teacher.

Another part of her shriveled instead. She'd have neither the time nor the money to invest in a second education for herself. She'd soon have a babe to care for, and she and Marko would be living paycheck to paycheck, she knew. The small savings they'd brought wouldn't last long, and they'd each spent a significant part of it just getting here. Once they had to factor in renting a house, buying their own food?

What a blessing Caroline had been. Unbidden, grateful tears stung Ana's eyes as she gave the table one last glance. Weeks with no rent, and Caroline wouldn't even let Ana contribute to the food budget—she had, of course, made up for it by doing the cooking as often as possible. They'd discovered that they had similar taste in food, which had made for delightful evenings spent at the stove together, tasting and testing.

A true friend, a true godsend.

"And this is Miz Ana, our teacher." Susie stole Ana's attention as she bounced into the dining room, her little friend's hand tucked in hers.

Ana smiled. She'd already met Jill before, but apparently being one's French tutor required a new round of introductions. Ana dipped into a curtsy, just to make the girls giggle. *"Enchante, mademoiselles."*

Where Susie had blond curls, Jill's hair was a straight red—closer to orange. But somehow as they giggled and grinned, they looked like two peas in a pod.

"Come get your sandwiches, girls," Caroline called from the kitchen. "Then you can start your lessons."

Ana trailed them into the kitchen, unable to keep the smile off her face. She knew that the novelty would wear off—it would go from being something exciting to a chore in a matter of days, as lessons generally did. But for now, she'd exchange a wink with Caroline over their enthusiasm and continue plotting how to keep the girls engaged.

Caroline had also made sandwiches for the adults and handed a plate to Ana, with some berries and veggies included as well. "In here with them or…?"

"That's fine. Jill can tell us how her little brother's walking is coming along."

"Oh, he's running around like crazy." Jill was already seated at the table, a small cup of water before her. "Mama says nothing's safe now."

Her first few days in America, Ana had found the speed of conversation difficult to follow, but after a couple weeks in the country, that had greatly improved. She had no trouble processing the girls' chatter—the drawl had taken a bit of getting used to, yes, but it was slower than the clipped accents she'd encountered in New York. A bit of a trade-off.

What, she had to wonder, would she and Marko sound like in a few years? How would their son or daughter speak? No doubt with this same accent, if they stayed here. But would hers and Marko's ever go away? Or, decades from now, would people still be able to tell after a few words that they were from Europe?

"Mama, you should read that one part out loud to us," Susie was saying, laughing even around her sandwich as she nudged *The Secret Garden* toward her mother. "What do they call it? The funny talking?"

"Yorkshire," Caroline said—she had, not surprisingly, ended up reading most of the novel with Susie, helping her with the odd spellings that the author had used to capture the dialect of the English moors. They'd passed a few delightful hours trying to perfect the accent just from the way it was written, the three of them collapsing into laughter more than once. "And we can read it after your lesson."

"There's even a place in the book where the cousin's daddy—the one who owns the estate—is in Italy! That's where Miz Ana's from!"

Ana merely smiled at that, not daring to correct her. It was technically true, these days, she supposed. Though it hadn't always been. Once, their area had been Croatia. Now it was Italy. Never was it allowed to be just what it was—Dalmatia. Always someone was clamoring for possession, trying to take them and rule them and bend them to their own ideals.

But those were subtleties she didn't expect any six-year-old to grasp. Certainly not one who had never been off this island she called home. It was simpler to smile and nod. "Perhaps sometime I can show you where I'm from on a map."

"Daddy has maps," Susie said.

Caroline smiled. "Not of Europe, sweetie. But I'm sure we can find one somewhere. For now, let's just finish up lunch, okay?"

A few minutes later, Ana was ushering the two girls into the dining room, where they each chose a seat in one of the chairs she'd arranged along with paper and pencils. "All right," she said, clapping her hands together. "We'll compare the first sentences of *The Secret Garden* in a bit, but first things first—you two lovely young ladies need to learn the alphabet in French. Did you know that, though they *look* the same as your letters in English, they're pronounced differently?"

The next hour flew by, the girls staying on task far more than Ana had expected. They went through the letters and their sounds and accents, she introduced numbers, and then they spent a bit of time on *The Secret Garden,* since the book had lured them into these lessons to begin with. By the time she closed the book and dismissed the children, she deemed the experiment a success.

The girls darted outside, off to play on the beach, and Ana took a minute to tidy up.

Her smile froze on her face when she heard another woman's voice from outside—Jill's mother, she was pretty sure. Miz Pauline.

"I'm just not sure what Greg'll say, that's all," Pauline was saying in an undertone. "What does Jilly need with anything but English?"

Caroline's huff sounded irritated. "What does she need with reading? With math? With history? Gracious, Pauline, it's *education*. Learning about other places and other languages has its own benefits. There's a whole world out there outside Hatteras Island, you know."

"Well sure, but let's be honest. She's never gonna go to France. She don't need to speak French."

"You don't know that. But even if she doesn't, that doesn't mean learning it won't be a benefit. Personally," Caroline said, her voice going up a notch, "I'm hoping to pick up a bit of it myself. I've always wanted to learn. And Ana is a fine teacher, I could tell that in a minute."

Her neighbor sighed. "I'm sure Miz Annie is all right, but she ain't a *teacher*, Carrie. She—"

"She is so."

Ana, still standing in the dining room, found herself gripping the back of the chair Susie had been sitting in. Her new friend shouldn't have to defend her like this. But what was Ana supposed to do? Storm into the kitchen and stick up for herself? Slink off to her borrowed room and pretend she hadn't heard?

"She went to college in Italy and has been teaching for five years—which is more than we could say about our own teacher, if you recall. She's a regular Anne Shirley."

Ana's brows knit. Who was Anne Shirley? A good or bad example? Coming from Caroline, she had to assume it was good.

"Firstly, you don't know it's true just because she says it. You ask me, you're taking a mighty risk, having some stranger in your house with just you and Susie here. Nextly, you think Greg's gonna care about some Italian college saying she can teach? He didn't much like that Mr. Walker went to school in Pennsylvania, and it was just the North, still America."

Was that a huff or a laugh? "It is hardly a risk. Ana is just a sweet young woman waiting for her husband to come back with ours—aren't we called to help our neighbors? She's just the newest one."

"But—"

"No, now never mind. We're not arguing about that. And I'm not saying you should argue with

Greg over the lessons when the fellas get home. If he really thinks it's a bad idea to let his daughter learn a little French and some good American literature over the summer, then who am I? I'm just saying that you'll be giving Jill a leg up by letting her learn along with Susie. Plus, it'll keep the girls occupied for a few hours a week. What's the harm?"

Pauline sighed. "I ain't never even heard of that book they're reading. But if they're so interested in gardening, there's plenty of weeds to be pulled. Seems like as fine a way of spending their days as this."

"Oh gracious, Pauline, they're little girls! They can weed and play and learn, all of it. You don't have to choose which. And if you let them mix it all up, I bet you'll hear far fewer complaints about the chores."

Another sigh. "I'm not gonna stop her—not right now. But if Greg don't like it when they get back…"

"That's weeks away yet. Just let them have fun in the meantime, and if they stick with it and can say 'polly-voo-on-fron-say' by the time their daddies get home, it should only make them proud. I know Jack will be. Probably insist we teach him everything we've learned. He's always wanted to go to Europe."

"Yeah, well, Greg hasn't." Pauline sounded resigned.

Resigned. Not excited or indulgent or even just amused. *Resigned* that her daughter would learn a few French phrases in the next few weeks. Ana pressed her lips together.

The screen door squeaked open. "Just send her home when you start supper, Caroline."

"I will."

Ana held her spot for a long moment, not wanting to walk into the kitchen and all but announce that she'd overheard every word.

Of course, Caroline beat her over the awkward hump, bustling in with a shake of her head. "Can you believe some people? Perfectly nice woman, now, don't get me wrong—I like Pauline just fine. We were in school together, you know, she's just a year older than me. But sometimes those Marshalls…"

"Marshalls?" Ana tried to remember if she'd met anyone with that name thus far but drew a blank.

Caroline waved a hand. "Pauline's maiden name—her parents live on the other side of her. The white house with the green roof? That's them. You probably noticed Miz Berta scowling at us in church on Sunday."

Ana's mouth opened, but no words came out. Honestly, she'd caught quite a few looks on Sunday, ranging from mild curiosity to dark suspicion. Mostly from the women. But she'd tried to tell herself it was her imagination.

Caroline moved to where Ana stood and placed her hands over Ana's on the back of the chair. They were similar in height, so her hostess didn't have to do anything but look her straight in the eye as she said, "Don't you let Pauline or Berta or anyone else get to you, Ana. You are *welcome* here, and I love having you as my guest, and I am tickled pink that you're willing to spend some of your summer teaching my little girl. Doesn't matter if Jill sits in or not. We appreciate this."

Ana summoned a smile and banished the clouds. Because she knew very well who was in whose debt, and there was no way she was the one doing a favor.

Chapter Nine

The busiest day of the week for the Island Bookshop was Monday—no question. Kennedy had lost track of the number of families that came in at the start of their vacations to stock up on reading material. And back when she worked here regularly, she even remembered many of the faces, since they returned year after year.

And when it came to the busiest week of the year, that was obvious to anyone in the Outer Banks. Fourth of July week always sold out from Corolla to Ocracoke, every house filled and every business booming.

Kennedy leaned into the rooftop deck railing and watched the sun stretch away from the horizon on the Monday of Fourth week, knowing this might be the last deep, peaceful breath she took until after the book signing at the shop on Friday.

She and Lara had been planning it for so long—a year, more or less. They'd worked with Wes to line up a house for the two *New York Times* bestselling authors and their families—they were friends, so the prospect of spending a week together in the same house had been a draw. Kennedy and her sister made flyers to leave in all the rental houses on Hatteras Island, and convinced the rental agencies to send out emails to this week's renters to let them know well in advance about the event.

But all their planning didn't guarantee success. She didn't even know whether to pray for rain—which would drive people off the beaches and into shops—or sunshine—which would allow the crowds to overflow from the small store into the large parking lot. So she just prayed that God would make of it all what He willed, and that it would go well. Whatever that meant.

Swallowing a last sip of coffee, Kennedy straightened and drew in a long breath. She'd already gone for a quick run. Now she just had to shower and hightail it to the shop.

She moved quietly in the house, hoping that she wouldn't wake Lara. Once upon a time, her sister had been up at the crack of dawn, but she'd been sleeping in whenever she could the last few weeks. And then napping midday, or at least lying down in the dark to try to ease the migraines that kept plaguing her.

When Kennedy emerged from the shower, she found Lara fixing a cup of coffee. Her sister offered a smile that tried to be bright but still looked pained around the edges. "Big week!"

Kennedy grinned and nodded. "We're ready." Even though getting ready had meant a lot of painstaking conversations with Lara, stretched out over days and weeks, to try to get up to date on accounts, and ordering and last-minute details for the event…without making her sister either frustrated or confused. There'd been more snapping and shouting than they'd indulged in since they were teenagers. And then plenty of tears and ice cream and hugs.

At this point, Kennedy was absolutely certain that everything was in good shape, but getting it there meant putting off the family research they needed to do. According to their lawyer, they needed documents proving that Grandma Janey was in fact Marija Horvat—something he seemed shocked to learn and swore he had no documentation to prove.

She and Aunt Grace had spent one Sunday afternoon looking through Grandma's files, but they'd lost a lot of what she'd brought with her in a hurricane over twenty years ago, along with many other family documents and memories. Proof had to exist somewhere...but she didn't know where, and they'd decided it would just have to wait until after the Fourth.

They had to bring this event off without a hitch. *Then* they would worry about settling the estate.

"I'm going to try to be there when they arrive today," Lara said, lifting her coffee cup and taking a sip.

Kennedy bit her tongue against the arguments that wanted to spring up. Not that she didn't want her sister there, but *getting* there... "Sure. I was thinking I'd pop home for lunch, so you can come back with me after."

Lara sent her a glare. "I can drive myself over."

What could she do but sigh? They hadn't gotten in to see the specialist yet, and while Lara's primary care doctor hadn't said she couldn't drive, she'd advised caution, especially while dealing with daily migraines. "I know you *can*. But you've been getting a pretty instant headache in the bright sun, and today's forecast looks clear. And you still get dizzy when you have to look from side to side, and you know how traffic is this week."

Lara hadn't seemed to draw the connection, but Kennedy had begun keeping a notebook account of every time her sister mentioned dizziness or nausea, and a lot of them seemed to be activities that involved moving her focus from one side to another quickly—whether reading something in columns, grocery shopping, or checking traffic.

A week ago, Lara told Kennedy she wouldn't drive, but then she'd hopped on her bike only to fall over halfway down the driveway. Just fell over. Which she clearly wouldn't have even mentioned to Kennedy if Aunt Grace hadn't ratted her out, having witnessed the incident.

Moving to her sister's side, Kennedy wrapped an arm around her waist. "Sis, I know this stinks. I know you just want to get back to normal. But I also know you're still in horrible pain and fighting nausea every day. You *will* get past this, I have to believe that. But why do things that make it worse?"

"Because it's my *life*, Kennedy! The shop, this signing..." Lara pulled away and turned to lean against the counter, tears clogging her voice. "You have no idea how it feels to be so useless."

Though Kennedy opened her mouth, she had to close it again. That was true. She'd never faced what her sister was going through now. She moved close to Lara again, leaning beside her. "You're right. I can only try to understand, but I'm not the one living it. Not like you are. And I absolutely agree that you should be there, Lara. But since we know how it's likely to tax you...let's do what we can to mitigate any discomfort. That's all I'm saying. Ride with me after lunch, so you can close your eyes during the drive. Save the effort for the important part."

The silence stretched, ticking along with the mermaid clock on the wall. Finally, Lara shifted so that their shoulders were touching. "Okay."

"Okay." Keeping her smile slight so that her sister wouldn't feel like it was a win/lose situation, she straightened. "I'll be back around eleven so I can grab a bite. Last I heard, the guest authors were planning to get here around one. I figure if we head back over at noon, that'll give us time to do one last check of the shop."

Lara nodded. "And Wes still plans to meet us there too, and lead the way to the...you know—the place they're staying?"

"Yep. He's looking forward to rolling out the red carpet. As much as everyone loves the convenience of keyless check-in, I think he really misses actually talking to all the renters as they come for keys." It had, in fact, been one of his stipulations for cutting a sweet deal on the rental—he'd let them basically steal the week at one of the properties the Armstrongs owned and rented, as long as he got to personally welcome the authors and their families to the house and show them around.

Kennedy had shouted "Deal!" so loud that he'd apparently dropped his phone.

And yeah, she was secretly looking forward to watching him glad-hand her authors this afternoon. It had been a while since she'd seen him in his element, doing the real estate agent thing.

After putting some coffee into a to-go mug and grabbing a breakfast bar she'd made yesterday, Kennedy said goodbye and headed out. They still had five days until the big signing, yes, and much of the prep had been done last week—dropping off all the flyers at the various rental agencies in time to be loaded into welcome bags and so on. But their shop wasn't set up for signings, generally speaking, and she had a lot of rearranging to do. Plus she needed to assemble the display—that was her big task for the morning. She wanted it done before the authors arrived, so they'd see that the shop would push their books all week long.

All before ten o'clock. Sure, no problem.

Once she arrived, Kennedy didn't waste time, her game plan already in place. She stowed her things in the office and got right to it, moving into what had once been Grandma's living room. It now housed gift and local interest books, along with other items made locally—soaps, jewelry, small pieces of beach-themed artwork, journals, tote bags, and beach-themed toys. This room was one of the newer additions to the shop, one that Grandma Janey hadn't been gung ho about. A bookstore, she had said, should sell *books*. Just books.

But given the number of whole families who shopped in their store, she and Lara had finally won the debate, arguing that it was good to have something for everyone. Toys for the kids who might not be readers yet, souvenirs that readers could take home to family, items to capture the attention of a reluctant spouse or friend. And it worked. They got to support local artisans, and they brought in some extra revenue.

For this week, all these things would find homes in other parts of the store. The plush pelicans and whales and other toys she moved into the room dedicated to juvenile and young adult fiction, nestling them into corners and windows. Not ideal for the long-term, but it would work for now. Much of the art had to find a temporary home in the kitchen, which had more open space than the other rooms. Wind chimes and stained glass had to be bunched together more than she liked in other windows.

By nine, the rest of the shop felt a bit too crowded, but that front room was mostly cleared out. She was just ripping open the first carton of *Black as the Sea* by Alyssa McDaniels when the door jangled open and Harper's "Good morning!" filled the shop.

"Hey," Kennedy called in reply. "Up to my elbows in book signing stuff, but go on back. Do you need a hand?"

"Do I ever?"

Hence why Kennedy hadn't put down the armful of books she was building into a spiral on one side of the table. On the other, she'd construct a matching display for *A Galaxy of Waves* by Justine Clayton.

It was *so* convenient that the two bestselling authors who were best friends and critique partners both had ocean-themed books releasing this month—though they were of very different genres. One was a fantasy, the second book in a series that had taken the world by storm and sold approximately a bajillion copies in the last year. The other was a contemporary psychological thriller, first in a new series. When she'd seen the announcements in *Publisher's Weekly*, she'd immediately started dreaming of getting them both down here for a joint signing. She'd met Justine at an event in DC three years ago and Alyssa at a different one a year later, and they had both been absolutely delightful. They followed her rare books channel now, and she exchanged messages with each author often enough that it hadn't felt like a horribly out-there ask, even given their ridiculous levels of popularity. Still, she'd done a lot of plotting with Lara—and, eventually, Wes—before braving the request.

Their typed shrieks of delight had made her glad she'd taken the risk. Apparently the friends were quite eager to take a week at the beach together in exchange for spending a day signing books in the store. Kennedy knew that they were each bringing their husbands and kids—they had five between them, aged six to fifteen—and she and Lara had some special things planned for their families too.

Harper emerged from the kitchen and scooped up one of the copies of *Black as the Sea* from a box. "I cannot wait to read this. You're reserving me a copy, right? What am I saying—I'm just going to buy this before I leave, and one of the others too, and if it's a total madhouse on Friday, you just slip them in for me. I'll leave them under the counter."

Kennedy laughed and placed another four books in the spiral. "I can have the copies signed for you this afternoon. You could even just come by when they get here. Around one or so."

"I don't want to butt in. But if they want to sign today, I'll pick them up tomorrow—that would be cool." She indicated the stack of unopened boxes. "Shall I?"

"Have at it."

"And of course, if by some weirdness this place *isn't* hopping on Friday, I'll stop by and bring everyone I know. But I anticipate no parking available and a line all the way down to the sound."

"I love your optimism."

Harper used the box cutter to slice open the carton of *A Galaxy of Waves* with the precision of someone used to performing the task countless times a day. "You've got some of their backlist too, right? I'm still missing a couple."

"Yep. We'll have those on the shelves there," Kennedy said, motioning to the shelves that still currently held the gift and local interest books. "That stuff will mostly be relocated to the kitchen with the cookbooks for the week."

"Sweet. So…" Harper sent her a glance as she pulled out one of the books. "Anything going on in DC that you're missing out on?"

At that, Kennedy had to sigh. Melissa was, of course, finishing the intake of the Kensington books on her own. Though Kennedy could admit that part of her had wanted to insist the job wait until she returned in September, that just wasn't logical. Or fair to Melissa, who was just as capable as she was of handling the grading and inspections.

"Melissa has kept me updated on the big stuff, sending along photos of the best books from the collection." Her lips twitched up. "Although the most recent video was far different—of her ancient neighbor vacuuming her lawn again."

"Wait, what?" Harper laughed around the question.

Kennedy pulled out her phone and showed her the evidence. "Seriously. You should see her in the fall. She's out there every day, sucking up the leaves with her household vacuum cleaner. I've seen it myself when we're hanging out at Melissa's place."

"That's just…I don't know what."

"Right?" It made her grin. "But otherwise things at work are just work as usual." Wonderful, beautiful, once-in-a-lifetime work that she was missing.

Harper straightened and moved toward the counter with her two books. "Do you have your computers up yet?"

"Yep."

"Then I'll ring myself up. Can't linger too long, I have ciabatta rising."

"Just tuck them under the counter with a sticky note."

A few minutes later she was alone again, working quickly so that at least the bulk would be done by ten. Not that she cared if the early morning customers saw her finishing the setup, but she liked to be able to give them her attention if they needed it.

As it was, by the time the bell over the door jangled again at 10:05 a.m., she had the giant posters for the signing on the authors' table for Friday, the spirals done, and was nearly finished stocking the shelves with all of Alyssa's and Justine's backlists. It put a smile in her voice as she called out, "Good morning."

"Good morning." A twentysomething woman entered the shop, a bright smile on her face as she moved her sunglasses from her nose to her spiraling dark curls. "Is Lara in?"

"Not until this afternoon, I'm afraid." Kennedy was willing to bet this wasn't just a local she hadn't met before, given the woman's casual tone as she asked about Lara. Every single person who lived on the island knew about the accident, she was sure. No exaggeration. She'd yet to run into a single local who didn't. But she saw no reason to launch into explanations for a visitor.

"Bummer. Maybe I'll pop back over." The woman wandered toward Kennedy, her eyes taking in the display without any real interest. "I wanted to give her an update."

Kennedy didn't have to work to keep her smile in place. She loved how many relationships the shop helped foster with visitors—even people who only came in once a year. "You are certainly welcome to swing by this afternoon, but you could also tell me and I'll pass it along to my sister."

"Sister. I guess you do kinda look alike." The woman held out a hand. "I'm Latisha."

"Kennedy." They shook, and Kennedy gave Latisha her undivided attention instead of turning back to the boxes of books.

"My family started vacationing here about ten years ago. My mom dragged me to the Island Bookshop against my will." Latisha chuckled, glancing around with obvious fondness. "I wasn't much of a reader, but I was totally sucked in by the dolphin stuffies."

See, Grandma Janey? Kennedy's grin settled comfortably on her mouth. "Our devious plan."

The young woman laughed. "It worked. And then your sister, she pointed me toward the kids' books on dolphins and other marine life. My mom is a fiction reader—she read stories to me every night but never really kept any non-fiction for me in the house. When I realized that books could have cool diagrams and facts…" She shook her head, eyes dancing. "Game changer. I mean, I obviously knew books like that existed, we had them in school. But I'd never paused to think that I could just buy one and keep it, you know?"

"I do. I think we all have moments when we discover books can do something for us we'd never considered before. Makes the whole world open up."

"That book opened up a whole new world for me all right. I became so fascinated with marine biology, and it never went away. I ended up going to college for it—that's why I wanted to update Lara. She encouraged me every year to chase that dream, always had a new book ready for me, and she somehow always knew what I'd need. Books I'd never heard of but which were just what I'd been wanting, or had learned of but couldn't find copies of. It's like she was this book savant."

Warmth spread through Kennedy's chest, making it feel beautifully tight. "That's Lara for you." And she did that for dozens of people every year. There was nothing mystical about it—the people Lara could get to know so well were the ones who tagged the shop on social media with their finds. She then followed them back and checked in on the accounts periodically. This young woman's mother had probably posted a victorious photo that first year, and Lara had kept up with the family ever since. She'd comment on their posts and note their interests and any books they mentioned, and when they came in the next year, she'd have a few recommendations in mind.

It was Lara's way. And it was a good way. A way made even easier when the families returned the same week every year—like Fourth week.

"I've just finished up my undergrad degree in marine biology," Latisha said, smiling with obvious pride. "I'll start my doctoral studies next month, but I had to stop in and tell her."

Gracious. Were Lara here, she'd be blubbering and smiling like an idiot and all the things in between. Kennedy nearly was, and she was just the sister. "Okay, you *have* to stop back in when she's here. I can give you her schedule for the week."

The accounts had proven too much for Lara's injured brain, but she *was* spending a couple hours at the shop every day again. She could manage the floor, and the check-out system was simple enough that she could handle it for a little while before the headaches kicked in.

Kennedy moved to the counter and pulled out a sheet of paper and a pen. She jotted down the hours Lara would be here and slipped it to Latisha with a smile. "And I'd bet she has another book here for you somewhere. I could call her and ask, but I imagine she'd like to show it to you herself."

Latisha glanced at the hours, her smile still lingering. "I'll just swing by again this afternoon, after I go windsurfing. Thanks, Kennedy." She turned to leave, then paused, a question in her brows. "Do you work here often? I don't remember seeing you before."

"I live in DC and work at the Library of Congress, actually." It was still true, right? Funny how it felt a little bit like a lie—or a dream. Another world, too many weeks removed from this one. "I'm helping Lara out this summer." Should she say why? Ordinarily she wouldn't mention it to a random shop patron, but her sister clearly had a relationship with this person. "She fell a few weeks back and gave herself a nasty concussion."

Latisha's eyes went wide. "Oh no! Is she okay?"

Not really. Words Kennedy could never say out loud, not to a stranger. "It's her third concussion, so recovery is proving slow, and she's having symptoms she never did before. She's fighting migraines every day, nausea, balance issues...but she's improving, and it would take more than a brain injury to keep her from the shop."

Latisha splayed a hand over her heart. "That is so horrible! I'll be thinking positive thoughts."

What she needed were prayers, but they'd long ago learned not to get into arguments about such things in the shop. They never hid their family's faith, but they didn't force it on people either. Better to pray that God would tug on this college student's heart even as He healed Lara. She kept her smile in place. "Thanks. Enjoy your windsurfing."

Another family entered as Latisha was leaving. Kennedy went back to the event space while they browsed, but her mind kept drifting to the young woman. To her sister, who had somehow nurtured a dream within another person, in ten minutes of face-to-face time per year. To this place, that did things like that every day.

She loved her work in the Library of Congress. She loved the life she'd built for herself.

But she loved what they'd built here too. The question was—what if she had to choose between the two?

Chapter Ten

"Pool and hot tub are both cleaned and cared for by one of our techs, so they're ready for you to enjoy. Any problems at all with any of it, just give us a call." Wes motioned toward a ground-level closet. "Pool and beach gear are in here."

Alyssa's brows lifted. "And it's not locked up, so we can use it?"

Gracious, this was bad news. The way Wes's eyes twinkled as he gave the doorknob a twist...it just wasn't fair. How was Kennedy ever supposed to fully shove him into friend territory when he looked so incredibly joyful about a closet full of beach chairs and pool noodles and boogie boards?

"Not every house provides gear, of course, but we like to keep the ones my family owns stocked. It makes it so much easier for families who don't have room in their cars to haul their own." He pulled the door wide so two of the kids could dart in, exclaiming the moment they entered that there were sand toys too, and an umbrella. "Just hose it all down before you put it away."

Justine peered into the closet as the two boys—one hers and one Alyssa's—darted out again, pool toys in their arms.

"Can we get in the pool, Mom? Can we?"

"As soon as we unpack enough to find your swimsuits, sure." Justine ran a hand over her son's hair absently as he darted for the fenced-in pool area, ready to deposit those toys and probably haul in all the luggage himself so he could get to the important stuff.

"This place is amazing," Alyssa said, surveying the pool and hot tub with her hands on her hips. "You said your family owns it?"

Wes nodded, his expression so contented and yet humble that Kennedy thought maybe she *shouldn't* have come along for the rolling out of the red carpet. It was wreaking havoc on her.

"My family's lived on Hatteras Island pretty much forever. There was a lot of property in the family before this became a tourist destination, and quite a few of my great-grandparents' siblings didn't have kids or moved away, so we ended up with a lot of houses to figure out what to do with. They started a real estate company right about the time people started coming here, just renting out the houses, selling now and then…but then buying other properties as they became available. We still have quite a few that we maintain solely as rentals." He flashed that smile of his. "We love being able to provide a week's escape for people who need a little taste of paradise."

"I love that you actually have landscaping," Alyssa's husband, Curtis, said, nodding to the garden. "Seems like that's missing from a lot of the houses around here."

"It's upkeep that a lot of owners don't want to fool with." Wes angled himself toward the giant pots of flowers, the seating area, the wind chimes. "But since we live here, we can take care of it ourselves. So if you see anyone snooping around with a watering can at any point, don't worry. It's just my mom. She feeds the island cats too."

Kennedy's eyes flicked to the miniature cedar shake house that stood between this rental and the next one over—also owned by the Armstrongs—that had THE SEA CAT MOTEL painted on it. It was basically just a roof over a dividing wall, with tins set up on both sides for the neighborhood cats. She knew that Wes's mom came by every day to put out food—there were similar feeding stations up and down the island, and local volunteers fed them with food donated by locals and visitors alike.

"Oh, and there's a Little Free Library!" Justine's daughter—the eldest of the crew of kids—pointed to the LFL across the lane. It was one of the many that the Marshalls had helped install. Dad built the enclosures, Kennedy and Lara painted them during one of Kennedy's weeks at home, and they'd gone together to install them. "Mom, you should totally leave one of your books."

Justine rolled her eyes even as she smiled. "This one is very generous with my books. She'd give them away to everyone."

The boys darted out from the pool area again and had the vans open. "Mom, where are the swimsuits?"

"Where's my suitcase?"

"Your stupid books are in the way!"

Alyssa shot Kennedy a look. "You see the glamorous life of a best-selling author?"

Kennedy grinned. Looked pretty perfect to her. "You brought books?" She would have assumed the boys were just referring to her reading material, but they were thumping on a cardboard box like the ones Kennedy had unpacked that morning.

"Not just any books," Justine was the one to say. "She brought you a case of special editions with sprayed edges."

"No way!" Kennedy sprang forward. "Let me help you with those, guys."

Alyssa laughed. "I didn't know if you'd managed to get any in or not, but I had a feeling you'd appreciate having some for the signing."

"Look at you, assuming I'm not just going to hoard them all for myself. And we tried, but apparently the first run all went to the big dogs. They assured us we were on the list for the next run, but that doesn't help us this week."

"I am so jealous of those," Justine said. "I keep trying to convince my publishers that more genres need to do sprayed edges. They're just so cool."

Kennedy no sooner extricated the box from the packed-tight van than Wes swooped in and took them from her. "I'll put this in your car, where I assume you'll rip it open here and now."

"Well *duh*." Not at all minding the laughter her excitement earned among the authors' families, Kennedy popped Mitzi's hatchback so he could put the box down there, rather than on the ground where it would pick up sand. She didn't have scissors or a box cutter handy, but she'd ripped open many a carton of books without such aids in the past and had no trouble peeling off the tape now.

It was totally worth it. She pulled out one of the hardcovers and gasped—actually gasped like a drama queen—when she saw the intricate sprayed-edge design. She'd been expecting a solid color, like the first book in the series had gotten, but no. This one had cut-outs of sea creatures, a trident, and a lighter drift of aqua over the main teal, making it look like undulating water.

"I am in love with a book."

Wes snorted. "Harper's muffins will be jealous."

"This is *so* beautiful." She turned her eyes, which felt round as sand dollars, on Alyssa. "Are you, like, jumping over the moon daily, or what?"

"Can't you tell by my bulging calves?" Alyssa grinned, and it was a lot like Wes's grin—content but humble. "And as you can also tell by the bruises all over me, I'm pinching myself daily too. I still can't believe this series has taken off like this."

"I can." Justine draped an arm around her friend's shoulders. "I *told* you it was awesomesauce."

"Lara will be pumped." Her sister had met the authors at the store already, but Latisha had returned just as they were getting ready to head to the rental house, so Lara opted to stay behind and chat with her friend. There would be plenty of time to visit with the McDaniels and Claytons over the week. They were going to join the Marshalls and Armstrongs on the Fourth, for one thing. "In fact, I'll get these over to her and let you guys get settled. I still need to film a video today."

For some reason, the authors' eyes went wide at that. "For real?" Justine said.

"Can we come?" Alyssa asked. "You've had guests before. I know our books aren't old and classic yet, but—"

"But Alyssa's will be soon. You can do one on these painted edges and find things that future collectors can look for." Justine grinned even as her friend rolled her eyes.

"That...sounds like a lot of fun, actually." Kennedy had planned to record something focusing on the copies of *The Secret Garden* from the attic, but she could do both. Having an extra in the bank wouldn't hurt, and dropping a video that tied in with the signing was a good idea. Not that her audience was likely to show up for the event, but still. It was content they could then post to the store's social media too.

She should have thought of it herself, but her schedule had been so crazy the last few weeks...

"Curt and Gabe and the kids can handle the unpacking. Right, honey?"

Curt gave a salute. "We got it. We'll pick up the grocery order too."

Kennedy slid the book back into its box and shut the hatch. "Well then. Hop in. I'll do the recording at my house." She'd set up a little studio in one of the spare bedrooms after bringing her equipment from DC, and had already filmed three episodes on the books she'd had waiting. In the meantime, she'd been doing some research on those versions of *The Secret Garden*. None were particularly collectible, given their much-used condition, but they were all first editions. And just so intriguing.

Either Justine and Alyssa were eager to see her setup, or they were just happy to escape for a few minutes after hours in the car with their families, because they clamored to get into the back, leaving the front passenger seat for Wes.

He met Kennedy's gaze over Mitzi's roof. "I can come too, right? I could help with cameras or whatever."

Her heart did a stupid little lurch. "Why? I mean, sure, but... why?"

He looked caught between bemused and insulted. "Because it's your *show*. It's the thing you've built. I would have asked to watch you make one before now, but I honestly didn't know if you'd be doing them this summer."

She didn't bother saying that she didn't dare stop. Her videos were finally making money from ads, and she'd gained enough of a reputation that it brought her freelance work too. Income she needed now more than ever. She had, in fact, just gotten a delivery on Friday of a book someone wanted her to appraise and then repair, in any way that wouldn't hurt its market value.

For Wes, she smiled. "I am, and you're welcome any time. I usually set up the cameras and then get in place and edit later, but it would be nice to have an extra set of hands." Melessa helped her once in a while in DC, but not often. Editing her videos always went so much faster when there was someone there to keep an eye on things during filming.

"Nice. If I prove myself useful enough, you can just have me come over whenever you do one."

She nearly opened her mouth to say that was asking too much… but she closed it again. Because there, hiding in the blues of Wes's eyes, was a truth she only glimpsed rarely. He needed this—something to do outside of work. Something to fill his evenings. Something that involved another person.

It shouldn't be her. She *knew* it shouldn't be her, but how was she supposed to deny him an hour or two of company once a week, when he clearly needed it? She pasted on a smirk. "Sure, let's pretend I'm doing you a favor instead of the other way around."

Twenty minutes later, they'd picked Lara up from the store—she squeezed into the back with Alyssa and Justine—and were on their way to the Marshall residence. Kennedy had originally planned on making her video after dinner, while Lara was lying down in the dark for a while to recover from her afternoon out. But a change of plans was clearly in order.

It was weird setting everything up with a chattering audience. An audience that examined every single prop she had out and asked insightful questions about them. She hadn't had room to bring the exact bookcase she had set up behind her at home, of course, but she'd duplicated it as best she could with a few of the shelves here, setting up her rare books, her loupe, her microscope, and the like.

"Am I allowed to touch this?" Justine asked, hands hovering over a leatherbound copy of *A Christmas Carol*.

Kennedy chuckled. "Absolutely. It's actually new, a recreation of the original printing. Much shinier for the camera, and no worries about damaging it as I move things around on the shelves. All of these are either reproductions or just not super valuable. I save the good stuff for featuring on the show but store them more securely."

"I am so fascinated by what you can learn about a book when you look closely at it." Alyssa picked up the loupe and held it toward the book in Justine's hands.

"*I* love how the typos in the original editions are what make them so valuable," Justine said. "Every time a reader emails me to let me know a mistake slipped through in one of my books, that's what I remind myself of. They'll fix it in the next printing—if there is one—and then those goofs will be how people like you will know it's a *real* first edition when it's a crazy collectible in a hundred years. It's just like *Huckleberry Finn*, that's what I say."

"She does, I've heard her." Alyssa laughed and picked up another of the books. "I'm still baffled by the microscope. I've never seen you use it."

"It's hard to record anything viewed that way with my current setup," Kennedy said. "And I don't have the funds for an upgrade that'll allow it. But they're especially handy for manuscripts—things that pre-date the printing press. When people hand-wrote books, they would scrape mistakes off, removing a thin layer of parchment. That's easiest to see under magnification, and often you can even see what they tried to remove."

"So cool," Alyssa whispered, as if it were a secret process not to be commented on at full volume.

Lara had joined the group too, despite the shadows in her eyes that said she was suffering from her daily headache, and she'd taken a seat on a daybed against the wall opposite the filming setup. The box of books from the shop's attic was there—well, okay, the variations of *The Secret Garden* were there, in a new, uncontaminated box. The moldy scent had dissipated with the pulp fiction from the '60s, so she hoped that these would be okay.

Her sister picked up the French copy and flipped it open. "Still wish I could remember finding these." Her voice was quiet too, but not with awe, like Alyssa's had been. Kennedy could sense Lara's regrets and invent her own interpretations. Lara's quiet voice came with sorrow not just for the missing time, but for the missing should-have-been. Lara should have been the one to tell Kennedy about the discovery, not the other way around. She should have been the one to drive to Manteo and find that same deed filed there. She should have been more focused on solving this mystery and less on simply staying on her feet for a few hours at a time.

It wasn't fair, how horribly life could go wrong in a single instant. And yet, it was the way life worked. Always, for everyone. There wasn't often foreshadowing or clues to point to that big twist. Just a random moment, a missed step, a slip, a fall. A split-second looking down at your phone instead of up at traffic. A twist of biology. A clot. And the whole world changed.

"What are they?" Justine slid the red leather copy of *A Christmas Carol* back into its place on the shelf and moved to peer at the books Lara held.

"Copies of *The Secret Garden* in a bunch of different…you know. The things we speak. Or read." She huffed out a frustrated breath.

"Languages," Kennedy supplied softly. She knew Lara hated it when she couldn't find a word she obviously *knew*, but it was worse when outsiders were around to witness it. When it was just the two of them, she could laugh it off and say how glad she was that Kennedy could always read her mind. "They were in the attic of the bookshop, along with the deed for the place. We're just not sure where they came from."

Or rather, *who* they came from. She'd taken her loupe to them, looking for any markings that might offer a clue as to their ownership. She'd found quite a few markings in faded pencil—further degrading the books, but that wasn't the point. She'd also found a faded name on the flyleaf of the Italian version. *A. Blazevic.*

Not helpful. Though a quick internet search told her that *Blazevic* was a Croatian surname, it was too common to give her any indication of who had owned this book. A first initial of *A* didn't help much either.

But *Horvat* was Croatian too—the name that was on both copies of that deed. Ana Horvat, and Marija Horvat. Maybe Horvat was Ana's married name, and her maiden had been Blazevic? Conjecture. Pure conjecture.

"Are you going to feature these in one of your shows?" Alyssa asked, picking up the Italian copy.

Kennedy nodded. "I found some interesting things in them. Namely, the same word in sentences of each version have faint marks—coordinating words. All throughout the books. It makes us think that someone was cross-referencing the sentences, perhaps for translation."

Justine sat on the bed too, on the other side of the box. "The French program I'm using with the kids uses dual-language picture books at the start. Maybe it's that same idea? Read a version in the language you know, then a version in the language you're learning?"

Lara smiled. "That's our theory."

"Lara came up with it, actually." Kennedy had been too set on the things she'd been trained to see—the books themselves, their condition—to get her mind out of the box enough to answer the question of *why*.

"And you noticed the marks. We make a good team." Her sister's smile aimed for bright, even if it appeared a bit too pained to pull it off.

"We do, at that." And Kennedy's half of the team wanted to gently prod her sister out of this room full of people and the lights she'd soon have to turn on, and into Lara's own room where she could pull the blinds and rest for a few minutes. Give her headache a chance to retreat. She knew if she said as much, though, in front of guests…

When she switched the lights on, maybe Lara would take her cue.

Wes, of course, had gone straight to the cameras she had set up on three different tripods. Given that the room was used for nothing else, she'd left them assembled after last week, just pulling their batteries and memory cards and putting the lens covers back on. "You've got a nice setup here, Kenni."

Coming from the guy who photographed rental houses for his website, she accepted the praise with a smile. "Thanks. I started with only a webcam, of course, but having three cameras makes it easier to make cuts when I screw up."

"Screw up? You?" Wes laughed and poked through the table of accoutrements she had set up beside the cameras. "What's all this?"

"Color cards for white balance, light meter, and that—is a measuring tape." For checking focal distance, but she left the instructive part off to make room for his snort of laughter.

"Measuring tape—amazing. Never seen the like."

"We're very high techy-techy around here." Figuring they'd better get to it so the ladies could rejoin their families, Kennedy held up a finger toward them. "Just a second while I grab some copies of your earlier books."

"Should we have brought makeup or anything?" Alyssa looked down at herself. "I didn't think this through when I volunteered us to be on camera."

Kennedy laughed. "You both look great, but if you want to freshen up, you're welcome to use anything in the bathroom down the hall there."

They were quick to take her up on that, and Lara stood too, lifting a hand to her temple. "I think I'd better lie down while you have the lights blazing in here. Don't take them back without saying goodbye though."

Phew. "You got it, Sis. Need me to get you anything before we start?"

Lara waved her away. "Just need quiet and dark."

Kennedy grabbed her laptop and a few books from the shelves in the living room before moving back to the spare room, where Wes was taking off lens covers and slipping in battery packs. She didn't bother giving him any instructions on the cameras—she'd asked his advice on which models to buy when she decided to upgrade from the webcam setup. She knew he'd researched what kind of camera he wanted for the agency and, being Wes, that meant he'd *over* researched. Sure enough, he'd sent her a list of the pros and cons of several different models, along with lenses and software. She'd ended up getting the same body he used. Just one at the start, then she'd bought the exact same thing again when she decided to expand.

Which meant he was perfectly capable of setting them up for her, even if he tended to use the still photography settings more than the video.

She positioned the books on the desk, pulled two folding chairs from the corner for Alyssa and Justine, and then opened her laptop. Ideally, she'd have had a week to do some research rather than ten minutes, but...well, she'd done a bit here and there anyway, after the authors accepted their invitation. Not because she'd thought to do a show, but because she couldn't resist learning everything she could about books.

Wes's phone pinged in his pocket, and he drew it out. "I'll mute that while I'm at it."

"Thanks. Wynn?" He had different noises set up for his main contacts, and that one sounded familiar.

He nodded, scrolling through something. "VaKayBo needs yet more information to get the initial offer to us." His tone said that VaKayBo had been asking for "more information" enough to make him wish he hadn't signed the non-disclosure at all.

She was more than a little surprised that they still hadn't seen an offer. "Do you need to get back to the office? You can take my car. I'll take the ladies back over in Lara's."

"Nope." He jabbed at his phone and tossed it onto the bed. "They can wait until tomorrow morning, which is what I told Wynn. I'm out with clients."

It was true, but it still made her laugh. "She knows very well where you are." With clients off whom he wasn't making any profit. He'd rented the house out for the week for expenses only. Because he was a fantastic friend.

"And she also knows that this is the tenth request they've sent. I swear they just want us to feel like our recordkeeping is screwed up so they can lowball us. But it *isn't*. They inevitably already have what they're asking for, they just want it in a separate file or something."

"Sounds like they're really buttering you up." Her laptop finished its startup, and Kennedy navigated to the document she'd started six months ago on a whim. "Are Wynn or your parents annoyed by how long it's taking?"

"Impatient, more than annoyed. But then, the requests keep coming to *me*." He shook his head and grabbed another chair from the corner, unfolding it behind the cameras. "But enough of that. This is Rare Book Talk time."

She might have pressed further, but she could hear her guests laughing their way back toward them, so she let it drop and turned her attention to the document on her computer: "How to know if you have a first printing of Alyssa McDaniel's blockbuster book, *White as Coral*."

Time to get to work.

Chapter Eleven

Wes scrolled through his online photo archive, but his frown only increased as he got to the dates he was looking for. He knew for a fact they'd taken photos of Kenni meeting Justine and Alyssa for the first time. He remembered thinking that their shirts were color-coordinated and looked like they'd planned for the photoshoot, just like when Mom made them take family photos.

No, wait. He scrolled down further, to a year later. There—that photo had been taken with Justine, not Alyssa. He and Britta had driven up to the event too, since Brit was a big fan of Justine's and she'd wanted an excuse to visit Kenni. He clicked through the pictures he'd taken of the event, of Kenni and Britta fangirling as they waited in line, candid snapshots of the two women finally getting to the front and introducing themselves.

Wes hadn't been *in* line, but he'd stood with them for a while and otherwise roamed around taking photos with his then-new camera. He had some fun coverage of the event, and of Britta and Kenni with Justine.

He clicked through the ones of Kenni with the author, downloading a few to print out. They'd been talking about that event at the big Fourth picnic last night, and he thought it would be fun to surprise Kenni and Justine with photos from when they first met.

Now...Alyssa. He knew Kenni had met her too, and he remembered seeing photos, but he hadn't been there to take them. Had she emailed them to him? Texted?

He searched his emails and texts from her—and wow, there were a lot. He hadn't really paused to realize that he communicated more with Kenni than anyone else. His search turned up nothing. But he *swore* he'd seen photos. And Britta had gone too, hadn't she? A couple months before that last trip—she and Lara had driven up together. She must have taken photos and just showed them to him on her phone.

A knock sounded on his door even as it opened. "Anyone home?"

"Back here, Beck." He pushed away from his computer and stepped into the hallway just in time to see Beckett Mills saunter through the living room and head his way. "What's up?"

Beckett looked like exactly what he was—a sun-bleached beach bum. By this time of year, his skin had taken on a deep bronze that wouldn't fade until the weather cooled, his hair had lightened to sunny, and even now he looked like he'd just stepped off his pride and joy—the *Ginger Lady*, which he kept docked at a marina in Buxton.

His friend followed him back into his home office with ease, carrying the scent of salt and sun with him. "Stopped by the office and Wynn said you'd taken a half-day so you could go to the big book signing. But since that doesn't start until three, I figured you must just be killing time at home. Which of course means you're bored."

Wes laughed and settled back into his chair. "Not yet, but that doesn't mean I mind company. I'm surprised you're back already. Don't you have, like, five charters a day this week?"

Beck made himself comfortable in a recliner in the corner. "Had a group that booked the whole day, but then half of them got so seasick they begged to turn back at lunchtime. All that chum made for some good fishing though." He cracked a smile, white teeth gleaming. "They were happy to get home, went home happy with their catch, and I got half a day off with full pay, giving me a long weekend. Life is good."

"Nice. I mean, not that they were sick, but..." Wes clicked on the photos he'd downloaded and opened a desk drawer. After pulling out a few sheets of glossy photo paper to feed into the manual tray of his printer, he sent the images to print.

"Whatcha printing? Anything good?"

"Just some pictures of Kenni with the authors who are visiting—from the first time they met, a couple years ago."

Beckett's blond brows rose. "Why do you say that like you're annoyed?"

"Hmm?" He snapped his attention back to his friend. "Oh, I'm not annoyed with these. I'm just trying to figure out where I have photos of her with the other author. I know I've seen them, but I think...I think they must still be on Britta's phone."

He'd already saved all the ones she'd uploaded to his own account, but she hadn't had her phone set up to back up to the cloud automatically—she said she took too many garbage photos. Instead, she'd go through every now and then, save the ones she wanted to keep, and delete the eight hundred selfies that were "so hideous." She must not have done it since the book signing.

Beck leaned forward, those brows now dropping into a frown. "You didn't ever clear her phone?"

He winced at the very mention. "I...no. They gave it to me with her personal effects, and the battery was dead. I just...left it in the box. Does that make me a coward?"

"Dude. That makes you a grieving husband. No judgment here."

And that was why Beckett and Asher were such good friends to Wes. Neither of them had ever tried to push him to grieve in any way but his own. He sighed and swiveled his chair around to face the closet. That's where he'd shoved the whole box of Britta's belongings. Her phone, her purse, everything else from her car. He hadn't even been able to unpack the suitcase she'd taken with her for the girls' weekend—it was in the master bedroom closet, still full of whatever she'd packed.

Not something he'd ever confessed to anyone. He'd just resigned that piece of luggage to a corner and used another whenever he needed one.

He didn't want to present photos of Kenni and Justine but none of Kenni and Alyssa. He sucked in a deep breath and stood, opened the closet door. Stared for a minute at that innocent looking white cardboard box like it was a sea serpent of lore ready to overturn his dingy.

Or maybe he'd stayed up too late last night reading *White as Coral*. He reached up and grabbed it, pulling it into his lap as he sat again.

So light. So light to have in it all the things that had surrounded her in her last minutes. The small "travel purse" she said was useless for daily stuff but was light and could be worn cross-body when she went into the city with Kenni. The phone with its sparkly pink case that he'd teased looked like a Barbie doll accessory. The lip balm she always kept in a cupholder—she was addicted to the stuff.

Beckett didn't ask if Wes was okay—he just moved over to the desk and sat on the edge. "You could just not give Kennedy any photos. Knowing you, you hadn't even mentioned it, and you were going to surprise her with them. She'll never know."

His grin felt weak. And yet grateful. Beck knew him well. "She wouldn't. But this is as good a time as any, right?" Better than most, given that Beckett was here.

Fishing the sparkly pink plastic from the box, he plugged it in. "I'll have to give it a few minutes to charge. Want some iced tea?"

"Got any of those cinnamon cookies left?" Beckett had always approved of Wes's baking and cooking habit, though he hadn't developed his own.

"No, but I've got some from Sunshine."

"That'll do." Beckett pushed off the desk and headed out of the office. "So…this Harper person. She's moved back for good?"

Wes's lips twitched. "Is that *interest* in your tone, Beck?"

"In her baking, sure." But his shoulders went stiff in that way they always did when someone suggested he give up his bachelor ways long enough for a date.

Wes still didn't know what his friend's hang-up was. He'd only moved to Avon six years ago after a stint in the Navy, so Beckett didn't know Wes's high school friends who had moved away, and he'd arrived with a boatload of baggage he never wanted to talk about.

Given the stuff Wes kept shoved in his own closet, he'd given up prodding his friend about it nearly two years ago. And since Beckett had just been so supportive, he could do the same. "It *is* some fine baking. I've got triple-chocolate, peanut butter, with peanut butter cups, and lemon." As they reached the kitchen, he moved to the counter where he'd put the cookies in an airtight container after bringing them home on Wednesday. "As for Harper—I don't think she knows if she'll go back to Savannah or not. Guess it depends on how her dad's doing and if they need her to stay."

Wes popped the lid off, and Beckett pursed his lips as he considered the options. "Her parents are great bakers—but I gotta say, their offerings have gone up a notch since she came home." He pulled out a peanut butter cookie.

"No arguments here." Wes selected an iced lemon and moved to the fridge with its ever-present pitcher of iced tea. "Grab a couple glasses down, will you?"

They planned their next sail, texting Asher to confirm dates and times, while they ate. The *Ginger Lady* was Beckett's sailboat, used only for his own pleasure. He had a motorized fishing boat too, which was what he took out for charters six days a week, weather permitting. One of his brochures was in every welcome bag that Armstrong Realty handed out.

By the time they'd taken their last swig of tea and returned to the office, Britta's phone was charged enough to turn on. Drawing in a deep breath, Wes eased into his chair and Beckett slid back onto the edge of the desk.

He'd seen her phone a million times, but rarely had he held it, aside from handing it to her. She'd always been weird about her phone, never wanting anyone else to use it. After dating her so long, he'd just gotten used to it. Britta's phone was *Britta's phone*. Everyone knew not to touch it without her permission.

Not that she'd had the same compunction about using other people's. He was all the time coming into the living room to find her using *his* phone while hers charged. He hadn't cared. But still, it felt weird to have the pink thing in his hands now. He watched the startup screen and drew in a deep breath when it displayed the lock screen.

She had a password set up, but he'd watched her tap it in enough to know what it was, so that was no problem. Soon he was staring at the home screen, his throat going tight.

She had twenty-four text messages waiting. Probably all from the days after she died, before friends had heard the news.

Not going there right now. He pulled up her photo gallery instead, telling himself not to look too closely, not until he'd thumbed his way to the right time period. He didn't have to scroll far—the signing had only been two months before her death.

There. She had quite a few shots of the event, some of Alyssa speaking—including a short video—and quite a lot of Lara and Kenni with Alyssa, then some with Britta too.

He hovered over one of those for a long moment, his gaze tracing her familiar face. He still saw it every day, in the wedding photos on his walls, but at some point he'd stopped *looking*. They were just there, like the painting she'd done of the sunrise over the dunes and the wooden cross his dad had made in one of his crafty phases. He hadn't really let himself look at her in…a while.

But no, it wasn't that he hadn't *let* himself—though it had started that way. It was that he hadn't felt the want to lately. No desire to stare at a photo of her and sob, like he'd done in the immediate aftermath of her death. Or to pull one up just to remind himself that he'd had a wife, once. Someone to come home to. He hadn't imagined it, his life truly had been full, if imperfect.

It was still too empty…but the throb had faded to an ache somewhere in the last few months.

He selected the photo, along with a slew of others from the event, and sent them all to himself. Then he set the phone down, picked up his own, and uploaded them to the cloud. "There we go. That wasn't so bad."

Beckett smiled. "Good. Well, I better get out of your hair then. You'll probably need to leave soon if you want a parking spot—the bookstore lot was already full up when I came by."

That seemed like a good sign. "I figured I'd just bike over anyway. So yeah, I could use the extra time. Glad you stopped by, man."

"Hey, I know which of my friends is likely to have cookies." Beckett slapped a hand to Wes's shoulder and moved toward the door. "See you at church if not before."

"Bye." He waited until he heard the door open and close and then reached for Britta's phone again. He should probably upload any other photos he wanted to keep. Grab anything now, and then just turn the phone off again.

He thumbed the gallery back to the newest photos and scanned the thumbnails, smiling a bit at the countless "hideous" selfies. Britta had definitely had a bit of a selfie addiction. Though his smile faded when he saw that she'd taken some in a bathing suit he'd never seen before.

The faded smile turned to something else entirely when he saw her face pressed to an unfamiliar one. He enlarged the photo, his stomach dropping. An unfamiliar *man's* face. He recognized the décor behind them as being one of the restaurants up in the Nags Head area—busy and full of people who wouldn't know her. As she pressed her cheek to some other guy's and smiled for her camera.

Maybe the air conditioner had kicked into overdrive. Or maybe summer had given way to winter in the blink of an eye. Maybe that's why he felt iced over, like his blood had frozen in his veins.

Not even thinking it through, he pulled up her messages. All those new, unread messages. He clicked on one from someone named Dan.

Hey, babe, why aren't you answering?

"Babe? *Dan*?" He ground the words out between teeth as frozen as the rest of him. Who was *Dan?* The guy in the photos?

Knowing he didn't actually want to read it, he opened the message thread anyway.

Now the melting ice gave way to nausea. He had to draw in even breaths, measure their release as he read the proof that Britta was having an affair. Places to meet up. More pictures of them together, arms around each other. Photos Wes had never seen that she'd sent this guy.

He nearly put the phone down. But he only got so far as backtracking out of that text thread when another with new messages caught his eye. *Kennedy.*

He opened it up.

We'll talk about this when you get here. What's your ETA?

This. What was *this*? He scrolled up to where this particular chain of texts seemed to begin, a day before her accident.

A message from Britta said, Hey BFF. Can I come up for a night tomorrow?

Kennedy, responded, Sure.

Then she added, Why? Do I want to know?

LOL prolly not!

He could all but see Kenni wincing at the "prolly." She was grammatically correct even in her texts.

Look I promise I won't tell you all about Dreamy Dan

You are NOT doing this again, Britta!!!!!!

Again? The nausea went heavier. Leaden.

Will you chill please?

Nope. You PROMISED you wouldn't do this again.

But that was before I met Dan! He's perfect!

He is not. Know why? Because he isn't YOUR HUSBAND. If you want to come up here to meet with some other guy, forget it. I told you I would never be party to that again, and I meant it. I will call Wes myself if you try it.

His jaw clenched. She hadn't, though. She hadn't called and told him about this *Dreamy Dan*, and she certainly hadn't told him about some other guy it sounded like Britta had rendezvoused with on a previous trip to DC.

Britta had replied, Relax! I'm not meeting him there. I just need a place 2 land for a night, k? Then I'm going 2 call Wes and tell him it's over. I'll be out of your hair again Saturday

AND YOU CAN TATTLE 2 MY HUSBAND ALL YOU WANT. I'LL BE GONE.

BRITTA...NO. YOU LOVE WES. YOU'RE NOT REALLY LEAVING HIM.

I AM. IT'S DIFFERENT THIS TIME.

IT'S NEVER DIFFERENT. BUT EVEN IF IT IS, IF YOU REALLY DO THIS, HAVE YOU PAUSED TO THINK WHAT IT'LL DO TO HIM?

HAVE YOU PAUSED 2 THINK WHAT BEING STUCK DOWN HERE IS DOING 2 ME? I NEED OUT KEN! YOU OF ALL PEOPLE SHOULD UNDERSTAND!

The texts had been scattered over a whole twenty-four-hour period, which had pushed into the Friday afternoon Britta left. The last message in the thread was the one he started with.

WE'LL TALK ABOUT THIS WHEN YOU GET HERE. WHAT'S YOUR ETA?

He set down the phone, eyes unfocused. Britta had told him she was visiting Kenni *weeks* before she went—at least two. He'd had time to plan the guys' weekend with Asher and Beckett, time to modify their plans a dozen times. But she hadn't let Kennedy know she was going—because she didn't actually care if she saw their friend.

Kenni was just a convenient layover. An excuse to give him.

She'd been...she was leaving him. Cheating on him—repeatedly, apparently—and *leaving* him.

And Kennedy had *known*. She'd known, not just about the real reason for Britta's trip, but about the affair—presumably about multiple affairs. And what had she done?

Nothing. Sure, she'd said something about Britta not deserving him right after they got engaged, but after they'd gotten married?

She never breathed a word. She'd done nothing but hold him while he sobbed like a baby at Britta's funeral. Thinking what? "Oh, the poor oblivious fool"?

He leapt from his seat, ignored the printed photos and the messenger bag already stocked with books he meant to get signed. He snatched his bike helmet from its place by the door and slammed outside, barely thinking to lock the door behind him.

Kennedy had some explaining to do. All the explaining that she'd apparently *threatened* to do before but never had. Not while Britta was alive, when it could have made a difference. They could have gone to counseling, they could have worked it out if she'd been forced to admit it! And certainly not in the two years since, when he kept turning to *her* because he thought she understood better than anyone what he'd lost. When he'd thought that Britta had loved them both.

Right now, he wasn't so sure Britta had loved anyone. Wasn't sure what it was he'd always felt for her, much less why she'd agreed to marry him. And certainly wasn't sure he could trust a thing Kennedy Marshall had ever said.

He grabbed his bike from where he stored it under the house and took off for the bookshop. Maybe if he pedaled fast enough, he wouldn't still be fuming when he got there.

But he had his doubts.

Chapter Twelve

The glow of success probably lit her up like a lightning bug. Kennedy pulled into the driveway with a smile still on her face. It didn't matter that she hadn't managed to get out of the shop until nine. Didn't matter that her back was screaming at her from all the bending to get more books out for the women to sign. Didn't matter that Lara had had to call a retreat at six and have Aunt Grace bring her home, or that Shaleen had ducked out an hour ago after the last of the guests left so she could babysit her niece.

It was the best book signing event of her life—and she'd been to many. She'd helped put together a few at the shop. But this…this had been *everything*.

Alyssa and Justine had been *on*, and they fed off each other so well they had the ever-changing line of people constantly laughing. There was a constant flood of people from three to eight o'clock, with twenty-five coming in at a time to listen to the ladies chat for a few minutes and get their books signed. The line hadn't been anywhere close to finished by their usual closing time of six o'clock, so the shop stayed open until the crowds dispersed. And they had sold out of books—both the new release and backlist titles!

That alone was amazing. But the fact that it had been such a joy for all involved—she might not come down from this high for a month.

Turning off the car, she hurried out while the headlights still illuminated the steps to the door.

"Kennedy."

She jumped, slapped a hand to her heart. And then frowned. It was Wes's voice, but he never called her Kennedy. Nor had she heard him sound like that—hard and cold—in more years than she cared to count. She closed Mizti's door, searching for him in the dusk. "Wes?"

He was on his rooftop deck. Or had been. Now he was coming down the stairs.

She leaned against the car to wait for him. She'd seen him arrive at the store a few minutes before the signing officially started, but he'd taken one look at the crowd, shaken his head, and pedaled on by. She'd expected him to come back after the initial rush had let up…but, well, it hadn't. She'd given up looking for him, figuring he'd decided to just let the visitors have their fun and get his own books signed tomorrow, when they were set to take the McDaniels and Claytons out for a celebratory brunch before they headed back up the road on Sunday.

Now, though, she wondered at his decision. Wes was never the type to shy away from a crowd, many of whom were likely Armstrong guests. He was the type to circle around to the back and lend a hand, working that crowd as effortlessly as Justine and Alyssa had.

And when she saw the storm on his face in the deepening night, she knew it hadn't been the overwhelming crowd that kept him away. "What's wrong?"

A muscle in his jaw ticked, and he jerked his head toward the dunes. "Walk with me."

It wasn't a question—which was also unlike Wes. She felt the firefly glow of success begin to dim. "Sure. Just let me toss my purse in the house and kick off my shoes." She'd worn sensible ones for the day, but they weren't sand-friendly.

He didn't answer, nor did he budge. Just stood there, hands shoved in the pockets of his cargo shorts, and waited for her to pad back down the steps after quietly closing the door behind her. Lara's door was closed, and hopefully her sister was sound asleep.

She rejoined Wes, offering him a smile that shouldn't have felt so tight and forced. Not today. "What's up?"

"Not here." To emphasize his point, he strode off toward the wooden walkway that led over the widest section of dunes.

Mosquitos buzzed around them as they hurried through the grass and scrub, though most of them vanished once they were on the beach, where the wind provided protection. The sun had sunk below the sound forty minutes ago, but a bit of light still stained the western sky. To the east, it was dark as ink, and stars were beginning to wink to life overhead.

One of her favorite sights, usually. The moon shone in the lapping waves, ghost crabs scuttled away from their footsteps, and the beach was an open, empty stretch of silver in the night. The wind danced between them, making her wish she'd grabbed something with sleeves.

She expected Wes to strike out either to the north or the south, but instead he walked to the water's edge and halted. Kennedy moved into place at his side, smiling at the warmth of the water that licked her toes.

The smile faded the moment he spoke. "How long did you know?"

She turned to face him, knowing her confusion was evident in her expression—not that he looked down to see it. "Know...what?"

That muscle pulsed in his jaw again. "That Britta was cheating."

All the joyful breath from the day gushed out of her as surely as if he'd punched her. "What?"

"I turned her phone on today—wanted to print some photos for you from that first signing of Alyssa's you went to. I found...things."

"Oh my goodness." She reached out to put a hand on his arm, but he jerked away like she'd burned him. Her hand fell back to her side, feeling rather burned itself. "Wes, I..."

"That last string of texts you had with her—she was leaving me, and she *told* you."

Another jolt. She pulled her feet free of the sucking sand so she could take a step back. "And I was trying to talk her out of it."

"That's your defense?" He finally turned to her, moonlight blazing in his eyes. "You *knew*! And from the sound of it, you knew about a lot more than *Dan*."

She backed up another step, and even though he didn't follow, she still felt him looming there. Too tall, too righteous, too furious.

Too right.

"What do you want me to say, Wes? Do you want me to tell you everything? Is that going to make it better?"

He made a sound too guttural for words and spun away. Stomped two steps, then pivoted and stormed back. "I thought you were my friend too."

Another punch. "I was your friend *first!* You know that. It was the two of us long before we ever met Britta in school!" That was why he should have fallen for—no. *Stop.*

"So, why?" His voice cracked, shattered like starlight on the waves. "Why wouldn't you *tell me*?"

"I tried!" That got his attention at least, brought his gaze to hers for the first time. "I tried to tell you before you ever married her!"

He took another step toward her, his brows lowering. "Wait. She...back *then*?"

Tears stormed her eyes out of nowhere, pulling her back ten years. To another night, on campus instead of here, but under the same stars. The same moonlight gleaming in his eyes.

She'd risked it all. Everything. Her heart, their friendship, her relationship with Britta. She'd risked *everything* to try to tell him that Britta didn't deserve the ring on her finger, and it had gotten her *nothing*. "After you proposed. She'd been seeing other guys all through college, Wes, and I *tried* to tell you—but you said..."

He winced, half-turning away with the force of it. "That you were just jealous. I didn't mean it like it sounded, I didn't mean to make you all but vanish for months. I only meant that you didn't like being the third wheel..."

She'd known what he meant—and she'd known that he was more right than he knew, even in how it sounded. "You shut me down, wouldn't listen. And how was I ever supposed to tell you after that, knowing what you'd chalk it up to?"

He lifted a hand, dug his fingers into his hair, held on as if those strands could tether him. His world must be spinning out of control; he'd question everything, *everything* he'd built his life on. It was one thing to realize your marriage wasn't perfect, which she knew he understood. It was another to realize your wife had betrayed you in the worst way possible.

Kennedy could understand why he wanted to blame her. She was here, and she'd known, and he could rail at her in a way he couldn't rail at Britta.

And maybe she should have insisted, over the years. Maybe she should have *made* him listen to the truth. But her own feelings had made everything all twisted and tangled up inside.

She folded her arms over her middle and did her own holding on. "Do you remember how she used to call me her conscience? Way back in middle school—I was always the one beside her saying 'Don't cheat on the test, Britta' or 'No, we're not having a séance, Britta' or 'You will *not* sneak out to meet that high school boy staying on your street, Britta.' She joked about it, and I think part of me, back then, was *proud* to be her conscience. To be the one to tell her to clean up her messes so her mom didn't have to or send a thank-you note to her grandmother or do the extra credit on the test. Because she *listened*, and it made me feel important. Like I mattered. Like she *needed* me."

Without meeting her gaze, Wes turned back to face the water. "She *did* need you."

"Maybe so—but here's the thing, Wes. No one can live with someone *else* as their conscience. I remember this time when we were seniors, when we all decided to go to UNC Chapel Hill together, but I realized how big it was and how, since we were all pursuing different studies, we'd see so little of each other…I just felt this bolt of fear. For Britta. Because I knew that I wouldn't be at her side nearly every hour of the day anymore, and I knew she had made *no* effort to make her *own* good decisions. And I thought, 'I've ruined her. I've done it for her so long that she doesn't even know how to make good choices without me. And she won't try. She won't find other friends to be what I've been to her. She'll just go merrily off the rails.'"

Wes's only response was to suck in a deep breath.

Kennedy moved slowly back to his side. "I still tried. But I was right. I wasn't there enough for her to run everything by me anymore, and even when she did, she stopped listening to what I'd say. I *tried*, Wes, I tried to help her be the girl you'd fallen for. But I couldn't make her do it. And I couldn't make you see it. And I couldn't—"

"It was never your job to be her conscience." He tilted his head back, face toward the sky. He sounded calm again, but not peaceful. The sort of calm that came from a storm having blown itself out, leaving nothing but debris in its wake. "And…and it isn't your fault I wouldn't listen. I'm sorry. I shouldn't blame any of this on you. It was her, us…I don't know. I just…I can't believe how blind I was. All those years, she'd never let me touch her phone. Her moods, her recklessness…I thought it was just *Britta*. I thought…I knew we weren't perfect, but I thought we'd work through it. I thought she loved me."

It was Kennedy's turn to wince. "She *did*. That was the worst part from my perspective. Because she *did* love you, you were the one she wanted to be with, and every time I threatened to tell you, she'd get this look on her face and accuse me of trying to ruin her life. To take away the one thing that mattered."

"She was *leaving* me!"

"She wouldn't have. Not for more than a week. She'd have called and told you she decided to stay with me a little longer, she'd have met that guy for a few days, and then she'd have panicked and come home, full of stories of all the made-up things she did with me in DC."

He went so still. So utterly, completely still. Remembering. Piecing it all together. "She'd done that before. Not just with you, either. She'd gone on trips to meet college friends, supposedly. Always after she'd been in one of her moods. I knew something was wrong, off, but...but I thought she just missed you. That some girl-time with you would fix it."

Her breath came out in a snort. "I don't know if she ever missed me, Wes. I don't know...I honestly don't know if she cared about me at all. I was her best friend when it was convenient. I was someone she knew she could turn to. But it was never about me. Just her. She made everything about her."

It sounded so harsh, so careless, so cruel. Especially since Britta wasn't there to defend herself, to explain anything, to unlock the mysteries of what really went on inside that beautiful head of hers.

Maybe she would have grown out of it, eventually. Maybe she'd have settled down. Regretted the way she'd treated Wes, all the other men. Maybe she'd even have come to Kennedy one day and apologized for being a craptastic friend.

Or maybe she wouldn't have. Kennedy would never know. She could only pray that somehow, there was a part of Britta's heart that truly was what she claimed to be—a woman who loved her husband, her family, her friends, and God. Pray that somewhere, somehow, that was true, just buried under the lies and the cheating and the selfishness and the backstabbing.

Kennedy prayed that somehow, when Britta stood before the Lord, He judged her for that kernel inside her friend that loved and believed, and not just for the sins she'd let rule her life.

Wes let out a long breath. "Did she—this is probably unfair to ask you—but, did she really want kids? She told me she did, and we were trying. I thought her unhappiness there at the end was because we weren't successful. But now...now I wonder if that was just one more manipulation."

Silence pulsed for a long moment, filled only with the rush of water, the song of the wind. She almost wished she didn't have the answers. That she could just shrug and leave something intact.

But she *did* know. And for the first time, he wanted to listen.

"She told me she never wanted kids." It was the truth, but admitting it felt like she was slapping him. That was what Britta had always done—made her feel like *she* was the one hurting Wes if she spoke the truth, even though Britta's actions were responsible. "She wanted to keep you happy, and, I think, liked the attention she got when she told everyone you guys were trying but hadn't been successful yet."

Britta had made such a mockery of their college friends who actually were trying and facing infertility. Kennedy had known real fury when Britta confessed that truth, when she'd come up to visit for Alyssa's signing. Only the week before, Kennedy had listened as a friend sobbed over the phone, when yet another month had passed and that friend wasn't pregnant. Then there was Britta, faking the same thing just to manipulate Wes and get her own way.

Wes heaved another sigh, turned toward the dunes, and walked a few steps. At first, she thought he might leave, the information having been too much to bear. But no, he just retreated to the drier sand and sat down.

She spared half a second's thought to the capri-length slacks she had on, then did the same, positioning herself at his side but with a little distance between them. "I'm sorry." Such pathetic words, but she didn't know what else to offer. And they were true. She was sorry for so much. For keeping Britta's secrets from him, for not somehow stopping her friend to begin with, for standing by while he asked her out. She was sorry for trying to manage Britta instead of...of...

What could she have done differently? She still didn't know. Didn't know why she'd always felt so responsible for her. Didn't know why she'd loved Britta like a sister, even through it all. Why she kept trying, kept advising, kept letting her turn to Kennedy when she needed something. Was it guilt, over those old feelings for Wes?

No. At least not entirely. It was that she really had loved her. Britta really had been one of her best friends. Because, despite the selfishness and lack of a moral compass, in spite of everything she did wrong, Britta was so *lovable*. When you were with her, she made you feel important. Smart. Beautiful. She listened to your stories and laughed at your jokes as if you were the funniest person in the world. She accepted all your quirks and made you feel like they were your superpowers.

Britta's attention had always been empowering, somehow. Heady. Kennedy had felt like the luckiest girl on the island when the beautiful, vivacious blond had singled *her* out to be her best friend in grade school. When she'd not even insisted Kennedy give up her friendship with Wes, despite the fact that boys were gross at the time. She'd accepted him too. Folded herself into their neighborly duo and turned them into a trio, and made them both feel like she'd given them an immeasurable gift.

She had. Sometimes Kennedy needed to remind herself of that. For all the ways Britta had broken them into pieces, she'd first built them into something they never would have been without her. She'd crafted them into the most magnificent sandcastle on the beach—then left them there to be destroyed by life's tides.

Loving Britta was like trying to embrace a hurricane.

Wes rubbed at his face. "How can I love her and hate her at the same time?"

Kennedy's laughter slipped out, joined hands with the wind. "Because she was so many bright and beautiful things. And she handled all the blessings God had given her so carelessly. Never imagining that her behavior would catch up with her. Never thinking she'd have to answer for any of it."

He wasn't just rubbing his face—he was wiping at his cheeks. "I've spent the whole evening stewing and thinking and going back over every day of those last few months. Going through her phone, trying to piece it all together. To sort out how much of our life together was a lie."

She let her eyes fall shut. Talk about a few hours of torture. "Wes...don't. That'll only hurt you, and the answers don't change anything. She loved you the best she knew how. She was unfaithful to you. But she's gone. We can't undo any of it."

"I just...I can't believe how stupid I was. How blind."

"You weren't. She was...this is going to sound horrible. But she was so good at lying. Sometimes I wondered what was wrong with her, that she was so good at it. Did she believe any of it? Was she a pathological liar?" Kennedy had wondered far more than that, but she couldn't bring herself to give voice to all the amateur psychology she'd tried to apply to her best friend over the years. It would only make the situation worse for Wes to know that she'd spent years asking all the questions he was only beginning to grapple with.

"But you knew." It didn't sound like an accusation this time. "You saw it, and I didn't."

"Only what she chose to show me. She could have been bashing me behind my back, and I'd never have guessed." Yet another thing she'd wondered about—why had Britta always confessed everything to Kennedy? Was doing so part of the game for her? Did it make her feel powerful somehow?

She'd wanted to believe it was a cry for help. That her friend told her everything because she knew what Kennedy would say, and she needed to hear it. That Britta *wanted* to change, to do the right thing, to repent, but couldn't do it alone.

Kennedy had no idea what the truth was.

"I was such a fool. All the hints…I just explained them away. Chose not to believe it, even though now it's perfectly clear." He set an elbow against his updrawn knees and rested his head against his hand.

"It's not foolish to believe in your wife. That's how it's *supposed* to be." She wanted to reach out, to comfort him like she'd done after the accident, but it felt too dangerous now. "Wes, I imagine you're going to run through the gamut of emotions as you process all of this. But remember one thing—her failures weren't your fault. If she were still alive, you'd have to decide how to move forward, whether you'd give her another chance or not. But God's taken that decision out of your hands."

He pinched the bridge of his nose. "Wanna hear something horrible? I thought, at one point tonight, that I'm glad she died. Glad I *don't* have to decide what to do about it. What kind of monster does that make me?"

"The human kind." She had to curl her fingers into her palm to keep them from reaching for him.

"So many things I wish I'd done differently now. So many things I can see that I could have changed, if I'd just known to look. I shouldn't have let her get away with so much. I shouldn't have accepted all her excuses, taken the easy way out and turned a blind eye just because I couldn't admit I'd made the wrong choice." He released a long breath, shoulders curling forward. "I shouldn't have married her. Wynn was right. I should have listened to what you tried to tell me in college, certainly shouldn't have tried to blame *you* for anything."

All those years of carefully built walls and warning systems blared at her, cautioning that she'd better slip out before the watertight door slid closed. She pushed to her feet and swiped the sand from the seat of her pants. "You don't need to feel any guilt for anything having to do with me. You have every right to be angry with me for knowing and not telling you."

"No I don't. Not given what I said to you."

She never should have brought up that night. "You do. And even then..." She shouldn't say it. She should just do what she'd trained herself to do and march right up the beach, scurry over the dunes, and lock herself in her house, away from him. But the words, so long pent-up, so long held back because she couldn't voice them while Britta occupied the space between them, pounded on that descending door, screamed for a chance to be spoken. "You were right. When you said I was jealous. You were right in how you meant it—and in how it sounded."

They hovered there, those words. Evading the wind that wanted to whip them away. Waiting for Wes to make it all better, for him to jump up, look at her in a whole new way. To make this about her.

But she was an idiot. This *wasn't* about her. It was about him, about the heart Britta had posthumously ripped to pieces, about the marriage Wes believed had been built on granite and just discovered to have been nothing but shifting sands.

He didn't so much as twitch. Didn't look up. His breath didn't hitch in sudden awareness. He just sat there for one beat, two.

She turned and walked away, knowing well he wouldn't chase after her. He never had. Never would.

Because she wasn't Britta. And as much as he hated Britta right now…she'd always been the one he loved.

Chapter Thirteen

Avon, North Carolina
July 5, 1938

Ana walked around the dining room table, a smile on her face as she leaned over to add the correct accent to the word Tommy had written on his slate. Eight children now showed up every day for lessons, though keeping them on track with French was proving a challenge. They were far more interested in reading the English version of *The Secret Garden* and then acting it out.

Each of the four little boys wanted to be Dickon, the boy in the story who could talk to animals and knew everything about nature. They had dubbed the dunes and beach their garden and were constantly collecting snails and sandfleas and crabs to "listen" to, and trying to convince each other that the sandpipers and seagulls were telling them secrets, that they were learning the intricacies of God's creation just as the character did in the story. They were only marginally less eager to play the role of Colin, who got to be carried about at first and then marched around giving lectures on what he deemed "magic," but which was really just the mystery of the natural world and people's determination to know it, to know the Creator through it. Whoever claimed neither of these roles would get to be the gardener, Ben Weatherstaff, or one of the servants—unless it was a scene in which Colin's father, Mary's uncle, was on the page.

The girls would alternate between the main character, Mary, Martha—Dickon's older sister and Mary's maid—their mother, and the housekeeper, Mrs. Medlock. Each character had their own bit of fun, and the children wanted to try them all, which made for a bit of chaos when they forgot which role they were playing that day.

Ana knew very well it was the playacting that brought them all to the table, not the French. Even

Susie and Jill, who were by far the most determined to learn the language, were distracted within five minutes.

Part of her wanted to chide them as she would have her students in Dalmatia, bringing them back to task. But another part silently whispered that it was their summer holiday, that this wasn't really school, and that if they wanted to focus on the story rather than the lesson, it was perfectly fine. Wonderful, even.

Let them lose themselves in Burnett's world as she had done so often as a girl—it was such a lovely world, with so many valuable lessons to be learned about God's world and the indomitable human spirit He had given them all. And the fact that so many children had now read her increasingly worn English copy? That was to be applauded. The idea warmed her as she crawled into bed every night.

When Marko returned, which should be any day now, he would glow with pride in her. He was always so proud of her teaching, saying that she enraptured the children just as she'd enraptured him. She couldn't wait to tell him all about it, to introduce him to the children, to tell him the funny stories she'd been storing up.

"How did you enjoy Independence Day, Miz Annie?"

The question came from the oldest of the girls—Gertrude, who was ten. Her blond hair was plaited down the sides of her head, her blue eyes always the first to wander from the French lesson. But she was a lovely girl, full of curiosity and questions.

Ana had given up trying to get the children to call her by her correct name. For whatever reason, *Ah-nah* was beyond them. They all turned that initial *A* into a long, drawling *ay*, and then changed the ending.

She smiled at Gertrude. "The picnic was delightful, even if we had to have it inside. I quite enjoyed the hotdogs. Though I was very disappointed that there were no fireworks because of the storm."

Caroline assured her they'd do them another night, even though that didn't seem quite as exciting. The storm had been a fierce one, and had raged for a full twenty-four hours, not letting up until early this morning. It was the first real storm Ana had seen from the Atlantic, but it had made clear why the ocean was known for its tempers.

She'd never heard such howling wind, and the rain had come down in driving sheets. She'd thought more than once that the roof was going to be picked up and tossed away like a paper hat, but it held firm.

Caroline had tried to laugh it off, but Ana hadn't missed the anxious looks she'd sent toward the sea.

The men ought to have been back in time for the holiday. The fact that they weren't meant they'd probably run into the same storm out at sea.

It was enough to strike fear into the heart of any fisherman's wife. Even now, the claws of anxiety hadn't fully loosened from Ana's chest, despite knowing that a day or two delay on a multi-week trip wasn't out of the ordinary.

Gertrude heaved a dramatic sigh. "Wasn't much of a picnic either. Most years, everyone gets together at the church. We play games all day and then watch the fireworks come evening. It's a real hoot. Not nearly the same when we're all stuck at home."

"Mama said we'll have the big picnic this coming Saturday," another of the girls, Nancy, put in.

Ana peeked over Nancy's shoulder at her work. "Well done on that vocabulary, Nancy."

And their own picnic, even if indoors, had still been nice. Caroline's parents and in-laws had both braved the storm to eat with them, and they were all such nice people. At one point, talk had even turned to houses that Ana and Marko might be able to purchase—apparently Jack's family had several in their possession that no one was living in right now, as various branches of the family either passed away or moved to the mainland to pursue better jobs. They seemed to think that "Aunt Kerry's place" would be perfect for a growing family. It sat soundside, about a mile away, and Caroline promised to take Ana to see it after the children left today.

The girls continued to chatter about Independence Day picnics and games, despite a few gentle attempts to get them back on task. Ana stood in the doorway to survey them, shaking her head. It was too much to ask after the excitement of the storm and the holiday, she suspected. So she clapped her hands and said, "Why don't we put away the French and move on to *The Secret Garden?*"

A chorus of approval sang out, and the eight children jumped up from their chairs, Susie grabbing the book and holding it aloft. Gertrude reached into the bag she'd brought over and pulled out a handful of papers, declaring, "I've made us scripts for this chapter!"

Whether the other children would follow them or not was debatable, but her weekend's work was met with cheerful admiration, regardless.

Ana, chuckling, drifted into the kitchen and out of their way. Caroline sat at the table, thumbing through a magazine. Before she could make any observations about the brevity of the lesson, a knock came on the screen door, though it screeched open in the next moment.

"Yoo-hoo." Berta Marshall let herself in, a container in hand. "I thought I'd bring a snack over for the children. Pauline said they have their lessons about now."

Had anyone asked, Ana wouldn't have been able to explain why her back went stiff every time she encountered Jill's grandmother. Maybe it was the way Caroline had warned her about the woman's closed-mindedness, but she didn't think so. It just felt as if there was always more to what she said behind her actual words.

The children, of course, came tearing out at that moment, scripts in hand, focused on the door. They didn't bowl into Miz Berta, which was good. But no one but Jill bothered to greet her, and even her granddaughter only tossed a hello over her shoulder as she zipped out the door. Was that the cause of the woman's frown?

Apparently not. "Pauline said their lessons began at ten. I would have thought they'd have lasted longer than fifteen minutes."

Heat surged into Ana's cheeks. "They were all a bit distracted after the holiday and the storm."

Berta smiled. But it wasn't a kind smile. "I suppose it *is* difficult for those not properly trained to keep rambunctious children in line."

Caroline pushed to her feet. "It has nothing to do with training, Miz Berta."

Ana tried to bite her tongue, but something about Caroline's quick defense made her want to stick up for herself, just to prove her friend wasn't wrong to do so. "I am keenly aware that this is not formal schooling, and that the children are here voluntarily. They are more eager to read together and act out scenes from the book than to learn French, which is a fine thing too, so I encouraged them to shift to an activity that would more fully engage them this morning."

Berta sniffed and patted her hair. "Playacting." Her opinion on that pastime was clear. "And what is this book they're so enthralled by, anyway? I've never heard of it."

A sentiment Ana had heard from quite a few parents over the last two weeks. Despite the author's international popularity, it seemed this particular title of hers wasn't all that widely read in America. "It was first serialized in *The American Magazine* back in 1911 by the author of *Little Lord Fauntleroy* and *A Little Princess*. Perhaps you're more familiar with those?"

"I've heard of them. But I don't put much stock in novels." Berta's chin went up. "I spend my reading time immersed in the Good Book."

Ana forced her smile to remain in place. "There is room for both."

"Perhaps for those who spend their days sponging off others instead of working for a living like decent folk."

Caroline had already been moving toward her guest. Now she snatched the bowl from her neighbor's hands with a glower. "I don't know *who* you're talking about with that comment, Berta Marshall. Certainly no one around these parts, though plenty of us enjoy whiling the evening away with a novel after the chores are done. Better pastime than gossiping, according to Reverend Porter." She met Ana's eye and jerked her head toward the door. "Let's see if they want this melon before they get too deep into things. They can pretend it's the breakfast Mrs. Medlock brings up."

Ana was grateful for a reason to trail her friend out the door. Even if Berta did follow them. Ana expected a retort from her, but it seemed that the moment she stepped outside, her attention went directly to her granddaughter. "Jillian, get off that table at once!"

The girl was standing on the wooden picnic table, no doubt as part of a scene-staging, given her bemused look at her grandmother's reprimand. "But—"

"This *instant*, young lady. You know better than to stand on a table."

"It's just part of the *playacting*." Caroline held a hand up toward Jill. "Your grandmother brought some melon, so hop down so y'all can eat some, sweetie."

Berta muttered something that included "shoes on the table!" though Ana didn't catch the rest, lost as it was among the children's opinions of the fragrant orange cantaloupe from which Caroline soon began handing out slices.

Ana took one, though her first bite told her it wasn't quite like the cantaloupes she'd tasted in Europe. Instead of the mild flavor she was used to, this all but assaulted her tongue. Yet another reminder that she was far from home.

The kids, of course, weren't to be distracted by a little thing like fresh fruit. They continued to chatter about today's chapter as they ate.

Tommy must have played the role of Colin today, because he ignored the melon altogether and was striding along the decking with his script in one hand, making grand gestures with the other. "'Of course, there must be lots of Magic in the world,'" he recited, "'but people don't know what it is like or how to make it. Perhaps the beginning—'"

"Magic!" Berta's screech was in the same octave as the screen door's squeal. She spun on Caroline and Ana. "What kind of trash are you letting this foreigner teach them, Caroline Harding?"

Caroline looked as bemused as Jill had a minute before. "What?"

"You know very well that magic is just another word for witchcraft and sorcery and is of the devil! I can't believe you'd let this woman fill your daughter's innocent young mind with such things that the Scriptures strictly forbid!"

Caroline shook her head. "No, Miz Berta, there's no actual *magic* in the book, it's just what the kids in the story call—"

"Jillian! Get over here right now. I'm taking you home, and I'll have a thing to say to your mother about this. I'll have something to say to *all* of their mothers!"

Was it frustration that sizzled through Ana? Panic? Dread?

It was all three, because, in a flash, she knew what would happen if Berta Marshall stormed off this deck and did as she threatened. She'd ruin Ana, ruin *everything*.

Ana didn't know all the other mothers very well. She'd met them, she could greet them by name, but when it came down to it, she was a stranger to them. They weren't going to believe her explanations over the objections of one of the pillars of their community; they'd simply snatch their children away from her and then view her with suspicion and distrust.

She'd be shunned by everyone but Caroline— which meant she'd drag Caroline down with her.

She'd never be able to teach here, never be able to integrate into the village.

Ana couldn't let that happen, not without so much as a squeak of protest. Grabbing the copy of the book Susie had set on the table, she hurried to put herself between Berta and the steps down from the deck. "Miz Berta, please, hear us out. There is no magic in this book, the children simply don't know what to call the workings of the Lord. The mother character explains later that—"

"A bunch of nonsense." Berta reached out, and Ana wasn't sure what she meant to do—push Ana aside, slap her? But she snatched the book out of her hands, and Ana got the distinct impression she didn't mean to read it. "This sort of trash ought to be burned, that's what. Or tossed into the ocean."

Jill's hand still in hers, Berta did push past Ana, giving her the option of grabbing hold of the railing and letting her squeeze by, or being shoved down the stairs. She opted for the railing.

Jill was tugging on her grandmother's hand, trying to dig in her heels but only putting herself at risk of falling down the stairs too. "Gramma, no! I don't want to go!"

"Berta, you give Ana back that book right now!" Caroline yelled, hurrying a step behind. "You have no right to take her property!"

Ana lost sense of who was yelling what, her eyes locked on that bright green cover with its sweet gilded words. It was in Berta's hands, then Caroline's, then Berta's again. The children had crowded around her, forcing Ana down a step, wondering what those two upstanding Christian women were going to do.

For a second, it looked like too many scenes she'd witnessed back home. Opposing sides, facing each other down. Shouting that so easily could turn to violence. And over what? A children's book about three kids and a robin redbreast and the garden that gave them hope?

It was ridiculous—but the things that broke people apart too often were. They were nothing, nothing worth fighting over. Even the book itself, much as she treasured it, wasn't irreplaceable. It was just a *book*. Caroline could let her neighbor toss it in the sea if she wanted. Ana would miss it, but they could buy another someday, sometime, when she had the money to spare.

"Please, stop!" She meant her voice to be authoritative, to cut through the squabble like she'd had to do many a time in her classroom. But maybe the wind snatched her voice away, because neither Caroline nor Berta seemed to hear her.

But then, they didn't seem to be fighting about the book anymore either.

Berta had gone red in the face. "I've had enough of you putting on airs just because you married the Armstrong boy. You're just a *Harding*, no better than your tramp of an aunt—"

"And *I've* had enough of you lording over everyone like you're the only person on the island who has the right to decide anything!"

"Caroline?"

"Mother!"

The two deep voices did what Ana had failed to do, bringing an immediate halt to the argument. From her perch halfway down the stairs, Ana saw not just the two men belonging to the voices, round the house, but a whole slew of them—seven or eight.

Jack Armstrong, it must be, given the way Caroline—book restored to her possession—flew into his arms. Which meant that the one who'd called out "Mother" must be Cliff Marshall, Jill's uncle, who Caroline had said was Jack's deck boss. And the others must be the rest of their crew.

Which meant... Ana flew down the rest of the stairs, even as she searched every face. Where was he? She saw men of various ages, various colorings, but no Marko. Her heart was still racing, even as it sank. Perhaps he hadn't known to come here to find her? That must be it. He'd have gone to the post office the very moment they reached shore, to see if she'd sent a wire or a letter for him. He'd learn there where she was, and follow in a few minutes.

Though Jack grinned as he held his wife, Cliff frowned at his mother. "What in the world is going on here?"

Berta's chin came up again. "That woman took in some foreign drifter woman and was letting her teach Jillian and the other children a bunch of unholy garbage."

Cliff's eyes cut over, found Ana. Something strange seemed to overtake him then. He straightened. Reached out and grabbed Jack's shoulder.

Jack released Caroline, his gaze moving to Ana as well. And his smile faded in a way that made her stomach go tight.

No.

She knew what it was to see bad news settle on someone who had to deliver it. She'd seen it after uprisings and massacres and beatings and burnings.

She'd seen it visit other houses, students' families, friends and neighbors. She'd known the dread every time someone with that expression strode along a street.

But this time he was looking at *her*.

With only a glance at Caroline, Jack moved toward Ana, the scent of brine and fish coming with him. Familiar scents. They should have comforted her. Instead they made her stomach churn. "Ana?" he asked softly.

She could only nod, too numb for words, and reach for something to ground her.

A little hand slipped into hers on one side, then another. She didn't even look to see which of the children had grabbed hold. She just squeezed back.

They knew that look too.

Jack pulled his cap from his head and wrung it in his hands. "Marko said you'd be here by now. He was so excited to see you again."

Was. He said he *was* excited. A ringing started in her ears, a silent cry in her mind, a litany of wordless prayers screaming their way to heaven.

Cliff stepped up beside Jack. "We got hit hard by a storm on our way back. Twenty-, thirty-foot seas.

Your husband, he knew what he was doing—he was a good fisherman."

"A good man," Jack said. "The best man. We got hit by a rogue wave, and the ship rolled. Engines cut out. Marko was the first in the engine room, doing everything he could to get them back up. We were getting battered, it was all I could do to keep us facing the right direction, but he did it. Restored power."

Cliff shook his head, that storm ravaging his face. "We'd have sunk if he hadn't. Greg got knocked out with the roll, and no else can ever get that engine restarted if it floods." He motioned toward another man, one who Ana hadn't even noticed. He had picked up Jill and held her on his hip. Pauline's husband, then. He had a dirty bandage wrapped around his head. "Marko saved us all."

"It happened when he was coming up to the bridge to report when the crane broke free. Caught him right in the head." Jack blinked, but Ana didn't miss the tears in his eyes. "It happened so fast, Ana. We all rushed to him, but it was too late. He was gone, just like that."

Gone. Marko, her Marko. She heard a keening and didn't know if it was the wind or Caroline or herself making the noise. The world tilted, and in the next moment she was sitting on the bottom step, sobbing into her knees. Hands rested on her back. Big hands. Small hands. Inside her, the baby kicked against the horrible truth.

He was gone. She and her baby were alone.

Chapter Fourteen

"So there we go." Wes leaned back in his chair and looked at the other three people who'd have a say in the decision. Mom, Dad, Wynn. They sat around a small conference room table at the office, door closed, with offer sheets from VaKayBo in front of them. "They gave us a month to decide."

It was a solid offer. Solid enough to make dread knot in his stomach. It would be tempting for the rest of them. Even given that the cash payout in the offer wasn't huge, the profit-sharing and stock they would earn from VaKayBo over the next decade, for doing none of the work, was sizable. His parents could retire and never need to worry. For that matter, he and Wynn could sit back and relax if they wanted to. They could run the sales division without fretting over whether it was enough to make ends meet, with earnings from VaKayBo still coming in at a generous rate. They'd have to downsize, but they could send off their staff with a generous severance package from the cash payout.

But it came with so many costs.

"Okay, so I think the pros are pretty obvious." Wynn's eyes bulged as she took in the bottom line. "That's a lot of money over the next ten years."

"It's what it's worth." Dad lifted the page and leaned back in his own chair, reaching for his glasses and settling them on his nose. "Sixty years of building a business, that's what it is." The pride in his tone for what his family had built came through loud and clear.

Wes got that. He felt it too. There was something affirming about seeing that big ol' dollar amount on the company his family had poured so many years of heart and soul into.

Mom shook her head. "We'd have to cut the staff by more than half. And this non-compete we're all required to sign?"

"It's standard," Wes heard himself say. Not that he wanted to defend VaKayBo or lobby for them—but it was the truth. "They have to be certain that one of us isn't going to go start up another agency and take all our clients with us. That would defeat their whole purpose."

"Yes, but you couldn't even move to another existing agency in the Outer Banks." Mom pursed her lips, those all-seeing green eyes of hers honing right in on him. Making it clear that *you* was *him*. "You're not going to be happy with only the sales side, Wes. We all know you're not."

Wynn tilted her head to the side. "Maybe they would consider rewording that part, with a contingency about working somewhere else if we didn't take our clients with us."

Was his family seriously suggesting he just go work for one of their competitors? It was a friendly enough market down here— they were family businesses, after all, and those families had known each other for generations. But they were also feeling the pinch as more and more homeowners took their rentals into their own hands with third-party sites similar to VaKayBo. Their rental listings had dropped from nearly seven hundred, when he first graduated college, to closer to six hundred, and they certainly weren't unique in that. "And what if one of the homeowners decides they don't like working with VaKayBo and checks out that other agency that I happen to work at? They get sued because of me?" He shook his head. "No one could risk hiring me. I'd paint a bullseye on them."

Wynn blustered out a breath.

Dad gave a thoughtful hum as his eyes moved back and forth over the offer sheet.

Mom tapped a fingernail on the table.

Wes rubbed at his eyes. He hadn't been sleeping well in the last week, since he'd turned on Britta's phone. Every time he tried, his brain just spun over the same useless details, looking for clues in every memory.

It was pointless. He knew it was. Britta was dead. Her betrayal was over. He didn't have to decide whether to give her another chance. He just had to figure out how to forgive someone who could never ask for it, someone who had made the same bad choices over and over again. Someone who had been so good at lying that he hadn't even realized all the times she'd hurt him.

Was it normal to feel every blow now, all these years later? He felt like he was bleeding, his life seeping from years-old wounds that were never seen before. It was like a bad dream, where you look down and see an injury and don't know how you got it. All the complaints he'd *thought* he had back then now seemed stupid and small. No, worse—tips of an iceberg he'd turned away from.

She'd told him in a million little ways that she wasn't happy. But he thought they could fix it. Thought that she, like him, would just live with the question of whether they'd made a mistake, and try to shore up their quaking foundation.

He thought she'd fight for them, choose to love him, just as he'd decided to do with her.

Wes had told his family about Britta's phone and the resulting revelations last weekend, when they asked why he'd bowed out of the farewell meal for the two visiting authors that the rest of the family attended. He hadn't wanted to confess what he found—despite Kenni's assurances, it still felt like his fault. He'd failed his wife. Failed their marriage. Failed...everything. But he couldn't *not* tell them. So he had. And Mom had cried and Dad had gotten all quiet and Wynn—Wynn had fumed and raged and reminded him that she'd *told* him he shouldn't marry Britta. She hadn't known about the cheating, but she'd known Britta wasn't right for her brother.

They'd been walking on eggshells around him all week, treating him like a mine waiting to go off.

Fair enough. That was why he'd been avoiding everyone he absolutely could—his family, Kenni and Lara, the guys. He knew he'd explode at some point, and he didn't want to leave little pieces of himself embedded in any innocent bystanders. Trying to blame Kenni for not telling him was the only one of those pieces he was willing to grant himself.

And her—he'd been doing his best to avoid even seeing her in passing. He didn't know how to grapple with the words she'd left him with. They'd wrecked him as much as that sparkly pink phone had done, and anger with *her* kept overtaking him at the oddest moments too.

What had Kenni been thinking, dropping a bomb like that and then just strolling away while he tried to decide if he'd heard her right?

What did she mean, that she'd been jealous—not just third-wheel jealous, but *actually* jealous?

Why would she say it now, in the wake of Britta's ugly truths coming out? His thoughts kept cycling through those questions when he should have been sleeping. Sending him down all sorts of pathways he'd long ago deemed impossible.

"Well, I think it's obvious what we need to do." Dad set the paper back on the table and took his glasses off again. "Sit with this for a while, pray on it. I say we each think it through, write up our individual pros and cons as well as the ones we see for the company, for all the people whose families rely on this business, and then we talk it over in a week. This isn't something we should rush to decide on. This affects all of us, and the next generation too, potentially."

The next generation—something Wynn had to consider already. Something Britta had never meant to give him.

"I think that's a great idea. And no hashing it out over and over again in the meantime, you two." Mom moved her pointing finger from Wynn to Wes. "I don't want to hear you debating anything at the fish fry tomorrow night, you hear me?"

Wynn rolled her eyes.

Wes sighed. "Mom, I don't know if I even—"

"You're coming, like you always do." Command given. No arguments brooked. He knew from experience that if he tried to disobey the order, she'd show up at his house and badger him until he gave in. She got up from her chair, moved over to his, and planted a kiss on the top of his head. "Family will help you heal. You know that. You don't have to talk about it, but you have to be near the people who love you."

Since she held out her hand, he gripped it, gave it a squeeze. And felt a little bit of comfort, despite it all. Because, of course, Mom was right. Wallowing alone would make it worse. Reminding himself that his life continued, that there were people who loved him enough to make sure he *didn't* wallow would help pull him out of the quicksand. Day by day, step by step. They'd been his rope before, and they would be again. Even the ones who didn't know.

Dad came over to give his shoulder a squeeze too, and then he and Mom exited, their printed sheets in hand. He wondered idly if they'd obey their own rules and not talk about it with each other over the weekend, or if that had been aimed solely at him and Wynn.

His sister dragged in a long breath and ran manicured fingers through her hair. She waited until the door clicked shut behind their parents and then leaned forward. "Have you talked to Kennedy again?"

He didn't even have the energy to roll his eyes. "Why are you so hung up on that?" He'd told her that he'd ambushed Kenni, all they'd said...up until that parting jab. *That* he'd kept to himself, but he was beginning to wonder if that twin-connection thing was finally rearing its head thirty-one years later, and Wynn was reading his mind.

"Because the fact that you've been avoiding her means that you either still blame her for not telling you before or...there's something else at work here that I'm missing. And you know how I feel about missing information."

"I don't blame her." How could he? Kenni tried to warn him before he even married Britta, just like Wynn had. His parents had asked him, when he told them he meant to propose, if he had prayed about it—which made him wonder now if they'd doubted his wisdom too. He'd told them he had. That he was sure.

He'd lied. He *hadn't* prayed about his relationship with Britta, not until well after they were married and the cracks in the foundation started showing up. Then he prayed that God would help him fix it—fix the thing he'd never asked His opinion on before. Because he'd been so sure. So certain he could make his own decisions. So confident that this was what he wanted.

So afraid to admit he'd invested years of his life with the wrong person already. Maybe he'd known all along that if he'd brought the question to God, he'd have gotten an answer he didn't want.

And Kenni. She admitted she'd been jealous. What did that mean? What had her intention really been that night, ten years ago? Just to warn him about Britta not being faithful even then or… something else? Something more? What had he cut off, after she got out no more than "She was flirting with Ryan last night"?

What would be different if he'd heard her out? Why hadn't she *made* him hear her out?

Wynn pulled her chair around to his side of the table and leaned an elbow on the shiny wooden surface, resting her head in her hand and batting her lashes at him in what she always called her "you have my undivided attention" pose.

It made him laugh, like it always did. And the laughter made him relax. And relaxing made him realize that he needed to talk this through with *someone*, and it wasn't a conversation he could imagine having with Asher or Beckett, neither of whom had been around at the time, and he certainly couldn't have it with Kenni. Which meant his sister was the most logical choice.

"You know how I said Kenni tried to tell me about Britta before we got married, but I cut her off?"

Wynn nodded, her thoughts on the matter clear in her eyes. *You should have listened.* But she kept the words to herself this time. "And you said she was just put out at being the third wheel."

Was that how he'd relayed the conversation to his sister? "Well, I accused her of being jealous. But that's what I meant. Well, the other night, she...she said she *was* jealous. Not just like I meant it, but *actually* jealous. And then she just walked away while I was trying to figure out if she meant *that* the way it sounded."

His sister's eyes went wide as she sat up straight. She slapped a hand to the table. "Oh my goodness! Kennedy's in love with you!"

It was so ridiculous he snorted a laugh. "She is not in love with me. She maybe had a crush on me ten years ago."

"No, she totally is!"

"Wynn." He shook his head. Maybe she *wasn't* the one to talk to about this.

"Let me walk you through this." Animation in every feature, she pressed a fingertip against the table in front of him. "So, clearly she had feelings for you back then, or she wouldn't have admitted to being jealous-jealous. Right?"

A weird feeling took root in his chest, one he had no words to describe. Not quite hope. Not quite fear. Not quite the vertigo that came with all he thought he knew realigning. Some combination, maybe, or some whole new thing. "Feelings...sure. But I don't think we can say she was in *love* with me. If she were, then..."

Wynn's brows rose. "Then what? She'd have tried to get over it when you first asked Britta out. Maybe put on a cheerful face sometimes and then other times made excuses to avoid you both?"

He blinked, trying to remember those days in high school. Was that what she'd done? It was so long ago at this point...the only thing he really remembered was that it had been awkward for a while. But that was to be expected when the three amigos turned into a couple, plus their mutual best friend. Right?

Wynn moved her finger an inch. "Right. In high school, Kenney might have just hoped your relationship with Britta wouldn't last. But you kept dating in college, and then the clincher. You proposed. Which triggered what?"

He stared at his sister's coral-painted fingernail. "She tried to tell me about Britta cheating."

"No doubt assuming that, if you knew, you'd end things. That was her first risk-it-all moment. Now, perhaps you could have argued that she'd have done that just because you were her friend and she didn't want you to get hurt, and I'd have granted that as a possibility, were it not for her admitting to being jealous. But you told her she was making it up because she was jealous, and what happened then?"

This he could remember more clearly. "She all but vanished for a few months, at least when I was around. But she had that internship—"

"Give the girl some credit, little bro," Wynn said, her expression telling him to think this through. "Kenni chose her moment thoughtfully. She knew it could go wrong, and if it did, she didn't want to have to see you daily. She tried to talk to you when she did so that she had an escape route already set up if it went badly. Which it did. So, cue the escape."

He winced and dropped his gaze back to her finger, which moved another step. "I should have listened. Heard her out. I should have...I should have at least started watching Britta more carefully."

"Agreed. But *should have* is irrelevant right now. We're talking about what Kennedy did, not what you should have done. So you and Britta were already engaged during your senior year of college. What did Kennedy do then?"

"She was so busy. We barely saw her—I mean, Britta still did, but I didn't much." It had nearly killed him, made him beat himself over and over for ever saying what he had. For making things awkward, when not having her in his life was the worst thing, the very thing he'd always feared. "Then there was the wedding. She was maid of honor. Then she moved to DC and pursued her master's up there and ended up getting on at the Library of Congress."

He had no idea what his sister could possibly point to in that sequence of events to back up her theory.

Wynn smirked. "Do you realize Kennedy didn't even *apply* for anything closer? I remember thinking at the time that you must have been right about her determination to get far away from here. But it makes sense now. She applied to graduate schools in DC, in New York City, in Boston, a couple other big northern cities I can't remember—"

"Where there are big museums and hence, rare books. Perfectly logical."

"Sure. Especially if she needed to stay far away from the guy she was in love with, who'd just married her best friend. We have plenty of museums in North Carolina too, Wes. She went to undergrad here, she could have continued to graduate level stuff a lot closer to home. But she didn't. Not with you married to Britta."

He just stared at her. "You're saying *I'm* the reason she moved away. But she'd *always* talked about moving away!"

"Much like I always talked about moving to NYC to be a Broadway star. Big dreams, little bro, but that doesn't mean we do it when it's actually time to make the choice. Much more likely is that we come home and take over the family business—and let's not forget that was the exact time when Kennedy's and Lara's grandmother stepped back, when the shop became too much for her. It would have been the perfect time for her to come home and help with that."

His weird feeling spread. Grew. "But Lara was doing it."

"You think Lara wouldn't have loved for her and her sister to do it together? That had always been the plan. Don't you remember how they'd joked about renaming it Two Sisters' Books?"

Now that she mentioned it, Kenni had even doodled the sign they'd someday hang above the shop. But that had been back in middle school, early high school. Before she started dreaming of bigger things.

He shook his head. "But she gave up on that before I ever asked Britta out. They went on that trip, and she saw those old illuminated manuscripts and became fascinated with old books. That was when we were fourteen. That was when she started talking about moving away. Long before I asked Britta out."

Wynn slanted a glance at him. "You sure about that timing?"

"One hundred percent."

She snorted. "No offense to your memory, but—"

"I'm not wrong about that." It came out a little more forcefully than he'd meant, which earned him another raised-brow look from his sister. He huffed. "I would have asked *her* out, if it weren't for that. Not Britta. But Kenni didn't want to stick around, and I always knew I did."

It was the first time he'd said it out loud, even to Wynn. Even just to himself. But it was true. Kenni had been his first friend. His *best* friend. Back then, he couldn't imagine life without her by his side every day. A part of him had always imagined *them* getting married, as if it were the most natural thing in the world.

But then she'd started dreaming dreams that didn't include him or his world. The thing she knew very well he wanted to do with his life. He'd never wanted anything but to stay here, to become a part of Armstrong Realty. But Kenni wanted to see the world, to explore the history only housed in big city museums, to work with the sorts of books no one in their right mind would keep in a flood-prone, hurricane magnet, hot and humid place like the Outer Banks.

But Britta had always said she just wanted to teach art and dabble with her painting right here. So as he grew up and realized he'd like a girlfriend, not just friends that were girls, Kenni might have been his first choice, but she wasn't the *right* choice. Britta made more sense. And it was easy to convince himself that he had a crush on her. She was a flashier kind of beautiful than any other girl in school. She was so outgoing and passionate about life. Every guy in their class had a thing for her, and yeah, that added to the allure, because he was a sixteen-year-old guy. In other words, he'd been stupid.

Wynn's mouth dropped open, and she reached out to slap him on the arm. "I am deeply hurt! You never once told me that! You've just denied that you ever even *considered* her."

"Because I didn't. I knew it wouldn't have worked."

She scowled. "You're an idiot. What you were was afraid. It was too big a risk. Too much at stake. Because you've loved *her* since we were kids."

The weirdness wriggled inside him. "Not like you mean. I was not in love with her when I was married to Britta."

"I didn't say you were. But love's a funny thing, Wes. It can shift and change and grow and morph into different forms, depending on what we need it to be. You've loved her as a friend all your life. You just admitted that it could have been a different kind of love, had you let it. Well guess what, little brother? You can let it now."

He had to look away from the gleeful hope in his sister's expression. But focusing on the window did nothing to stop that weirdness. It...*bloomed*. In a way that made him fill at once with hope and the same kind of fear that had led him to Britta instead, all those years ago. "You're still assuming her feelings are present tense."

"Right. I need to continue my points." She repositioned herself, fingertip to the table again. "I maintain that all Kennedy's dreams of rare books and big city museums *could* have just been like my Broadway dreams, had you given her a reason to stay. Instead, you gave her a reason to leave—so she did. She pursued those dreams, and she was very careful never to so much as get close to any lines while you and Britta were married. Despite the fact that she apparently knew Britta didn't deserve you. You loved her. Not Kennedy. That's what she would have seen."

Wes's chair felt suddenly uncomfortable. He shifted. "All right. I'm willing to grant that at least in theory, given her admittance of jealousy. She *did* feel something. But that was a lot of years ago. She's dated plenty since then." Yet, even as he said it, he remembered his own questioning before she came home for the summer. Her social life wasn't exactly burgeoning. Never had been. He'd thought she was just too focused on work. But was that it?

Wynn waved his point away with a flick of her fingers. "Of course she hopes to fall in love with someone else, so she can forget about you. But it clearly hasn't happened, because here she is, still single. Which brings us to the present. She has no reason to think you've ever seen her as anything but a friend, so she's clearly never going to make a first move. But she admitted to that jealousy."

"And then walked away." It irked him again just to think about it.

"Well *duh*, Wes! What else could she have done? You just sat there like a mute moron, which would have made her think that you found the whole idea ridiculous. You'd just been talking about the wife you clearly loved. She puts herself out there with that admission, you do nothing, so she runs away. And you didn't stop her."

"What was I supposed to do?" He pushed away from the table so he could stand, pace to the window. "It came out of left field. We'd just been talking about how the woman I'd put all my hopes in apparently didn't find me good enough to stay faithful, which Kenni knew all along. I feel like my guts are hanging out, and then she admits she had a thing for me ten years ago?"

He spun back to face his sister, feeling as though she could see every bit of his devastation. "Don't you get it? She might as well have said that this was all my fault—all of it. Because I could have had *her*, had I just listened. But instead, I steamrolled over her and ruined all our lives in the process. I married the wrong girl, the one who slept around and made a mockery of everything I value. A girl who ended up *dead* because she was leaving me and got in a car accident, probably while she was texting her lover or something. A girl who apparently felt *trapped* in this life that I thought she wanted. Meanwhile, Kenni felt unseen and unloved and was constantly put in the worst possible position, forced to keep Britta's nasty little secrets and yet still play the part of friend to me." His chest ached. His stomach roiled. His head felt like it was about to explode.

Three lives ruined because he'd been too proud to hear her when she tried to tell him he wasn't enough to keep Britta's attention. Too willful to ask God if he was doing the right thing.

Three lives ruined because Wynn was right—he'd been too afraid to risk the thing he really wanted. Too afraid of being rejected and losing the friendship he needed like air. Too afraid that *she* could never love him, so it had been easier to never let his own love grow.

He was a coward and a fool, and even though he *had* given everything to his relationship with Britta, clearly it had never fit quite right. They'd just been an easy answer for each other.

"Oh, Wes." Wynn was there at his side, wrapping her arms around him and holding on tight. "I'm so sorry. So sorry life dealt you this hand." She gave him a squeeze, then pulled away enough to look him in the eye. "But your life's not over yet. And neither is Kennedy's. She's probably kicking herself for ever admitting that to you, and you haven't so much as spoken to her since. Maybe it's time to give it a chance. See what happens."

The same old fears reared up. "What if doesn't work?"

"You think trying's going to ruin things more than you already did by letting her walk away? Could they get *more* awkward?"

A breath of laughter slipped out, unknotted him a bit. "Fair point." Yet the frown was quick to reclaim his face. "But she still lives in DC."

"And you," she said, pulling away altogether and tapping his copy of the offer sheet, "aren't necessarily tied here anymore. I know you love the business, Wes. You love Avon. You love helping people find their perfect getaway for a week. But maybe it's time to discover if you love Kennedy *more*. You were always afraid she loved her dreams more than she could ever love you, right? Well, flip that question around. Do you love *your* dreams more than you could love her?"

Wynn lifted her shoulders, effectively pushing the question from her to him. Then, apparently knowing he'd have to chew on it in silence, she slipped out of the room.

Chapter Fifteen

Though the table in the bookshop kitchen was completely covered in documents, Kennedy was keenly aware of all that was missing. Papers and records she'd seen before, when she was too young to care about the details of her family history. But she had a memory of seeing it all spread out on this very table when the shop was Grandma Janey's house. Of poking through the stacks, wondering if there were any treasure maps or interesting photos, or maybe secret diaries that would say she was really a long-lost princess.

Most of the things here now were either new copies of legal documents that had been filed with the state, or from a single box that had escaped Hurricane Isabel when the storm hit more than twenty years ago, which Dad had dug out and brought over from the house. The family had lost nearly everything in the flooding, including photos and records which Grandma Janey had, ironically, just moved to their house from her own.

Ironic, because the newly created bookshop hadn't flooded at all. That house never had and likely never would. Kennedy's and Lara's, on the other hand, being oceanside and at sea level...

Beside her, Lara sighed and took a sip of her sweet tea. "I just don't get it. How did Grandma never mention any of this?" She had the deed in front of her—the one with *Marija Horvat* on it. "How could she be both Janey Marshall and Marija Horvat?"

Dad and Deanne had ferried over to have dinner with Kennedy and Lara, and then they'd all come over to the shop to unload book orders that had just been delivered with the evening UPS drop-off, figuring they could talk and unpack at the same time. New books shelved, they now occupied the four chairs at the table, stacks of documents before them. They'd pulled out everything they still had access to, but it was just so *little*. Mom and Dad's marriage license, Kennedy's and Lara's birth certificates—copies, mind you, all three. All the stuff from Mom's death, and then from Grandma's death.

But items from Grandma's earlier life? Gone in the flood.

Dad shook his head. "Maybe she legally changed her name. Where would we go to find that out? Think there are any digital archives or anything?"

They all looked to Kennedy, which made her laugh. "Hey, I deal with old books, not ancestry stuff. But...I think the county superior court would be the place to go. I'm not sure what information we'd need to bring though. Is having the two names enough, or would we need to know the year of the change? I have no idea how their records are kept."

Dad shrugged and made a note on the pad of paper he'd gotten out. "I can call on Monday and ask."

Lara pulled forward a photo they'd unearthed from behind another of Grandma in its frame. She was in her early twenties in the snapshot, hair in a bouffant that screamed early 1960s, the brown-tinted photo accentuating her dark hair and eyes. She'd been a beauty, her Italian heritage obvious.

Or what they'd always *thought* was her Italian heritage, from her mother's side. If Horvat had been her real last name, then it seemed she was Croatian, not Italian. Why would she have hidden that?

Deanne had a piece of paper in front of her too. "Okay, so what do we know about Janey's mother? All I have here is that she'd mentioned her mother was Italian—and that's why they were both such great cooks."

They all chuckled at that.

Deanne went on. "What was your grandmother's name, honey?"

"Annie," Dad said. "Though that's not an Italian name. Maybe it's short for something with 'Ann' or 'Anna' in it. There are lots of Italian names that end with *ana*. But that's all anyone ever called her. Annie Marshall."

"Have we looked for death certificates for her?" Deanne asked. "That might give us her actual given name, maybe even have her maiden name. She died when you were how old?"

"Two. I don't remember her at all." Dad jotted another note on his Action Items list. "I just remember asking Mom once if she knew any Italian, and she got this weird look on her face and said that speaking anything other than English at home wasn't exactly a popular thing when she was a kid—especially languages that belonged to the Axis. In the forties, when she was growing up, All American was the only way to be."

Kennedy sighed and let her gaze drift to the shelves full of kitchen and house and gardening books. The ones displayed face-out showed picture-perfect scenes. But was life ever really like that?

"It's sad. So much culture was lost because people felt uncomfortable talking about their backgrounds. They just wanted to blend in."

Lara looked as though she was about to reply, but before she could say anything, the bell jangled at the front door. The sign on the door still said Closed, and they'd turned the lights out in the main room when they adjourned to the kitchen for sweet tea and cake, after shelving all the books. So who'd be coming in? Kennedy stood, her eyes drifting to the clock on the wall. It was nearly eight—Dad and Deanne would have to leave soon to catch the last ferry to Ocracoke. Two full hours after closing.

She shouldn't have been surprised, then, when Wes's familiar voice called out a hello moments before he appeared in the kitchen. But given his week of complete avoidance, *surprise* was putting it mildly. Her heart flipped, her stomach clenched, and it took every last bit of willpower she had to drum up a smile and pretend like she hadn't spent the last seven days wishing she could redo their last conversation. "Hey."

"Hey." He moved toward them, lifting a hand in hello to Dad and Deanne, who of course called out greetings with oblivion.

Lara, not quite so oblivious but also good at pretending, stood. "Want some tea, Wes? Or dessert? Deanne brought her famous cookies-and-cream cake."

Earlier, Lara hadn't been able to get the word *cake* out. She'd first described it as "like a pie but with layers and not a pie." They'd offered *cake*, but she still hadn't been able to make her tongue say it. She'd managed to say *pake*, and then finally *cake*. But she'd laughed over it instead of getting frustrated, which had felt like a victory.

Wes waved Lara back to her seat. "Nah, I'm fine. Wow, this looks like quite a thing y'all are doing."

"Trying to figure out Mom's history," Dad said. "Feel free to take a stack."

"Gee, that sounds like bushels of fun." He moved to Kennedy's empty chair and rested against its back. She tried not to notice how comfortable he seemed here among her family. Or the way his hair was tousled as though the wind had run its fingers through. Or the way his T-shirt stretched over his muscled back as he leaned closer to Dad's stack of papers.

It had been a long, long week, full of far too many thoughts about Wesley Armstrong.

"We're currently making a list of things we can look for in state or county records, like maybe an official name change document. Her mother's death certificate," Dad said.

"Her marriage license," Wes added. "Bet you could find some of that at the church, if you wanted to save yourselves a drive to the court archives. They have baptism records, birth records, death records."

Dad hurriedly wrote that down, though Deanne's brow creased. "Think they'll have survived? The church is on low ground—it's probably flooded quite a few times."

"Worth a shot," Dad said.

Wes straightened and reached into his pocket, pulling out his phone. "Hold on. I remember Wynn saying something about coming across old church documents in some of the boxes stored in the attic of Nana's house when she was cleaning it out. She was baffled as to why they'd have been there, but we figured maybe Granny

Caro had moved them to her house when a storm went through or something. She was the church secretary back in the day." He typed as he talked, presumably sending a text to his sister.

"Do you think Wynn kept them?" Deanne asked, her tone dubious. They all knew Wynn had gone on a big "simplify your space" purge when she was pregnant.

Wes granted the point with a tilt of his head. "I doubt it, but she wouldn't have tossed them out, just returned them to the church. Probably."

Why had he come to the shop? Clearly *not* to help them unravel their family mystery. Maybe he saw their cars in the lot on his way home from the office and just wanted to say hello and see what they were doing here so late, but even that seemed a bit weird this week. Kennedy fidgeted from her spot near the counter. His presence made her antsy.

Lara sent her a look saying she was clearly wondering the same thing. Kennedy had, of course, told her all about last Friday's nighttime conversation, though she'd waited until Saturday morning to do so. A nod to her sister's injury—any other time, she'd have woken her up to gush it all out. Of course, Aunt Grace had come by in the middle of their discussion and overheard enough that she'd had to be filled in on *everything*, which, to Kennedy, had felt a little like stripping herself bare.

Even if it *had* been a much-needed balm to have her aunt wrap her in a fierce embrace and hold her close. To whisper in her ear, *"You do not need to carry this alone. You should have told me ages ago, sweet girl. I would have been praying more specifically than I knew to do. Like I'll be praying now."*

She'd felt those prayers, these last few days. She was pretty sure they were the only thing keeping her on her feet when thoughts of Wes clanged around in her overactive brain.

Dad checked his watch. "We better skedaddle soon, unless you girls want overnight guests."

Lara grinned. "You know you guys are always welcome. You might have to share a room with your younger daughter's old book obsession, but..."

"Hey, I left the bigger guest room totally free." Kennedy paused, considered. "I mean, aside from the boxes I haven't unpacked yet that I shoved in there. But they're not on the bed."

"No offense, but I'd prefer my *own* bed." Deanne rose, smiling.

Wes's phone pinged. "Wynn says she moved the boxes to her attic and they're presumably still up there—she didn't get that far in her simplifying. She'll look when she has a chance." Wes looked up, met Kennedy's gaze. Was it her imagination, or was it not quite the look he usually gave her? "Just text her any names you want her to keep an eye out for, and any years you know."

She couldn't seem to find any words, so she simply nodded.

Deanne put the lid back on her plastic cake carrier while Dad and Wes chatted about the record-setting marlin an angler had brought in on Beckett's boat Wednesday. The process of leaving took the fifteen minutes it always seemed to, but once they got out the door, she'd have her escape. Dad and Deanne would have to drop Lara off at their house, and Wes had his own car.

Except that Wes, hands in his pockets, looked over at her and said, "I was hoping maybe we could take a walk? I can drive you home afterward."

Her breath came out in a gush. She knew Wes. He would apologize again for blaming her last week, apologize for his week of silence as he tried to absorb the magnitude of what Britta had done, apologize even for letting her walk away without a word.

But he wouldn't address the elephant in the room. He'd just reestablish their friendship so they could go back to how things always were. That's what he always did.

It's what she should want him to do. Except it just wasn't.

Lara was already hurrying out behind Dad and Deanne, tossing "Have fun!" over her shoulder.

Wes edged closer, pitched his voice down. "Please? I could really use a do-over."

If she refused, she might as well admit that she was *still* jealous of how he'd always felt about Britta. Avoiding him for the rest of the summer was unlikely, but she was still weeks away from the possibility of escape, so what choice did she have? She summoned up another smile. "Sure."

Being soundside, they had a lovely view of the sunset as they walked toward the water that was so much calmer than the ocean. The colorful sky gave her something to focus on as they wove along a path leading to the waterline and the dock that no longer held any boats. There really wasn't anywhere to walk here, not like on the beach. But Wes didn't seem to mind that his stated purpose would be foiled unless they headed for the sidewalk. He sat down on the end of the dock, taking off his flip-flops and dangling his feet in the water.

Kennedy sat beside him and did the same, letting silence settle into the place between them. By her way of thinking, Wes had asked for the do-over, so he could figure out how to start it. No doubt he'd go through some long explanation of working through his feelings for Britta. Maybe he'd have more questions, or want some of the details they hadn't gotten into last week. Or maybe he'd start with an apology for pulling into his shell all week, citing heartbreaking betrayal as the reason.

He reached over and picked up her hand, weaving their fingers together.

This was new. The confusion of it settled in her brows as she turned to face him, expecting him to drop her fingers again once he had her attention. She prayed he couldn't tell how the simple touch made warmth surge up her arm and settle in her chest. But he didn't let go. "What you said, before you went back inside. About being jealous."

Oh, Lord, help me. It was a selfish prayer, maybe, but the one that flew from her heart. She didn't know how to talk about *that* with him. He was supposed to ignore it, like he'd always done.

She drew in a sharp breath, but it didn't give her any magic words to use to deflect him.

And his fingers were *still* holding hers. "That...that wrecked me, Kenni. More even than the truth about Britta."

The water warmed her ankles, and she felt as though the gentle currents had washed her right out to sea.

He'd called her *Kenni* again. But why did the thought of her having feelings for him wreck him? Was it that horrifying? She looked away, toward the wide expanse of water that lay between their island and the mainland.

He scooted closer, touched his free hand to her chin, a silent bid for her to look at him again. She did, and found his eyes close and deep and gleaming. "That probably didn't sound right. What I mean is...I chose her because she was the safe choice. You were the risk. I didn't think you could ever see me like that. You had such big dreams, and I just wanted to stay here. Had I known, I...I would have done things differently. Everything. Every single thing, but I didn't, and I ruined it all instead."

He ruined it all? And even more baffling..."Britta was *safe*? You're kidding, right? She was the adventurous one, the outgoing one, the one everyone wanted." Not to mention the reckless one, the faithless one, the one who played with men's hearts like it was all a game.

His gaze didn't waver from hers. "She was safe. Because if it didn't work, it didn't matter. If I lost her as a friend, I'd just go on with my life, and I'd be fine, because I still had *you*."

Too many emotions clogged her throat for her to form any response, beyond squeezing the fingers that still held hers.

"Then, to hear you say that if I'd been brave enough to go after what I really wanted, you wouldn't have turned me down?" He shook his head, his eyes clouded. "*That's* what wrecked me. That my choices not only meant not knowing what could have been, but knowing what *was*. That I forced you away, that Britta felt trapped in a life she hated, that she *died* trying to get away from me..."

"That was *not* your fault." Of its own accord, her free hand reached up and settled on his chest, trying to instill peace. "You gave her exactly the life she said she always wanted. You loved her, you were an amazing husband."

Was that amusement now, sparkling in his eyes? "I appreciate the reassurance, Kenni. But that's not my point in all this. I guess what I really need to know is…if…well, if you're still jealous. If I should be brave and go after what I want, or if it's just going to make you run away again."

Her heart thudded so hard, he could probably hear it over the waves and the wind. But then, she could feel his heart racing under her hand too. For *her*. And the fingers that had touched her chin traced her jaw now, feathered through her hair. It made the admission easy. "I'm still jealous."

He must have been holding his breath, because it came out in a soft *whoosh*. A smile flashed over his lips, into his eyes, and then his gaze dropped to her mouth. Lifted to her eyes again, his intentions clear. His brows forming the question.

Yes, yes, yes! She leaned closer, tilting her face toward his, and then his lips were moving over hers.

She'd kept herself from dreaming of this for so many years. Hadn't let herself wonder what it would be like for his arms to come around her, to slide hers around him. And she was glad there weren't fifteen years' worth of dreams crowding her mind—even as she knew the kiss would have shattered them all.

They'd hugged countless times over the years, but his arms felt different now. They cradled her to him, held her like she was something precious. His lips were soft, coaxing, but she could taste the edge of need there too—the need to be sure this was real, that it was worth the risk.

He pulled her closer as he deepened the kiss, and her pulse kicked up another notch in response. She let her fingers brush over the short hair at the back of his neck, to feel the tension in the muscles there.

He was really kissing her. Really *wanted* to. Really saying he wanted more than friendship. It was that realization, as much as his kiss, that made her head spin.

A boat went by way too fast, kicking up more water than it should have in the no-wake zone and splashing them. She and Wes both jumped to their feet, laughing, hands catching each other again.

Wes patted his pocket—probably to make sure his phone hadn't fallen out as he jumped up—and then slid an arm around her waist and pressed another kiss to her lips. Soft this time, but still lingering. When he pulled away, his eyes were just as gentle, just as content to hold her gaze. He wove their hands together again.

It felt weird. And warm. And right.

"Are you overthinking everything yet? Because I am." He grinned at her. "So, you know...give me some help here. Should we *date*? Or is that weird, given that we've known each other since we were in diapers?"

Laughter bubbled up again. "Talk of diapers. You are *so* romantic."

"I'm as romantic as you are mysterious, what can I say." He lifted their joined hands, pressed a kiss to her knuckles. "You knew that before you said you were jealous."

Her hand actually tingled where he'd kissed her, like some sort of teenage heroine in a book. And man, did it feel good. "Dating...is kinda silly, but also kinda sounds nice. I like eating."

"Look at that, something we have in common," he said with feigned shock. His thumb stroked over hers. "Well then, it's settled. We shall eat together sometime. At a restaurant, if you like, or I can cook for you. Or, hey, both. Different nights."

Her smile was big enough to make her cheeks ache a little. "I'm okay with that."

"Kenni." He gave her fingers a long squeeze. "Wynn said I should see where this goes. But I'm not a causal dating kind of guy. You know that, right? This isn't just for fun, or just to see if we could make things work."

She knew that. And yet, what did it mean? "I know. But, so... what *is* it?"

He just looked into her eyes for a moment, his thumb still moving over hers. Then his lips quirked up. "I guess it's figuring out *how* it can work. But I'm all in. I need you to know that. I'm not just going to decide in a week or a month that I like us better as friends. I want you in my life. Like this. Permanently."

She didn't know why she found herself grinning. Teasing. An hour ago, she wouldn't have thought it possible, not about this. "You seem to be dancing around something here, Wes."

"I'm not dancing, I'm just giving you a chance to run away if this isn't what you want."

She reached up, settled her hand against his cheek. "I only ever ran from you *because* this was what I wanted."

His eyes slid closed, but even so, she could see the self-recrimination in his features. They'd have to talk everything through, sometime. Their decisions back then, all the Britta stuff. But that wasn't for now. Now was for hope. Now was this joy that wanted to burst free.

His eyes opened again, and his face cleared. "I love you, Kenni."

And there it went—joy soaring like the birds, whipping like the wind, rushing like the sea. "I'm going to need you to say that about a billion more times. Because I've loved you all my life. Even when I tried really hard not to."

He laughed, leaned in for another soft kiss. "I can do that. And everything else? We'll figure it out. Whatever it takes."

She might have just floated across the sound, if her hand wasn't tethered to his.

Chapter Sixteen

Her sister was silent in the back of Mitzi for most of the drive home from the appointment. Kennedy didn't try to force her to talk, to process what they'd just been told at Lara's first consult with a brain therapist, nor did Aunt Grace from the passenger seat. Kennedy knew how *she* would feel, if she'd been told she couldn't drive or do much else independently until her reflex and vision scores significantly improved. If she'd just been told that it could be *years* before that happened.

Lara would talk when she was ready. Aunt Grace kept looking out the window and dabbing surreptitiously at her eyes.

And Kennedy...her fingers tightened on the wheel. She had her own thoughts to grapple with. The weight of decisions she didn't feel ready to make. She wanted to say what she knew she *should* say—that she would be here. She'd stay. She'd move home. Take over all the tasks of running the shop that Lara couldn't handle right now.

It made sense. Her main reason for wanting to stay away from Avon no longer existed. Seeing Wes daily had become a highlight, not the thing to dread these last three weeks.

But part of her didn't want to say goodbye to the career she'd built. Was that horrible of her? She didn't think she'd miss the hustle and bustle of DC itself—what Lara had always called the "soul-sucking" you couldn't help but feel the minute you neared the beltway. She didn't mind it like her sister did, but that had never been what fueled her.

Melessa, though. Pam. Her friends from church up there. And the Library of Congress itself. The towering floors of books, the back rooms you couldn't enter without a keycard, the labs she worked in every day, white gloves on.

She'd made a career doing things so few people ever got to do. Seeing texts so few people ever got to see. Handling books that so few people ever got to turn the pages of.

She *loved* her job.

She loved her sister too. She loved her aunt and uncle and dad and stepmom. She loved the Island Bookshop. She loved Wes, who loved Avon more than she loved DC.

The decision ought to be easy. So why was it so hard?

It wasn't until they were crossing the bridge onto Bodie Island that Lara finally spoke. "Going out with Wes tonight?"

Her voice sounded like she was trying really hard not to be raw. Not to cry. Not to pout. Strained, pulled taut, near to breaking.

Kennedy cast her gaze up to the dark clouds roiling to the east. "If by 'out' you mean outside to put up the storm shutters, sure. He already said he was going to check on the rental houses with the maintenance crews all day again. I said I'd help when we get home."

Aunt Grace made the dismissive sort of gesture that only a coastal native could make in the face of a tropical storm. "Winds won't be *that* bad."

"Yeah," Lara agreed. "It's not even a…you know. No evacuation required."

Hurricane. Kennedy didn't feel the need to fill in that particular word, given that Lara had moved on from it. "I know, but better safe than sorry on the storm shutters. We'll take care of ours and the shop's too, while we're out."

"Tim could do that," Aunt Grace objected. "There's no need for you to go out in all this."

Kennedy laughed a little. "If it's the only date I'm gonna get tonight, I'll gladly be the one to help Wes. I'll be okay. It's just a little rain, and as my dear sister has so kindly informed me on many an occasion, I'm not made of sugar. I won't melt."

In the rearview mirror, she saw Lara grin, though it looked pained. "I'm just glad you two…"

Kennedy smiled too, knowing Lara's pain had nothing to do with *that*, and everything to do with *this*—the reason they were all on the road right now instead of at home, preparing for the storm that was set to make landfall tonight. The traumatic brain injury that wasn't getting better, not significantly. The thing that made Lara's every day pain-filled, her every word hard to grapple with, some hours so bad she could do nothing but curl up in a ball in the dark of her room and wait for another headache to ebb.

More than once during these last weeks, Kennedy had felt a strange sort of guilt for being happy while her sister was so miserable. Even though she knew very well Lara was happy for her. She sent her sister a smile in the mirror. "I'm glad too."

Lara smiled back and leaned against the headrest. She had dark glasses on, even while the afternoon light looked closer to twilight with those clouds. "We'll soon get to break out all those books of wedding plans we made as kids."

Aunt Grace laughed at the memory. "I remember you girls making those. Do you really still have them?"

Kennedy's stomach did a little flip.

Lara nodded. "They were in the top of my...you know. Storage thing. Escaped all the floods."

"Closet." Kennedy shook her head. The sisters spent countless stormy days as kids cutting wedding dresses and flowers from out-of-date bridal magazines that Grandma had been about to toss out of the shop, gluing them onto paper and writing commentary. They then stapled the pages together to create their own "magazines." "Man, we never would have guessed back then that we'd both still be single into our thirties, would we have?"

"Now, you girls still have plenty of time." Aunt Grace grinned. "They keep telling me fifty is the new forty, so surely that means thirty is the new twenty or something. Right?"

Lara snorted what might have been a laugh. Or derision. Hard to tell which. "Let's hope so. Because we had no idea how complicated life could be."

"So true." At age twelve, Kennedy had assumed that life would work out perfectly. That she and Wes would fall in love and marry young and live happily ever after with a few perfect children and their every dream coming true. She'd assumed that Lara would meet Prince Charming in college—since she didn't have a neighbor boy to fill the role—and get married right after.

Lara *had* met the guy Kennedy had thought she'd marry her senior year of college—but she'd broken up with him right after

Mom died. Kennedy still wasn't sure whether anything but grief had contributed to that decision, but Lara had never once said she regretted it. Maybe something had happened that her sister never wanted to talk about—or maybe Tyler just hadn't proved himself capable of handling the hard stuff, like losing a parent.

So Britta had been the one to live out Kennedy's dream.

It still seemed unbelievable, when she paused to think about it, that she and Wes were getting a second chance. Despite Wes's words from the start, she still half-expected him to wake up one day and say he preferred her as a friend. Most days, that thought would niggle until she saw him. Until he smiled at her in a way he never used to. Until he pulled her close and kissed her—sometimes softly, sometimes greedily, each way saying that he'd been thinking about doing it all day.

Even so, they hadn't talked about the future yet. Despite Wes's claim that all they had to figure out was *how*, there'd been too much *now* to dwell on. Lara, plus the VaKayBo offer, and Wes had been spending most of the last couple days helping with storm prep.

And there was too much of the past to sort through. It seemed wise to get it all out of the way—all the secrets Britta made her keep, all the running away Kennedy had done, all the dreams Wes hadn't dared to dream.

She still couldn't believe he'd thought Britta was the *safe* choice. That she was the one he'd settled for. That Kennedy had been the one he thought was out of reach.

"Kennedy."

After she halted at the first stoplight on the island, Kennedy looked back at her sister, brows raised at her tone. "Yeah?"

Lara met her gaze. "Don't give up DC for me. Because of *this*." She motioned to her head. "I can't be the reason you give up your dreams. I *can't*."

"Lara—"

"No. I know...I *know* I'll be part of your decision. And there's Wes, who might be reason enough for you to come home. But I just..." She shook her head, reached up to squeeze Kennedy's shoulder, and then let go. "It's bad enough this stupid injury is stealing *my* life. It can't steal yours. You can't let it."

"Lara." Tears wanted to crowd her eyes, but driving through heavy summer traffic wasn't the time to indulge them.

Aunt Grace craned around enough that she could reach for Lara's hand. "It's not going to steal your life, sweetheart."

Lara choked on a laugh. "I can't run the bookshop. I can't drive. I can't even *read* without wanting to puke."

"It'll get better," their aunt said.

"It might not!" Lara's shout filled the car, hung there suspended in the air.

Kennedy eased off the brake when the light turned. Another horrible something the therapist had said today. Some things would get better...some things might not. And they couldn't know, right now, which was which. They could only work to heal and improve and use workarounds where possible. The therapist had given Lara a pair of prism glasses to help with some of her vision issues, exercises she needed to do at home, recommended apps for her phone and computer.

Otherwise? She'd prescribed rest from the things that hurt most.

The things that had been Lara's whole life.

"I know." Kennedy's admission sounded quiet in the wake of Lara's shout. "I know it might not. But we still have to believe it can. And that, if not...then you'll adjust. You'll dream new dreams. You'll find new ways to be *you*, because we will *not* let it steal *you*, Lara."

"Your sister's right," Aunt Grace said. "You're more than the things you do."

Lara sniffed and turned her face to the window.

Kennedy let the words sink into her own heart. She, too, was more than the things she did. More than the career she'd chosen. More than the life she'd built. Her identity was attached to the people she loved—and more, she was the one God loved. Even when she lost the people, she still had that reassurance. Always had that.

It was a truth she'd clung to as a heartbroken twentysomething who fled to DC to escape. God loved her, even when her dreams shattered. God loved her, even when He took her mother home too soon. God loved her, even when she waited year after year for new dreams that never came.

And when those old dreams reignited? When the cost of them meant giving up what she'd forged for herself from their previous ashes?

He still asked to be her foundation, her resting place, her shelter from all the storms, but also the true source of joy. Him, not Wes. Him, not Lara. Him, not her career.

The rain started shortly after they crossed onto Hatteras Island. Silence had fallen in the car again, which Kennedy was thankful for as the wipers came on. She never loved driving in the rain, but Aunt Grace loved it even less, so she'd insisted on being the one to drive today.

As she flicked the blinker on to turn down their lane, Lara said, "When you secure the shutters at the shop, will you check on the roof leak too?"

They'd had rain since then—but not like what was to come, and not with the wind sure to accompany it. "Absolutely."

Their aunt frowned. "Just be careful on the ladder. Maybe make Wes do it."

"Nah, I'll just make him stand at the bottom and catch me if I fall."

Lara gave a weak laugh at the joke. "I'm glad you have him to do that. Seriously. You know that, right? I am so, so glad you finally have your shot."

"I know." Kennedy pulled into their driveway but didn't bother getting out of the car. "Go on in. I'll see where Wes is." She already had her rain gear in the back seat.

Lara set her hand on the back door handle but didn't pull. "Be careful. Not just on the ladder. Everywhere."

"I will, I promise."

"It's been years since you've—"

"Lara. I haven't forgotten how to be careful in a storm." She gave a reassuring smile both to her sister and to Aunt Grace, and then texted Wes.

Lara huffed but then shot her a smile and got out. Aunt Grace sent her a wink. "I'll make sure she gets in safely."

"Thanks."

Her aunt let herself out and hurried up the steps with Lara, out of the rain.

Kennedy's phone chimed seconds after the two were safely inside.

PERFECT TIMING. I'M ON DOLPHIN, IF YOU WANT TO JUST RUN OVER HERE AND RIDE WITH ME.

Perfect indeed—he was one street over.

SEE YOU IN A FLASH.

She pulled her long rain jacket and boots on before she got out, then sent Lara a text letting her know why she was leaving Mitzi in the driveway. It only took a minute to hurry over to the next street and find Wes's SUV parked behind the renters' vehicles at one of the houses.

He stood at the front door—under the protection of the porch roof—chatting with a middle-aged couple, so Kennedy climbed the stairs and smiled a greeting.

"So if we decide to leave, there's no refund?" the man was saying as she approached. He barely glanced at her.

Wes welcomed her to his side with a hand on her back, though he kept his smile aimed at the renters. "Not if you didn't purchase the travel insurance. That changes, of course, if there's a mandatory evacuation—we issue pro-rated refunds for everyone in those cases. But this shouldn't last more than a day. Of course, there's always a chance we'll lose power. I'd recommend you search through all the cabinets and drawers now. You should find candles and flashlights and maybe even an electric lantern, depending on what the owners have left."

The man was still frowning, but the woman rested a hand on his arm. "Just a little adventure, right, honey?"

The man pursed his lips.

Wes grinned. "Hopefully not too much of one, but if you need anything, don't hesitate to give the office a call. And of course, if there's any storm damage, let us know right away. We don't anticipate much, but there are always a few surprises." He motioned to the ocean-facing windows. "Won't take us but a few minutes to get all the shutters down, and we'll come by again after it passes to raise them. Sorry for the loss of view in the meantime."

"Oh, we understand and are grateful," the woman said.

Her husband nodded, though he still looked a little grumpy. "Yeah. Thanks. We'll let you get to it."

Wes's smile didn't relax until they'd closed the door, and then he turned to Kennedy with a look that said *Inlanders, am I right?*

She grinned and followed him around to the east-facing side of the house. "And how many times have you delivered that speech in the last two days?"

"Lost count. How was the appointment?"

"Educational but depressing. I'll update you when we're someplace dry." For now, they moved to separate windows, drawing down the metal storm shutters much like a blind and securing them into place at the bottom. Not every house had them, and usually only on the windows facing east, but even so, she knew it took a ridiculous amount of time for the agency to prep all their houses.

But the fact that Wes was working on a street so close to the home office meant they were almost done. They always dispatched people to the farthest-away houses first and worked their way homeward from both northern and southern points, each team with designated streets.

Even so, they worked for a solid two hours, driving from house to house and street to street, before Wes finally said, "And that was it! Now, the shop?"

"Sounds good. Lara wants me to check on the roof patch too—so long as you're poised at the bottom of the attic ladder, ready to catch me if I fall."

Wes flashed her a grin. "Happy to be your knight in shining armor. Oh, before I forget, there's a box of church records in the back from Wynn. She gave up trying to find the time to go through it."

Kennedy put out her bottom lip—in sympathy, not as a complaint of going through the church records herself. "Hannah still coughing and not sleeping?"

"And teething on top of it. I don't think Wynn and Ev have slept more than two hours at a clip for the last two weeks."

She'd even called in sick a couple days last week, Kennedy knew. Just one of those miserable summer viruses that didn't want to let go of their household, it seemed. "I'll keep praying."

"Rain's getting heavier," he observed as they pulled into the shop's parking lot a few minutes later.

Shaleen would have closed up fifteen minutes before, but she'd wasted no time in clearing out, given the empty state of the lot. Kennedy couldn't blame her. She'd be hurrying home in earnest before the storm hit. "Let's get the shutters first, and then I'll brave the attic."

"I can go up if you want."

She couldn't help but smile at him as they unlatched their seatbelts. "What, and leave me to catch *you* if you fall? I don't like those odds."

He laughed and, when she reached for the door, stopped her with a hand on her arm. "Hey."

"Hmm?" She turned back to him, her insides going mushy at the soft look on his face.

He leaned over and pressed a sweet kiss to her lips. "That's all. For now."

They made short work of the few shutters, and Kennedy was soon using her key to let them inside. It was cool and dark, darker than usual given the shutters, even after she flipped the lights on.

She shrugged out of her raincoat and toed off her boots too, rather than making puddles she'd have to clean up. Wes followed suit, then trailed her back through the hall to where the attic access was hidden in the ceiling.

They had bookshelves even in the hallway, making it a tight squeeze to lower the ladder, and Wes had to be the one to jump up and pull on the shortened cord. "Do you need a flashlight?" he asked.

"There's a bulb at the top of the stairs. I'll be fine." She climbed up the first three steps before a wave of heat billowed down and hit her in the face. "Whew. August is not my favorite time to come up here."

"Want me to come up too? Can't have my girl suffering alone."

She laughed, even as her heart did a silly dance at being called *his girl*. He'd even started introducing her as his girlfriend, and when she'd shown up each Saturday at his parents' fish fry, he'd greeted her with a soft kiss, right in front of everyone.

Needless to say, the whole island knew they were an item, and it had taken about two seconds for people to start asking when the wedding would be, knowing glints in their eyes.

"I'll be fine." She cleared the attic floor with her head, the rest of her soon following. The string for the bare bulb dangled right in front of her, so she switched it on and looked around.

The place where the leak had been was immediately evident—not because anything had been stained, but because Lara had moved items away from the area, and it was the one open spot. Good grief, she hadn't realized Grandma left so much stuff here. Had she brought *anything* from the attic?

Maybe not. Which kinda made sense. They didn't have room for all this stuff at their house, but it wasn't as though she'd sold this place. It remained a fine location to store things.

Something fluttered inside her. "On second thought," she aimed down the stairs, "come on up. It occurs to me that there could be useful stuff for the search somewhere up here."

She didn't know why they hadn't thought of it before—except that she honestly hadn't realized there were so many things still stored up here, and Lara couldn't remember what she'd seen. Not to mention that no one had wanted to return to the scene of the accident.

While Wes climbed up, Kennedy checked the place where the leak had been. Sam's patch seemed to be holding up fine, so she turned her attention to the boxes.

"Wow." Wes had to stoop a bit to keep from whacking his head on the slanted beams as he moved to take stock of the boxes. "At least Grandma Janey was organized. Everything's labeled. Christmas decorations, albums, dishes…I'm not seeing anything labeled 'helpful old documents.'"

"Well, the deed was in a box of books for some reason, so if you see any of *those*…"

He laughed. "You mean like all of these?" He motioned to several stacks.

She didn't know whether to groan—it was a lot to look through—or clap her hands in glee—*more books*. "I'm not looking through those up here. I'll melt before I get through a single crate."

"So let's haul them down."

A simple suggestion, but it made sudden fear claw at her. That was how Lara had fallen, trying to carry a heavy box down those rickety stairs.

Her silence must have spoken pretty loudly. Wes moved to her side and dropped a kiss on her forehead. "You just scoot them toward the ladder. I'll carry them down."

"But—"

"Not to pull the manly-man card, sweetheart, but I'm a lot bigger than Lara and can manage the boxes one-handed better than she'd have been able to."

Because she knew it was true, Kennedy exhaled, willing away her anxiety. "All right."

The boxes weren't huge, but as she moved each of them off the stack and carried them to Wes on the ladder, she was more than a little grateful he was there to help. Because what he easily hefted in one hand would have been a struggle for her, as it no doubt had been for Lara. But within a few minutes, they'd relocated each of the eight boxes to the main floor, turned out the light, and closed the attic back up.

Thunder rolled through the sky as she surveyed the roadblock they'd made. "Usually I'd say let's look through them here and now, but—"

"We still need to get the shutters down on our houses. Let me back the car up to the porch, and we'll load them." He grinned. "Good storm reading, right?"

Was it any wonder she loved this man? "Perfect."

By the time they got home, they'd decided to unload all the boxes into Wes's house, since his parking area was covered. Had she wanted them at her house, it would have meant carrying them through the rain. Given the way the rainfall slanted, even an umbrella wouldn't have been enough to keep them dry.

"I'll let Lara know we're home and what we brought." Kennedy drew her phone out of her pocket after taking off her rain gear in Wes's entryway. "I don't know if she'll feel up to going through any of it tonight or not."

"If she does, tell her to just come over now and we'll make dinner too."

She flashed him a smile and sent the text.

Chapter Seventeen

As Wes moved around the kitchen, he snuck occasional glances at Kennedy as she talked to Lara in the living room. They'd both been over here countless times through the years, and rather often in the last few weeks—Kennedy more than Lara.

The first time he'd cooked for her, he wondered how it would feel. Having her here, in the house he'd shared with Britta. Would it be weird?

But how could it have been? This was the house he'd grown up in, and Kennedy had been there every day when they were kids. The furniture had changed since then, the art on the walls, the paint and some of the drywall. But despite his parents giving him and his late wife this larger house upon their wedding, and moving to a smaller bungalow, the place didn't scream "Britta." It never had. She'd left nearly all the redecorating choices up to him, which he'd found odd at the time.

She'd been the artsy one. Shouldn't she have wanted to decorate her own house? But she'd waved him away, insisting that, this way, if his mom disapproved of any of the changes, she could only blame *him*.

As if Mom was the disapproving sort.

Now he wondered if, even at the start, Britta had not wanted to invest too much of herself. If she'd never really meant for this to be home.

The thought didn't make him as sad as it would have that first week after learning the truth about her. How could it, when he looked over and saw Kennedy and knew that, this way, it wasn't so awkward? She looked at home here.

Soon he had chicken sizzling for fajitas, and Kennedy joined him with a smile after leaving her sister with one of the boxes. Her hair looked more frazzled than usual, thanks to the rain and the hood of her jacket, and seeing it like that made him smile too.

"Put me to work," she said.

He nodded toward the lettuce he'd pulled out. "You can shred that. It's all that needs done now." Knowing the sounds of the skillet would cover their voices, he finally brought up what he'd been thinking for days, as their VaKayBo deadline drew ever nearer—one more week. He'd been praying, asking God for clarity, for Him to make it clear what the right decision was.

But a strange thing had happened. When he considered not selling, staying here, making a life with Kennedy if she chose to move home, he felt complete peace. And yet, when he considered selling, moving to DC instead and working for a different agency there, he also felt peace.

For a while, that peace had made him strangely unsettled—oxymoronic and amusing. But he was beginning to understand it.

The important thing was exactly what his sister had said—that he had his priorities straight. He loved Kennedy. He always had, even if he hadn't let it bloom into romance. But the moment he realized he *could*...that bloom had been full, complete, all-encompassing. He had known from the moment she admitted to still having feelings for him that this would be it for him. He wanted to marry her. Have a family with her. He wanted her to be his forever.

Wherever that forever might be. He'd be happy if it were here—but he'd be happy if it were there too. He would be happy anywhere with her.

According to what she'd told him about the appointment before Lara joined them, though, her sister really couldn't manage the shop on her own anymore, which meant Kennedy would feel pressure to move home.

He needed to make sure she knew that none of that pressure would come from him—which meant saying something now, before she had time to worry herself into the decision. "Hey. You know what you told me Lara said, about not giving up your dreams for her?"

Kennedy set the lettuce she'd just rinsed on the cutting board, brows arched. "Yeah..."

"You're not going to give them up for me either. Just need to throw that out there." He flipped a few strips of chicken, then met her gaze again. "If you want to stay in DC, I'll move, find a job up there with some fancy real estate firm. Then you can hire someone to run the shop."

She'd reached for the knife but didn't start chopping. Probably good, since she was looking at him rather than the lettuce. "I appreciate the thought. But we can't afford to pay someone else to run it while still giving Lara a salary, which she'll need. Unless she can qualify for disability, and I have no idea about that..."

"I'm sorry, that was unclear." He eased a little closer to where she stood. "I meant *we* can hire someone. I'll have the money, if we sell the rental side of the agency. I'd be honored to invest it in the Island Bookshop and taking care of our family."

"Wes." She set the knife down altogether and turned to face him. Her eyes looked damp, and when she blinked a few times, she had to reach up to dash at them. "You're selling?"

"We haven't decided." Actually, they'd all said that it was a matter of what *he* decided. If he wanted to move to follow Kennedy's dreams, then they would accept the offer. There were plenty of good things that would come of it, and the rental side was Wes's domain. No one else wanted to take it on full-time. But if Kennedy wanted to move home, if she was going to stay in Avon, then his family agreed to refuse. "But it's a strong option, and I am perfectly willing to do that."

She shook her head, eyes not getting any less glassy. "I can't ask you to give up everything you ever dreamed of for me."

"You're not asking." He reached over and caught the next tear that spilled. "I'm offering. All I need is you, Kenni. The where doesn't matter. I love what I do, yes—but I can do it somewhere else. It's working with people that I love, and there are plenty of those in DC, I hear. There's no Library of Congress here, though."

She laughed a little, then turned her face into his hand, eyes sliding shut. She drew in a deep breath that shuddered on its way out. Her shoulders relaxed. When she blinked her eyes open again, some of the unease he'd seen building in them, as the summer waned to a close and her leave of absence ran out, was gone. "It means the world that you'd offer. But...that's not who I want to be.

The girl who sacrifices family and everyone else's dreams for her own. That's not the story I want to tell my kids someday. I want them to know that family's more important. That dreams built together are better than dreams built alone."

She reached up, wrapped her hands around his, and leaned into him. "I want to come home, Wes. I do. There are things I'll miss, but I can still stay in the rare book world through my video channel and the grading I do on the side. I already do that through the mail more than in-person anyway. All I'd be giving up is the Library of Congress and a rather ghastly thirty-year mortgage. What I'd be gaining is far more."

"That's a pretty big 'all,' Kenni." He grinned. "Well. The library job. The mortgage isn't exactly a thing to cling to, even if your townhouse *is* nice."

"It is," she agreed. "And I could have kept on being happy there. But I don't need it to be happy." She looked over her shoulder, toward the living room, where her sister sat on Wes's floor, poking through the old church records. "This is the right decision. I was struggling with it, but when you offered me another way...funny how that's when I knew. I want to come home. For good. I want our kids to grow up with family nearby. I want to keep my grandmother's dream alive. I want to help my sister get better, however I can. And I want to watch you make the company you love grow and thrive—not watch you hand it to someone else."

Our kids. Their future. Hearing her talk about it felt so incredibly *right*. He couldn't resist leaning down and capturing her lips. Because if she was sure, then he was too. They'd make their life here.

"You two lovebirds better not be burning my dinner," Lara called out.

Wes pulled away with a chuckle. "We're just deciding our fates over here, that's all. Thanks for the interruption."

"I don't see a diamond flashing, so my point remains," Lara teased. "I'm starving, and that smells fantastic. If you burn it, I'm going to be really put out."

"Well, we can't have that." He kissed Kennedy once more, then pushed her back toward the lettuce.

Dinner was enjoyed and cleaned up, and the three of them moved back over to the boxes that were taking up much of Wes's living room. Kennedy took a seat on the floor between her sister and her boyfriend—that was still a little weird to think—and opened one of the boxes Lara hadn't gotten to yet.

Her sister had spent the hours between drop-off and Kennedy's call resting, so she was doing pretty well now, despite the fact that reading seemed guaranteed to give her a headache after a while.

And Kennedy...Kennedy was doing well too. Despite all the uncertainty she'd been dealing with in the car, things truly had come into alignment the moment Wes offered to move. To invest his family's money in her family's dream. Realizing he'd do that, seeing absolutely no hesitation in his eyes, knowing very well he'd never begrudge her any of it and would throw himself into thriving there...

He was so achingly wonderful. And he saw *her* dreams as having that much value. Knowing as much, feeling that validation, seeing the love and willingness in his eyes had made it clear.

It wasn't the thought of giving up her job in DC that had been bothering her—it was feeling like she *had* to, like it was the only real choice. But when he gave her another choice, it changed everything. Somehow, choosing to stay here freely was so much easier than making the decision under duress.

"Well, here's something," Lara said, tapping a finger against an entry in one of the church registry books. "A mention of a Horvat—baptism."

"Yeah?" Kennedy and Wes both leaned in from opposite sides.

The ink was faded, looping, but there it was, the name they'd become so familiar with—Marija Horvat, baptized in October of 1938. Grandma Janey would have been about a month old at the time.

However, in the space to note the child's parents, it read: *Ana Horvat and Marko Horvat (deceased, July 4, 1938).*

Kennedy blew out a breath. "That's so sad. Her father died before she was born."

"Ana must have married into the Marshall family later." Wes poked through the remaining books from the church but shook his head. "I'm not seeing any marriage records here. Maybe we'll find something in Janey's things."

"Let's hope so." Kennedy shifted back to the box she'd selected. She wrinkled her nose at the stale smell that greeted her when she opened it, though it wasn't a full-on moldy odor. Then her pulse kicked up a notch, as it always did, when she saw gilded letters on cloth spines.

Old. That's what those details meant. She pulled a stack of the books out, breath catching when she realized they weren't in English. "I may have something here. These look like they're in Italian." She flipped open the hardcover of the one on top, bypassing her usual training to look for any identifying marks.

"Is there a name?"

"There is! Ana Horvat. And the copyright is 1936—that doesn't mean it's when Ana bought it, but I'm guessing it came from Europe with her." Kennedy got out her phone, pulling up a feature that would translate Italian into English. The translated title soon appeared on her screen, though it meant nothing to her. "Don't recognize it, but it's definitely Italian. This one, on the other hand…definitely a Slavic alphabet," she said as she moved to the next book in the stack.

"Croatian?" Lara asked.

Kennedy waited for her phone app to catch up. It kept twitching between a few possible translations in different languages but finally settled on one. "Looks like it. Not the same title as the Italian, let it be noted."

"Here, see what your app can make of this." Wes handed over an old-looking piece of paper. "Looks like a letter, but definitely not in English. There's a whole stack of letters here—some still in envelopes, addressed to Ana Horvat. Looks like they're from… Dalmatia?" He gave her a goofy look. "I'm guessing that's where the breed of dog comes from, but that is literally the only thing I can associate with it. Where's Dalmatia?"

"Uh…you can look that up while I try to translate this letter."

Lara released a breath. "If this is our great-grandmother, and we don't even know where she's from…that's really sad."

It was. But not nearly as sad as the letter that appeared on Kennedy's screen as she scrolled the phone over the text. She fetched blank paper and pen and transcribed it.

September 7, 1938

Dear Marko,

It has been two months, and still I cannot believe you are gone. Still I awake every morning and long to see your face, to hear your voice. Still I go to sleep every night, crying for you. Wishing that I had at least seen you again before you died. That our farewell in Dubrovnik hadn't been our final one. But then I think, no goodbye should have been the final one. We should have had years together yet. I wasn't ready to let you go and wouldn't have been, even had I kissed you farewell the morning you set off on that trawler.

Today, I gave birth to our daughter. I named her Marija, after your mother, and I've written our parents letters announcing the birth. I haven't written them since the last letters I sent, announcing your death. I should have. But it hurt too much, to face the people who knew you and loved you, even in writing. I will do better. I promise you and our daughter and our families, I will do better.

I have been but a shadow of myself these two months, washed around by the tides. When I opened my eyes this morning, the pains upon me, I had a moment where I could not even place the walls of my bedroom. Could not remember how I came to be in this pretty little cottage, all alone, about to bring a new life into the world. I was supposed to be here with you. I was supposed to greet this day with joy instead of dread.

Our daughter is beautiful, my love. She has your eyes, your perfect nose. Please do not think for a moment that my dread was over her—it was not. Even as I write this, she is but a breath away, sleeping in a bassinet beside the table. To be her mother is everything I could ever have dreamed. But I was supposed to be her mother with you by my side. So long we prayed for this babe, this family, this new life...how can it be that you are not here to live it with me?

I know that in heaven, you are not worried for me. I know that there, with our Father, you have perfect trust that He holds us in His hand. But down here, I admit that I cannot see it so clearly. And so, as this new blessing sleeps beside me, I think I need to write out the ways He has provided and blessed me, so that I can see them. Too often, all I see is your loss.

But I have Caroline Armstrong—a friend I did nothing to deserve but who has been steadfast. Sometimes I forget that I've not even known her three months. She feels like a sister, so quickly did we bond. Not a day goes by that one or the other of us doesn't stop by to visit.

Through Caroline, I have this house, which her husband's family sold to me for next to nothing. Jack said that had you lived, he would have done the same, to guarantee that we stayed nearby. You were too good a sailor, he said, too quick a friend for him to risk losing you to another house farther away. He said he'd even told you about it on that trip, promised to show it to you as soon as you returned.

Caroline's brother even helped me find an "old jalopy" to drive around—had you heard that term? I hadn't, and I still laugh whenever I say it. It's just an old Ford, more replacement parts than original. But it gets me where I need to go.

I have a job, which is how I can afford to put fuel in my jalopy and food on our table. At first, after you died, I couldn't see past my grief and lived solely on the charity of Caroline and her family. But thanks to Jack's doing—did you know the Armstrongs were such a prominent family when you signed on with Jack's crew?—my education has been recognized, and I'm now a teacher at the grade school. Well, I only taught one day, and now I'll be taking time off with Marija. But they have already agreed to let me come back in a few weeks, and Caroline will babysit for me. I hate the thought of being away from our little one so much, but I don't know what else to do. You would understand, I tell myself.

Last week, an unexpected gift arrived from home—a box of my beloved books! Papa sent them, of course, despite the cost. I chided him for the extravagance when I wrote to them of Marija. But you know Vito Blazevic—he values books above all and said that his grandchild should enter the world with books surrounding her. There was never a question as to where I came by my love of books. I hope to instill that love in our daughter, but never worry. I will instill your love too. We will be out in nature every day. I will teach her how to fish... or let Jack or Cliff Marshall or one of the others do it, perhaps.

All the men from your crew have been stopping by regularly, to make sure we are well—and well fed.

It was so like you, to earn their trust and regard so quickly. To become their friend and brother in a few short weeks. And the fact that your last action on this earth was to save them—they will never forget that. That, I know, is why those men keep stopping by. Doing every chore they see and bringing by vegetables from their gardens or a side of bacon they claim not to need. They take care of us because you gave everything for them. For my own pride, I would refuse. But to honor you? To honor you, I accept. And I thank God for the provision.

We will make it, Marija and I. We will make it here in this place you chose for us. I admit that I have considered giving up, going home...but then I think of all the reasons we left, and I cannot stomach taking her back to all that turmoil. So we will stay here. We will live this life you fought for. We will make a place for ourselves among these people.

Which reminds me. Perhaps the greatest miracle of all, the greatest sign of God's provision...I have another regular guest, one I nearly slammed the door on the first time she stopped by. You never met the harsh side of Berta Marshall's tongue, but I feared she'd force me from this place. Make life difficult, because we are "foreign."

I don't know what her son said to her when they returned without you, but it was a different woman who stepped into my kitchen on the day I moved in here. A woman with tears in her eyes, who gathered me into her arms and cried with me. I wonder what loss she has known, that turned her into the woman she was, so quick to judge, halfway to bitter. Perhaps someday she'll tell me. For now, I think it is just that she knows her son lives because of you. That it could have been him. That is enough to make her my friend instead of my enemy. And I am glad for it. She chides me like a mother and tries to tell me I'm cooking everything wrong, but there's a strange sort of comfort in that. Between her and Caroline, I know I am not alone.

I will always miss you, Marko. Every day of my life. But I will keep on living it, for Marija. We will make you proud. We will become Americans, just as we dreamed of. Our daughter will know no other way. She will be a child of the island, like the other children, one of them. She will grow up tasting freedom and unafraid of the sort of violence that constantly overshadowed us. So help me God.

Yours always,
Ana

Kennedy had to wipe tears from the corners of her eyes by the time she finished reading the translation aloud to Lara and Wes.

Lara, leaning back against the sofa, was sniffling too. Wes, elbows resting on the coffee table, let out a long breath. "Wow. Well, to add a bit of history—seems that Dalmatia was a region between Croatia and Italy that was constantly disputed. It was given to Italy after the First World War, but Mussolini's regime proved violent for it—they weren't 'Italian enough' for Italy. Before that, they were often oppressed by the Croats, being not 'Croatian enough' for them."

"So her passport would have been Italian in the '30s." Kennedy gave her eyes one more wipe. "And I daresay no one here really cared about any differentiation."

"They got out just in time too, didn't they?" Lara held the pages of the letter, though she wasn't trying to read them. "I can't imagine things got any better there once World War II broke out. I wonder what happened to the rest of the family?"

"The letters might tell us." Wes unloaded stacks of them onto the coffee table. "I mean, translating them all's going to take some time, even with the wonders of technology."

"I wonder if they'll answer our questions about Grandma Janey too. Her name, I mean."

"If not..." Wes pulled out another clothbound book; this one definitely did not have the look of a published work. No—it looked like a journal. And *Janey* was written on the front in marker. "Maybe this will."

Kennedy and Lara were both moving to snatch it from his hands when the lights went out.

Chapter Eighteen

Avon, North Carolina
July 5, 1939

A day of quiet was a solace after the busyness of the day before. Ana eased onto the porch swing with a contented sigh, praying its clinking and squeaking wouldn't wake up Marija. The baby had been a bear to get down last night, too overexcited by the church picnic and the noise of the fireworks, and she needed a good, long nap today.

Which usually meant she'd take a too-short one and then be a grump until bedtime. But that was all right. Even a day with a grumpy Marija was a beautiful day. Much as Ana loved teaching, the best moment of every day was when she got to rush up the steps of Caroline's house and cover her baby with kisses. She'd been enjoying each moment of the summer so far, when it was just her and Marija.

Okay, so it was rarely just them all day long. Caroline would bring Susie and little Johnnie by, or she and Marija would visit them, or Berta would pop in with a batch of cookies, or Pauline to ask Ana's opinion on something. In the evenings, after the fishing boats returned from the day runs, one fisherman or another would pop in to see if there were any chores that needed done. Their wives were regular visitors too.

A year since she learned of Marko's death. A year and, somehow, this had become home, even without him. Somehow, this was the only world she could imagine Marija growing up in.

Footsteps sounded, drawing her attention to the drive. Her lips tugged up when she saw Cliff Marshall approaching the house, a basket in hand. He came more often than the others—no doubt sent on errands by his mother. Often enough that he knew— when she merely waved instead of calling out a greeting—he should approach the porch quietly.

He did so with a smile of his own. "Mary Jane asleep?"

She laughed softly at the name. Last week, since she had time on her hands without lessons to plan, she'd finally finished the baby quilt she'd started in the winter months, embroidering *Marija* into a corner square, along with her birthday. Cliff had asked to see it, and when he saw the spelling, he'd declared that the J was just too much for a North Carolinian to handle and that she was bound to end up as Mary Jane.

She thought he was joking, but he'd been calling her that ever since. "You're going to confuse the poor little thing, Cliff."

He grinned and set his basket down. Surprisingly, she didn't see fresh vegetables in it, nor paper-wrapped fish. "I'll stop if you want."

She waved off his comment and leaned to peer into the basket. She'd gotten used to everyone calling her *Annie*, after all. "I don't mind. We'll see what she likes as she gets older. And are those *books?*"

He pulled the top one off with a flourish and held it up for her to see. "New book for kids that Barney said his boys want him to read every day. It rhymes."

"*The 500 Hats of Bartholomew Cubbins*." Ana had never heard of an author by the name of

Dr. Suess, but she reached for it. "The illustrations are darling."

"I figured you needed something other than *The Secret Garden* to read to her—she'll have it memorized by the time she's two at your current rate."

Ana laughed. She read to Marija for at least a few minutes every day, even though the baby wasn't old enough yet to really know what she was hearing. She would be soon. "Thank you, Cliff. This is—"

A cry interrupted, making Cliff wince and whisper, "Sorry."

"It's all right. She's been down for an hour." Ana had been hoping for two, but there was little chance Marija would go back to sleep if she woke up now. She'd gotten her cleaning done, at least. Who needed time to relax anyway? She drew in a breath, setting the book down and bracing her hands on the porch swing.

Cliff waved her down. "I'll get her. You sit."

She wasn't going to argue. Cliff had gone in and out of the house enough to know the way to the nursery, and she smiled as she heard him through its open window.

"Hey there, pretty girl. Are you awake already? Oh, you still look so sleepy. Come here, darlin'. We'll go swing with your mama. Maybe you'll just go back to sleep, hmm?"

She loved hearing the way Cliff spoke to Marija. If she squinted, she could hear Marko saying those things—or nearly those things. He wouldn't have said *darlin'*, and he never would have said anything with that lowland drawl. But the sentiment would have been the same. He'd have cradled her against him just as Cliff did whenever he visited—or when he saw them at Caroline's or his mother's, or his sister's, or at church. Marija loved him, was always lunging for him.

It had given Ana a few pangs at first. Her daughter was surrounded by so many people who loved her, but none of them were her father. But then it had begun to fill her with gratitude. She wouldn't lack for father figures. And maybe, perhaps, someday...

Cliff came back onto the porch, a sleepy baby snuggled onto his shoulder. He gave Ana a smile and sat beside her on the swing. She moved the book out of the way, flipping through a few pages and smiling at the clever verse. Then she put it aside, her attention snagged by her daughter.

Part of her itched to take Marija from him, to get those cuddles for herself. But her little one was perfectly content, there on his big shoulder, eyes closed and thumb stuck in her mouth. Ana reached out only to smooth back one of the dark locks just getting long enough to curl.

"Don said you had another letter from Italy today," he said, fingers rubbing soft circles against Marija's back. "How's your family?"

The postmaster was without question the biggest busybody on Hatteras—but Ana had long ago gotten over everyone knowing the minute she heard from home. "They are well, but worried. Ever since Hitler invaded Czechoslovakia in March...and life under Mussolini gets ever worse. I wish they could all come here, but I know they wouldn't leave, even if I had money enough to send for all their fares."

Cliff sighed. "I can imagine how that makes *you* worry. I wish there was something I could do to help."

That was Cliff. Even more than the others, he had a heart that just yearned to make everything better. She'd learned that about him quickly and had been the recipient of his aid all too often. "You do all you can, Cliff. Not for them directly, but for us.

They know that and, according to my father, sleep easier knowing Marija and I have a friend like you."

He was a fisherman, one who spent most of his days out on the water. Despite the sun-bleached hair, his skin was as dark as her own this time of year, though of a different hue. Even so, she saw the red that flushed his neck and ears at the statement.

Maybe she shouldn't have said it. It was indeed what her father had said, but what if he thought she meant something more? Something else?

He cleared his throat. "I would do more. I would..." He glanced over at her, then back to Marija. "I would *be* more. Someday. When you're ready, if you...if you ever wanted. Not that..." He shook his head, looking off toward the sound. "Forget I said anything. It's only been a year, I know that. I know a year isn't long enough to mourn a man like Marko."

Her chest went tight, and yes, there was sorrow there. Still so much of it. But there was something else too. Something soft and warm, like the sunshine sneaking out of the clouds in May. She rested her fingers on his arm, there where it curved around her daughter. "Cliff—you've become a dear friend—"

"And I'm happy to stay that." The red deepened. His gaze stayed averted. "I am. I don't want you to think I'm pressuring you to change anything. I love being your friend, and I know you have Mary Jane to consider, and you're doing a fine job raising her on your own."

A breath of laughter puffed out. "I'm *not* raising her on my own. And I thank God for that." Which wasn't the part she should have latched onto. "And I thank Him for you too. When I see you with her..."

His eyes slid shut for a second, then finally turned to her again. "I'd be a daddy to her, and I'd love every minute. But I...I don't want you to think that's all this is. I could make you promises—that you wouldn't have to work if you didn't want to, if you married me. But you could, if you wanted. All the sensible things. But what it comes to, Ana, is that this last year, as I've gotten to know you...well, you've stolen my heart. I didn't mean for it to happen, I just wanted to be your friend. But when I see how strong you are, how fiercely you love your little girl, how you work for her, how you've opened your heart to all of us here...and of course, it doesn't hurt that you're so beautiful."

She didn't feel beautiful most days—she just felt like a frazzled mother, a harried teacher. But when Cliff looked at her like he was doing now, like he did so often, when he didn't think she was paying attention...well, she remembered that she was a woman too.

Ana had known his feelings were growing. There were times she could have tamped down his interest, discouraged him.

She hadn't. She wasn't ready quite yet to say yes to all he was offering. But she certainly didn't want to say no.

So she smiled and reached up to smooth down *his* hair. "We're going to have to take this slow. At least to start. My heart still feels like a few pieces are missing, most days. But you've been gathering up those pieces all year, Cliff Marshall. Offering them back to me, one by one. Proving how tenderly you can care for us. And I'll admit that my days are brighter whenever you're in them."

It wasn't, perhaps, a profession of love. But she understood herself well enough to know that's where it would go. A few more months of healing, more time spent with him, shared laughter, conversation... that was all it would take. He'd already become a friend, someone she depended on. Someone she loved seeing with her baby.

And when he smiled at her like that, like she'd just handed him a piece of the sun...well, how could it do anything but melt her? "We can take things as slow as you like. I'm not going anywhere. I intend to be right here, guarding your heart, as long as you'll let me."

She intended to let him as long as he wanted. To prove it, she let herself do something she never had before. She rested her head against his shoulder, leaned into his side.

It felt…it felt like they were a family. And she knew that feeling would only grow. Eventually, he'd ask her formally to marry him, and she'd say yes. She'd become Ana Marshall—or, more likely, *Annie* Marshall.

And Marija? Would she be known as Mary Jane Marshall?

Even as she wanted her little girl to have a father in Cliff, part of her rejected that. Marko, too, deserved to be remembered. Honored.

She'd just have to pray the Lord would give them wisdom.

In the light of day, the journal sang a siren song in Kennedy's ears, mocking her from where it sat on the table. Trying to read it by lantern light would have been doable, but Lara's headache had made its appearance, so instead, they'd gathered up what they could carry under their raincoats and carted it back to their own house.

Kennedy had promised she wouldn't look at it without Lara, but that promise was chafing right about now. The power was back already, and the rain still coming down convinced her that it wasn't a great morning for a jog. But she had more than an hour before she had to leave for work.

Maybe she should wake up Lara.

No. That would be cruel. But...she hadn't promised not to look at any of the books they'd brought over, from the same box where they'd discovered the journal.

The box was full of kids' books, ranging from some early Dr. Seuss to *The Chronicles of Narnia*...all of which looked at first glance like first editions. She itched to examine them more closely, and she didn't think Lara would mind.

First she picked up *The 500 Hats of Bartholomew Cubbins*. She'd done a quick search on her phone last night and knew that if it were in good condition, it could go at auction for several thousand dollars. Ironically, the second editions were worth more, since they had dust jackets—she'd seen some that went for more than fifteen grand.

This one, of course, was too well-loved for any big price tag, and it wasn't like she meant to sell them anyway. The corners were ragged, the pages yellowed, a few of them bent, one missing a piece of its corner. This was a book that had been read many, many times.

That was its own treasure. She flipped back to the first page, not at all surprised to see a name penciled into the top outside corner—right where Ana had put her name in *The Secret Garden*.

Marija.

She traced the letters with her fingernail. They were written in the same hand as the letter she'd translated last night—Ana's hand. And this book came out the same year Marija was born. She could imagine the young mother reading the story to her little girl over and over again.

When she picked up *The Lion, the Witch, and the Wardrobe*, however, the name written inside was different. This one looked like a child had written it, and it said *Mary Jane.*

Kennedy pursed her lips. Grandma Janey was twelve when this came out, a perfect age to read and love it—which she knew very well she had. Grandma had always adored the entire series and had read it to her and Lara when they were kids, too, then bought them a set to read themselves when they were a little older. So many conversations they'd had about all the Christian symbolism worked into Lewis's Narnia. Kennedy's faith had been hugely shaped by it, especially *The Last Battle*.

Grandma had told them about how she'd waited eagerly for each new book in the series to release and even said she had her copies "somewhere"...but she'd never bothered searching for them, apparently, or had forgotten where they'd been stored.

Her eyes moved from one inscription to the next. *Marija. Mary Jane.*

They didn't sound similar but, visually, she could see it. She could see how the Dalmatian spelling of *Maria* could shift. That *J*... followed by an *A*. Mari Ja could easily become Mary Jane.

And it wasn't a big leap from Mary Jane to Janey. It didn't answer the why, or even exactly the when, but it explained a bit of the how.

"You're not reading that without me, are you?"

Kennedy jumped at Lara's voice, then laughed. "Not the journal. I'm just looking at the kids' books. Looks like there was a stop between Marija and Janey. Mary Jane. That's what Grandma wrote in the front of *The Lion, the Witch, and the Wardrobe*."

"Interesting." Lara joined her at the table, still blinking sleep from her eyes. She looked at the book while Kennedy reached for the next one in the series.

Prince Caspian, too, had an inscription reading *Mary Jane*. But *The Voyage of the Dawn Treader* read: *Janey*. "Hold on," she muttered, more to herself than to her sister. She pushed back from her chair and darted to the spare room with all her supplies, emerging again a moment later with her loupe and microscope in hand.

Lara laughed. "Seriously? You're going all...you know, CSI stuff on it?"

"Forensics? Why not?" Grinning, she sat down again, taking the loupe to *Dawn Treader*. "There was definitely something erased here, under *Janey*. I can't quite make out what it is though—she did too good a job. Look and see what name's in *The Silver Chair*, will you?"

Kennedy turned her microscope on and carefully positioned the book under the bulk of the machine, moving only the corner of the page in question under the lens so that the light shone up through it.

"*Silver Chair* has *Janey*."

The original writing sprang to life. "Aha! As I suspected. *Mary Jane*. Which she'd erased and written over with *Janey*. That must have been when she started going by that nickname—when she was...fourteen or so."

Perhaps it was an answer Kennedy didn't really *need*. But still, it felt good to have. To see the evolution, and not have to wonder at all the things Grandma had never told them.

Lara was laughing. "I cannot believe you brought your microscope out here for that. You are such a...you know."

"Scholar? Academic? Brilliant sleuth?"

"Dork." She gave Kennedy's shoulder a teasing shove. "Put away your dork stuff and let's look at the journal before you have to leave."

Though she sighed, it was just for dramatic effect. She was eager to see what the journal said. They'd gotten just enough of a glimpse last night to learn that it started in 1956—the year before the house was deeded to her grandma. Surely it would mention the event.

"You do the reading," Lara said. "Out loud, if it seems relevant. I'll pour us some coffee while you get started."

"Deal." She skimmed through the first few entries, summarizing more than reading. "Looks like it starts with her high school graduation. Excited to go to college, wanted to start writing this to chronicle her life as an adult." The thought made Kennedy grin, but it faded. "Wait. Looks like she deferred college for a year because her mother was sick. Oh, here we go. 'Mom wants to put the house in my name, she says, when she and Dad move into Aunt Pauline's house to take care of Gran. I still can't believe Aunt Pauline and Uncle Greg moved to the mainland! Didn't think I'd ever see the day. And I'm okay with keeping this house for me someday, but it still seems weird, thinking of them not being here. It's the only place I've ever lived. Even weirder to think that when I finally start classes next fall, it'll be as a homeowner! Bet none of my classmates will be able to say that.'"

Lara returned to the table with two mugs of coffee, setting one in front of Kennedy. "So this house used to be Aunt Pauline's. She moved, so Grandma's parents moved in."

"I think someone in the family owned the one that used to be next door too—before it was torn down and that new one built in its place. That makes sense with this. Must have been Gran's house." Kennedy took a sip of her coffee and flipped to the next entry, skimming, then going back to the beginning. "I think this is the one we're looking for."

Lara sat back down, her expression eager. "Read, read."

"'I think I've finally won the fight. I sat Mom and Dad down last night and told them I wanted to change my name. I know I'm eighteen now and there's no point in Dad officially adopting me at this point—just like I know that he's been my father, whether my last name is *really* Marshall or not. And I get that Mom didn't want me to forget my real dad—but I never knew Marko Horvat. I know her stories, and Dad's. I know he was a wonderful man, that I look like him. I know he died saving the lives of Dad and Uncle Jack and all the others on the trawler, back when Mom was still pregnant with me, right after she got here from Italy.'"

"She called it Italy," Lara interrupted.

"It *was* Italy. Dubrovnik might be in what we call Croatia again now, but it was Italy when Ana emigrated."

Her sister smiled and rolled a hand through the air. "I'm only saying that it's a consistent narrative."

"Point taken." She looked back to the text. "'I told her that I respected her for preserving my father's memory, and that I've never forgotten where we came from—but that we were now the only Marshalls left on Hatteras, and I want to truly *be* one. It's what people have called me all my life, even if it wasn't technically my name. And I explained to her how strange that feels to me—to have Marija Horvat on the deed she'd just drawn up, but to be known by absolutely everyone here as Janey Marshall. Explained that I want to *be* Janey Marshall. I want to carry on the legacy of that family too, the one that took us in. I want to honor the man who raised me, not just the one who helped create me. And yes, I may have gotten a bit childish and said it was no fair that she got to choose to marry Cliff when I was two and take his name and let everyone call her Annie instead of Ana, but she tried to tell me I couldn't do the same.

"'Dad looked about to argue, which makes me think he was the one that had insisted on keeping Horvat. But Mom started laughing and said, "Well honey, we said from the start that she'd get to pick what she was called. That's why she was Mary Jane for a decade, and that's why we didn't put up a fuss when she wanted to be Janey instead. Guess it would be a bit arbitrary to put our foot down now, wouldn't it?" And you know, I almost relented, when I realized it was Dad that wanted to preserve the memory of the friend he'd only known for a month or two, but who had had such an impact on him. But then it made me even more determined. I know Marko must have been a wonderful man—but so is Cliff. He's Dad. And I want to really own his name, not just claim it falsely. So...we're driving up to Manteo tomorrow! I will finally and officially be Janey Marshall.'"

"Aww." Lara made a that's-so-sweet face. "Nothing dark and secretive there at all. Though I'm still baffled that she never talked about the Horvats."

Kennedy lowered the journal and reached for her coffee again. "I daresay there were a lot of things that factored into her silence. Not least of which was that the Horvat family wasn't the one she knew. I mean, the letters make it plain Ana kept in touch with them, but they clearly never went back to Europe. This became their world." Kennedy reached over and covered Lara's hand with hers. "And I can't blame them for that. I'm looking forward to making it my world again too."

She expected a smile. Maybe a little surprise. Certainly not the frown Lara gave her. "No. I told you, you're not giving up your dreams to move back here and take care of me."

Gracious—the Marshalls sure were a stubborn family too, weren't they? Another trait that clearly went back generations. Kennedy rolled her eyes. "Don't give yourself so much credit. It's not for you." Well, not *only* for her. "And it's not for Wes. It's for me, Lara." She gave the hand under hers a little shake. "I'm done running away from home. This is where I want to be, where I want to raise kids someday. Where you're next door to babysit, and Dad and Deanne are just a ferry ride away, and the Armstrongs are a five-minute drive. This is the future I want. So don't you tell me I can't have it just because you're all hung up on not pulling me from something I'm happy to give up."

For a long moment, Lara just stared at her sister, face impassive. Then, finally, she lurched forward to wrap Kennedy in a hug. "Having you next door forever sounds pretty perfect to me."

Epilogue

September had long been Wes's favorite month in the Outer Banks. The sun was a little less scorching, the water still summer-warm, the crowds had dispersed...but the people who came for vacation were no less happy to be there. They got a lot of older couples this time of year, along with homeschooling families, and some couples without children too. The pace slowed down, but it didn't drop to winter levels.

Pretty perfect, by his way of thinking. And this year, September was even more special.

This year, he drove away from Armstrong Realty each evening feeling unspeakably blessed that he was still doing just that. He'd given VaKayBo their answer two weeks ago, before the deadline, and he'd been more than a little touched when his family had rejoiced with him over that "no" with a party they'd clearly all planned behind his back. He'd come out of his office to find streamers hung, a cake in the break room, and every single employee present and clapping.

He pulled into his driveway now, smiling again to remember it. There hadn't been much time for more than that quick celebration—they still had the end of summer rush to get through. But now that Labor Day had come and gone, he could breathe a little easier.

And turn his mind to the Next Thing.

He'd beaten Kenni home, from the looks of it—good. The weather was perfect this evening, cooperating with his plan to turn the dinner he'd promised her into a romantic rooftop event. He hurried inside, popping the food he'd already prepped into the oven, then turning his attention to preparing the space.

He carried up a table and two chairs, a tablecloth and dishes to anchor it down. The chances of an exposed candle staying lit in the constant wind was slim to none, but he had one in one of those glass chimney things—he carried it up and put it in the center of the table.

The weathered deck up here didn't exactly scream "perfect place to propose," with its graying color and windblown sand in all the cracks and crevices, but there was only so much a guy could do about that. He'd taken inspiration from that impromptu party, anyway, and grabbed some streamers to wrap around the railing. Wynn had foisted twinkle lights on him, which he admitted begrudgingly were a nice touch. A *really* nice touch.

He'd have to thank her tomorrow.

Nah, he'd thank her now.

Lights really make it! Best sister ever.

She replied almost immediately.

Get off the phone and onto your knee! What are you doing texting me??

She's not even home yet!

Do you have the ring? Don't forget the ring. And don't put it in her glass or food, we don't need her choking.

You have no faith in me.

How could I? You tried to tell me you didn't need the lights.

Chuckling, he signed off when he saw Mitzi pull in next door and rushed down to call to Kenni from the main deck. "Hey, beautiful."

She looked up, a smile lighting her face. "Hey, yourself. I'll be over in a minute."

"We're eating topside, since the weather's so nice. Come on up when you're ready."

"Sounds good."

He watched her until she disappeared inside, then went inside himself. The smell of dinner met him when he opened the door, making his stomach growl. He grabbed hot pads and took the pan out of the oven, covering it with foil and carrying the whole thing up to the deck. A couple more trips with the sides and iced tea and he was ready.

Well. Almost ready. He dashed back into his bedroom, where a red velvet box sat on his dresser.

He'd already looked at it a dozen times, wondering if this was the right choice, but he had to open it again now. The box was old, the white lining yellowed with time. And the diamond was nothing flashy. A half-carat round solitaire in a yellow gold band.

It wasn't what he would have picked out for her, had he gone to a store. He hadn't even considered giving it to Britta—she'd made it clear long before he proposed that he was to get her a marquis cut with baguettes on the sides.

But he thought Kenni would appreciate this one. The story of it. The years behind it. He closed the box, slipped it into his pocket, and headed up.

She'd beat him up there this time and stood in front of the table, turning to him when he approached.

"Wow," she said, motioning to the setup. "This is beautiful."

She knew what it meant. The shimmer in her eyes said she did, as did the tremble in the hands she lifted to try to reclaim her hair from the wind.

Which meant there was no point in waiting until after dinner. Wes moved over to her, took those hands in his, and gave them a squeeze as he dropped to one knee, per Wynn's orders. "I'm really not very romantic, Kenni. I know this isn't a big surprise and not so grand a gesture...but I love you. I want to spend forever with you. Will you marry me?"

He pulled out the jewelry case and opened it up.

Kenni looked at him instead of the ring, resting a hand on his cheek. "It's perfectly romantic. But I'm still not mysterious—you know very well that my answer is *yes, yes, yes*."

Maybe he knew her too well for her to be mysterious in some ways—but part of him still couldn't believe she wanted to be his, that she wanted him to be hers. He pulled the ring out of its holder and slid it onto her finger. It was a little loose, but not so bad that it would fall off. "This was my great-grandma Caroline's ring. When I realized that she and your great-grandmother Ana were such good friends, I thought..."

Kennedy drew in a breath and raised her hand to study the gem. "Really? This was hers? That is so stinking cool!"

He laughed and stood again, pulling her close. "I love that you think so. And I think that if our great-grands could see us now, they'd be over the moon. The Marshalls and the Armstrongs, finally becoming family."

She looped her arms around his neck. "Our families have always been family. But…I guess I see Grandma Janey's point. There's something wonderful about making it official."

There was nothing to do but seal it with a kiss.

From the Author

Dear Reader,

The Outer Banks of North Carolina have long held a place in my heart. My family started vacationing there when I was twelve, and my husband's family always did too. When we got engaged, we at first thought we'd have a December wedding...but then his mom said, "You should get married at the beach!" So we changed our plans to June and said our vows on a deck overlooking the Atlantic in Kitty Hawk. Needless to say, we kept up the tradition and continued to vacation there nearly every year of our married life too.

We've stayed all up and down the islands, but once we discovered the little village of Avon on Hatteras Island, there was no going anywhere else. Avon stole our hearts, and when my awesome editor at Guideposts asked if I would consider writing a beach book, I knew exactly where I wanted to set it. I've written stories set in the Outer Banks before, but never a contemporary. So to write this book was really me inviting you into *my* world, taking you to my favorite place and seeing the way it is today through my own eyes.

I, of course, am only a vacationer, a visitor. But I love chatting with people who actually call the islands home. When I got the news that *The Island Bookshop* was a go, the first thing I did was email two bookshop owners in the Outer Banks and ask them to regale me with all the details of owning such a store in a vacation spot. And oh, how I loved every exchange! Books and the beach are two of my very favorite things, after all, so to combine them is pure joy. The Island Bookshop you see in these pages is a loving combination of Buxton Village Books (Buxton is just a few miles from Avon, which does not actually have a bookshop of its own) and Books To Be Red in Ocracoke (the next island down the chain).

I pray that you enjoyed this little island getaway too, from the picturesque setting to the glimpses behind the scenes at those locals who make paradise so welcoming for us visitors. Most of all, I pray that the story of Kennedy and Wes and Ana brings a bit of the feeling of *home* to your heart. I know that's what I felt as I wrote their story.

Signed,
Roseanna

About the Author

Roseanna M. White is a bestselling, Christy Award–winning author who has long claimed that words are the air she breathes. When not writing fiction, she's homeschooling, editing, designing book covers, and pretending her house will clean itself. Roseanna is the author of a slew of historical novels whose stories span several continents and thousands of years. Spies and war and mayhem always seem to find their way into her books…to offset her real life, which is blessedly ordinary.

A Note from the Editors

We hope you enjoyed *The Island Bookshop*, published by Guideposts. For over seventy-five years, Guideposts, a nonprofit organization, has been driven by a vision of a world filled with hope. We aspire to be the voice of a trusted friend, a friend who makes you feel more hopeful and connected.

By making a purchase from Guideposts, you join our community in touching millions of lives, inspiring them to believe that all things are possible through faith, hope, and prayer. Your continued support allows us to provide uplifting resources to those in need. Whether through our communities, websites, apps, or publications, we inspire our audiences, bring them together, and comfort, uplift, entertain, and guide them. Visit us at guideposts.org to learn more.

We would love to hear from you. Write us at Guideposts, P.O. Box 5815, Harlan, Iowa 51593 or call us at (800) 932-2145. Did you love *The Island Bookshop*? Leave a review for this product on guideposts.org/shop. Your feedback helps others in our community find relevant products.

Find inspiration, find faith, find Guideposts.

Shop our best sellers and favorites at guideposts.org/shop

Or scan the QR code to go directly to our Shop.

More Great Mysteries Are Waiting For Readers Like *You*!

Whistle Stop Café Mysteries

"Memories of a lifetime...I loved reading this story. Could not put the book down...." —ROSE H.

Mystery and WWII historical fiction fans will love these intriguing novels where two close friends piece together clues to solve mysteries past and present. Set in the real town of Dennison, Ohio, at a historic train depot where many soldiers once set off for war, these stories are filled with faithful, relatable characters you'll love spending time with.

Mysteries & Wonders of the Bible

"I so enjoyed this book....What a great insight into the life of the women who wove the veil for the Temple." —SHIRLEYN J.

Have you ever wondered what it might have been like to live back in Bible times to experience miraculous Bible events firsthand? Then you'll LOVE the fascinating **Mysteries & Wonders of the Bible** novels! Each Scripture-inspired story whisks you back to the ancient Holy Land, where you'll accompany ordinary men and women in their search for the hidden truths behind some of the most pivotal moments in the Bible. Each volume includes insights from a respected biblical scholar to help you ponder the significance of each story to your own life.

Mysteries of Cobble Hill Farm

"Wonderful series. Great story. Spellbinding. Could not put it down once I started reading." —BONNIE C.

Escape to the charming English countryside with **Mysteries of Cobble Hill Farm**, a heartwarming series of faith-filled mysteries. Harriet Bailey relocates to Yorkshire, England, to take over her late grandfather's veterinary practice, hoping it's the fresh start she needs. As she builds a new life, Harriet uncovers modern mysteries and long-buried secrets in the village and among the rolling hills and castle ruins. Each book is an inspiring puzzle where God's gentlest messengers—the animals in her care—help Harriet save the day.

Learn More & Shop These Exciting Mysteries, Biblical Stories, & Other Uplifting Fiction at **guideposts.org/fiction**